I0614591

Sweet Dreams
at
The Palace Hotel

by

Stella Jayne Phillips

Creekside Dreams, Book One

This is a work of fiction. Names, characters, places, and incidents are either the product of the author's imagination or are used fictitiously, and any resemblance to actual persons living or dead, business establishments, events, or locales, is entirely coincidental.

Sweet Dreams at The Palace Hotel

COPYRIGHT © 2019 by Stella Jayne Phillips

All rights reserved. No part of this book may be used or reproduced in any manner whatsoever without written permission of the author or The Wild Rose Press, Inc. except in the case of brief quotations embodied in critical articles or reviews.
Contact Information: info@thewildrosepress.com

Cover Art by *Abigail Owen*

The Wild Rose Press, Inc.
PO Box 708
Adams Basin, NY 14410-0708
Visit us at www.thewildrosepress.com

Publishing History
First Fantasy Rose Edition, 2019
Print ISBN 978-1-5092-2685-6
Digital ISBN 978-1-5092-2686-3

Creekside Dreams, Book One
Published in the United States of America

Dedication

Dedicated to
Christina, Sabrina, Mary, Penny, and Barb,
who read the various drafts and offered support;
Melanie Billings, editor, who cared enough
to offer feedback and suggestions;
and generations of women in my family, who provided
inspiration with their personal stories of starting over.

Chapter One

"March 1, 1917, Donaldson builders completed The Palace Hotel on Beatrice Street. Within a few days, owner and innkeeper Mrs. Victoria Wyatt moved into the hotel, residing in room 15 on the second floor. The first hotel of its kind, The Palace included a bar in the lobby."
~A Brief History of The Palace by Arthur Welles

The Palace waited. A sleeping, three-story lady, her windows dressed in shadows and lace curtains, dozing in the very early morning. Up three stone steps, a weathered wood veranda surrounded her. Creaking in the breeze, a lone rocking chair rested near the weather-beaten front doors. A slamming truck door punctured the quiet. Nikki Benton's black boots hit the ground. Thirty days since she last saw The Palace and arranged a few renovations, sixty days since Patrick, James, and Nikki pooled their resources to form Sweet Dreams LLC and purchase the hotel. A second car door slammed and the Realtor, Jackson Caulkins, joined Nikki on the sidewalk.

"Congratulations on your new business venture," said Jackson, his hand outstretched. Three steps and they stood before double doors. Hand trembling slightly from a potent mixture of fear and anticipation, Nikki inserted the key and opened the antique door into a shadowed lobby. Jackson reached behind the front desk, flipped a switch, and the shadows disappeared. "Room keys in the safe behind the painting in the manager's office. Directions for changing the combination inside the safe." He handed her the combination and grinned. "You'll find Creekside's excited to have The Palace open again, Nikki. Call if I can help."

With a wave, Nikki watched his car pull away.

A biting January wind burned her cheeks when Nikki dashed to her truck and lifted a small white dog from the back seat. Georgie whined, eyes focused on The Palace. Nikki searched the area for the source of Georgie's distress. A woman stood silhouetted in the window of room 15 on the second floor. Victoria?

Nikki whispered, "Georgie, it's okay. She's welcoming us. I'll bet she was lonely while the hotel was vacant." Nikki slammed the truck door shut, and the silhouette disappeared. They walked the short sidewalk. Georgie sat down and whimpered. "Legs too short?"

Cuddling Georgie against her chest, Nikki climbed three steps, walked across the wide veranda, and opened the front door. Her future beckoned. Offering a welcoming warmth to travelers, running a successful business, becoming a vital part of the community, creating a network of friends all in the company of her resident ghost. New dreams, new hope, new life starting this moment.

Under keys and combination instructions in the safe lay a small red leather book, *A Brief History of The Palace Hotel,* written by Arthur Welles. Nikki skimmed a few pages, the book focused on Mrs. Victoria Wyatt, original owner of The Palace and hotel resident from 1917 to her death on April 24, 1949. The hotel's resident ghost. Nikki closed the book and slid it back inside the safe. Would history repeat itself since she and Victoria had a common history, two previously married women living in and operating the hotel alone?

Nikki and Georgie strolled through the three empty rooms combined into a two-bedroom suite. At a knock on the back door, Nikki greeted the movers, and a short four hours later, furniture filled Nikki's suite and the lobby. She unpacked kibble for Georgie and poured it into her bowl, setting a filled water bowl beside it in the sitting room. The chorus of "Wasted Time" announced a call from her brother.

"Hey, James. Before you ask, I arrived safely and so did my furniture." She laughed. "And I love it!"

"Exactly what I wanted to hear." He chuckled. "What's Georgie think of the hotel?"

Nikki gazed at Georgie, now nestled in her small dog bed. "She can't get up the front steps without help, and she let me know her feet were cold when we walked."

"At least you won't have to worry about her running out the front door if she can't do the steps. What about you? You handling the cold okay?"

"No problem. I wore a jacket and boots. Poor dog was barefoot." Nikki plopped down on a small settee, reached over, and scratched Georgie's ears. "I brought boots for her and a jacket; she just wasn't wearing them."

"Figures." He chuckled. "The contractor finished the changes? You're satisfied with the suite and the library?"

"Absolutely. It looks exactly like I pictured." She scanned the room and admired the cozy reading nook. "Come up next weekend and see for yourself." She pushed off her shoes and curled her legs under her.

"An invitation already? Why?"

"Let's see. You own one-third of Sweet Dreams? You know, the corporation we formed to buy The Palace?"

Georgie uncurled from the dog bed and hopped gracefully onto the settee, laying her head on Nikki's feet.

"So you're encouraging me to check on my investment? After you made such a big deal about being in charge of The Palace? I don't think so. Why the invitation?"

"You know me too well. Georgie needs a fence built around part of the back patio. While you check on your investment, you can build one."

"Okay. That I believe." He chuckled. "You're looking for cheap labor."

"Next week is my birthday. Think of the fence as a gift."

"That's what you want Nikki? A fence for your thirty-second birthday?"

"Yep. A fence." She lifted Georgie onto her lap and fluffed the dog's silky ears.

"How times change. I remember when you wanted a car."

"Yeah, but I was sixteen. You and Patrick gave me a car, sort of."

"We did, a classic car because we're so generous."

"A framed picture of a 1954 red Corvette convertible. Beautiful, but not what I wanted." A

4

picture propped against the wall waited to be hung above her desk in the office. A 1954 red Corvette convertible. "So this birthday I'll see you and a real fence. Please not a photo."

"No photo," James agreed. "Next week a real fence. Bye, Nik."

A cold wind slapped Nikki's cheeks as she and Georgie, both wearing boots and jacket, walked out the hotel's back door. Nikki's mind filled with tasks undone and decisions still unmade. She strolled from the parking lot onto the sidewalk and collided with a hard chest. Scents of aftershave and soap surrounded her, and Nikki gazed into chocolate brown eyes lit with humor.

"Whoa," her human wall commented as he grabbed her arms, stopping her fall.

"My fault, I'm so sorry. Wasn't watching where I was going," Nikki babbled, embarrassed. Steady now, she stepped back, and he released her arms. "Thanks for the rescue."

"My pleasure." He held out his hand. "Police Chief Alexander Stark."

"Nikki Benton, nice to meet you." She shook his gloved hand.

"New owner of The Palace." He released her hand. "Welcome to Creekside, Ms. Benton."

"Thank you, Chief."

He tipped his Stetson. "Have a safe evening. I'm sure I'll bump into you soon."

Nikki laughed and watched him walk away and disappear around a corner.

****

James, paintbrush in hand, plopped in the redwood

chair on the back patio and admired his building project, a custom fence for Georgie. The artificial turf on this section glowed bright green against the white fence. The dog door, installed exactly ten minutes ago by the home improvement store, opened with a flap and a clap and out came Georgie. She pranced over and sat down next to James' feet.

"Well, Georgie, what do you think? Does it meet with your approval?"

"It meets with mine," Nikki commented as she climbed the steps to the patio and exchanged the paintbrush for a bottle of beer. "Thanks for the birthday present. Your timing was perfect." She kissed him on the cheek.

He shook his head. "Would have finished sooner without your supervision. Matching the existing railing was tricky."

"But it's my birthday present. A gift." Nikki wrapped the paintbrush in a plastic bag. "Don't I deserve perfect?"

He rolled his eyes. "Of course. You're a Benton. Only the best for Bentons."

Later, showered and changed, James joined Nikki for dinner in the sitting room. He dropped into a dining chair and commented, "Mom's furniture looks good in here. Who knew her collection of estate sale finds would fit in a historic hotel."

"I'm happy I didn't have to part with her treasures when we sold the house."

"How did you decide what to keep?"

"Did you look in the basement?" Nikki asked. "I didn't decide, I just moved everything I couldn't seem to part with and stored what I didn't need in the basement."

James lifted his glass and stared into his sister's eyes. "Any sightings of your resident ghost?"

"If I say yes, are you going to give me a bad time?"

James shook his head no.

"I see her mostly in the evening. Between Georgie and Victoria, I never feel alone even in a palace full of empty rooms."

Time raced as Nikki readied The Palace for the soft opening. Contractors built shelves in the library. Nikki unpacked her eclectic collection of fiction and non-fiction books. She filled every shelf. Standing on the threshold of the library, she commented, "Instead of an innkeeper, I could have been a librarian."

****

Friday, Nikki woke to a sunny winter day and glanced over at Georgie, sleeping soundly in her bed. Opening day. Behind the front desk, Nikki stood dressed in pleated wool pants and long-sleeved purple shirt with The Palace logo. Everything was ready for the soft opening.

Leather duffle on his shoulder, James, first to arrive, wrapped his sister in a hug. "The place looks great, what can I do to help?"

"Welcome to your palace." Nikki hugged him back. "I'm glad you asked. You're on bar duty in Victoria's."

"I'll keep the wine pours small and make sure no one gets out of line."

"Perfect. Coffee's behind the bar and the number of our lone taxi service is stuck to the wine cooler."

"Is this how you treat your partners? Master's degree in accounting and all I'm good for is bartending?" James retorted, a twinkle in his hazel eyes.

"Look at it this way; you could be on dish duty." Nikki smirked. "Or you could be my waiter who boasts a law degree."

Blond hair mussed by the February wind, Patrick climbed the steps to the front door with a smile lighting his face. Patrick's sixteen-year-old son Scott trailed behind with his usual distracted gait.

"Welcome to your palace, brother dear." Nikki greeted Patrick with a hug, then grabbed Scott. "Thanks for volunteering."

"So, what did we volunteer for?" Patrick teased, his blue eyes twinkling.

"Waiter for you, Patrick; busboy for Scott."

Taking his key, Scott asked, "Can I talk to you later, Aunt Nikki?"

"Of course." She frowned. "But you're okay with being a busboy?"

"Sure." Scott and Patrick climbed the stairs, disappearing at the first landing.

During a brief lull before the party began, James poured wine for Nikki and Patrick, soda for Scott. "Here's to the success of our Sweet Dreams," he toasted.

"To Sweet Dreams," they echoed. Nikki cast a final admiring glance around the lobby. Lamps on their lowest setting cast a welcome glow; furniture gleamed with polish, even the old oak floors shone. Rudy Vallee crooned, "The world will always welcome lovers as time goes by."

Standing in shadow behind the front desk, Victoria appeared, a smile lighting her face. Footsteps rang on the wooden stairs, and the spirit disappeared.

Within a few minutes, the lobby rang with guests' animated conversation accompanied by the instrumental sounds of Benny Goodman, Duke Ellington, and Tommy Dorsey. When the guests wandered down the street toward the town square and restaurants, Patrick and Scott walked two blocks to Willie's Pizza, returning with dinner for the hotel staff.

After dinner and clean up, Nikki and her brothers met in Nikki's sitting room. "Did you meet Eric and Charlotte?" Nikki asked Patrick as she poured him a glass of wine.

"They introduced themselves as your assistant managers. How'd that happen?" He relaxed against the back of the sofa and sipped the wine.

"At the interview they came in together with excellent resumes and a complete plan for sharing the job." Nikki poured wine for James.

"If one's sick," questioned Patrick, "will the other cover?"

"We're still ironing out the details." Nikki moved to the wingback chair and plopped her feet on a small ottoman.

"Did you meet Jackson's wife, Maggie?" James asked as he lounged in the Morris chair.

"We've met. She stopped by the first week and introduced herself."

"Met the police chief," commented Patrick.

"And what did you think?" inquired Nikki. She remembered tingles of attraction when she'd collided with Alex Stark's hard chest.

"Decent guy, single father of two boys, lives with his mother." Patrick shrugged.

Nikki grimaced. "I bet he figured you for a lawyer.

Sounds like you cross-examined him."

"Just checking him out for you," Patrick admitted. "Wanted to be sure you're safe in Creekside."

James shook his head. "That's why I'm the favorite brother."

"Am I safe, oh protective ancient brother?"

"Too soon to tell." Patrick winked.

"Change of subject, since Scott's upstairs, do you know what he wants to talk about?" Nikki frowned. "Wanting to talk to me was almost the first words out of his mouth."

"Summer work. Scott wants to work at The Palace."

Nikki sipped her wine. "Won't he be with Amy when school gets out?"

"Nope. Amy planned yet another honeymoon to Europe," Patrick answered. "Scott spent only a week with her last summer and even that didn't go well according to either of them."

"Why not? Scott's always been pretty flexible, even for a teenager."

"Amy says he's spoiled. Not grateful for anything she gives him, complains about everything, and didn't get along with her boyfriend or his children."

"That doesn't sound like Scott." James shook his head. "He gets along with everyone."

"According to Scott, Amy treated him like an on-call babysitter. She was rarely home and planned no time with just the two of them. The boyfriend, Brandon, was with them or his children or both." Patrick shrugged. "Amy let me know she won't have time for Scott this summer. If you're willing to have him live here and work, I think he would enjoy the change."

"Sure. We should be busy enough to support paying him something," Nikki responded. "I'll find time tomorrow to talk to Scott."

****

Morning rolled around. Coffee dripped into a carafe, filling the lobby with its welcome scent, toasters lined the bar, and Nikki gathered the balance of the continental breakfast. Eric arrived. As he yanked off his jacket, Nikki noticed they wore identical green Palace shirts. "Good morning. I didn't mean we were dressing exactly alike."

He shrugged. "Great minds and all that."

George Strait promised he'd make "Amarillo By Morning," and guests clattered down the stairs into the lobby for breakfast, the first guest breakfast served at The Palace by Sweet Dreams.

By five o'clock, Frank Sinatra extolled the virtues of being "Young at Heart," and the lobby brimmed with the hum of conversation and sounds of glasses clinking. Four teenagers, including Scott, huddled over the game table playing Monopoly. Eventually, guests drifted away, and Nikki put the games away and loaded the dishwasher.

Finally, Nikki dressed her dog in a miniature puffy jacket and boots, and they strolled toward the back door for Georgie's nightly walk.

****

Patrick and James sat in the library with a final glass of wine. As the back door latched, James commented, "Nikki seems happy, don't you think? For the first time in way too long tonight she laughed and sounded like the Nikki we raised."

"If The Palace makes our baby sister happy, it was

worth every penny." Patrick took a final sip of wine. "For the last few years, she couldn't get a break."

"Big challenge running a hotel alone."

"Yeah but she's never been afraid of hard work. Her enthusiasm for the town and the hotel is refreshing."

James nodded and finished his wine. "Cheers, brother." He rose and started for his room. "Sweet dreams."

Patrick chuckled, finishing his wine. "You too."

****

"Wouldn't you enjoy the walk more out front rather than in the alley and parking lot?" Police Chief Alexander Stark asked when he caught up with Nikki and Georgie as they stepped from the parking lot onto the sidewalk in front of the hotel.

"We're still searching for the perfect route." She gazed into Alex's warm brown eyes. "Georgie seems to like the parking lot. Especially the motion sensitive lights. I think she feels powerful when they light up as we pass."

"A dog with a love of clothes and power." Chief Stark nodded toward Georgie's purple puffer jacket bearing The Palace logo. They turned down Beatrice Street toward the square, their breath making small white clouds in the frosty air.

"Yep and she's going to need more outfits living in Creekside." Nikki shivered. "The weather's too cold for a little Scottsdale dog." Side by side, they walked toward the square.

"How's life at The Palace? This your first hotel experience?" he questioned as they crossed the street.

"So far it's great. As a fanciful child, I dreamed of

living in a hotel where someone else made my bed, washed the dishes, brought me food, and generally made my life one long vacation." She shook her head. "Inn keeping is not exactly like that, but I got the living in a hotel part right. Did you dream of being a police chief?"

"I had lots of dreams as a child, but I can't think of even one that had to do with being police chief in Creekside." A smile crossed his face. He nodded his head in farewell and strolled across the street, disappearing behind the county building.

"He seems like a nice man. Definitely a good looking one," Nikki commented as Alex disappeared around the corner. "But you and I, Georgie, are not getting involved with any man. Insanity is doing the same thing over and over and expecting a new result, and I am no longer insane."

They returned through the back door of The Palace, made one last check of locked doors, verified everything was ready for tomorrow's breakfast, and headed to the suite.

As she drifted off to sleep, Nikki's last thought was of Victoria Wyatt. What would she think of the changes to The Palace? The hotel came full circle when Nikki moved in and a previously married woman became the innkeeper and The Palace was her home. Sleeping soundly, Nikki dreamed of Victoria, dressed in clothing of the 1900s, standing halfway up the stairs, looking back over her shoulder with a sly smile.

****

Waking moments before the alarm, Nikki dressed quickly and woke Georgie, and they left the suite. Headed toward the back door, Georgie whined and

Nikki stopped at the sight of a woman standing before room 11, her hand raised to knock. No sound echoed from her knock, yet her form glided through the door. Victoria. Who waited inside room 11?

Although the sun just barely peeked over the horizon, Nikki exited the hotel and found Creekside awake. The rumble of voices as workers at the neighboring coffee house arrived, car doors slamming, accompanied her on her walk. Nikki waved to Mary Beth Wright, owner of Cuppa Joe.

"Excellent breakfast, Nikki. The soft opening went well," Patrick commented as he checked out. "Looks like you're a success."

Scott pulled Nikki into a hug. "Thanks, Aunt Nikki." He stepped back. "I can hardly wait for summer."

"Little sister, you make an excellent bread pudding," James added, giving Nikki a hug. "Remember, if you need me, call. I'm only a couple of hours away."

From the lobby window, Nikki watched them drive away. Once upon a time, she dreamed of love, marriage, children, and a glowing career in the corporate world. Those dreams were gone now, replaced with the sweet dream of making The Palace successful, becoming part of a community, and enjoying the independence of having no one to answer to except herself. She turned toward the stairs. Standing on the first landing, Victoria gazed directly at Nikki. The faint scent of lavender drifted in the air. The ghost smiled, then vanished.

Chapter Two

"According to the Creekside Reporter, when asked the significance of the Hotel's name, Mrs. Wyatt responded, 'If a man's home is his castle, then a woman's home should be a palace.'"
~*A Brief History of The Palace by Arthur Welles*

Heart racing, Nikki woke to a shadowy room. The desk clock blinked five thirty, still an hour until sunrise. She pulled her tired body up and tossed her legs over the side of the bed, planting her feet firmly on the floor. Nikki's gaze darted around the room, searching for the cause of her anxiety. Quiet, only the sound of her own breathing. Georgie slept curled at the foot of her bed. Thinking her cell phone might be the culprit, Nikki grabbed it from the desk. No message, but an answer. The date, March 21. One year ago today she'd held her mother's hand for the last time. Nikki brushed the tears from her cheeks and plopped down in a chair. Georgie woke and jumped from the bed, rubbing herself against Nikki's legs. Lifting Georgie in her arms, Nikki felt her dog's heartbeat and heard her soft whine. Wishing for dawn, Nikki glanced toward the window. Victoria appeared in the arms of a young man wearing a military uniform. He stepped back. They disappeared.

Nikki's eyes drifted shut and, in the place between sleep and wakefulness, the happy memories returned.

Family trips, holiday fun, Mom's calm voice from the passenger seat when Nikki learned to drive. Tears gone, she opened her eyes. Coffee's welcome smell finally drew Nikki out of the chair and forward with the day.

****

"Those came for you a couple of minutes ago, Nikki." Eric pointed toward a bakery box on the front desk. Nikki peeled a card off the top.

Chin up, little sister. She's in a better place now. Love, Patrick. Inside, a dozen mixed cookies lay in a blue tissue paper bed. Nikki's heart lifted. Munching on the mix of chocolate and sweetness of her favorite cookie, she headed to the office. An unfamiliar green plant filled the corner of her desk. She pulled a card from beneath the plant.

Eric poked his head in the office and nodded. "That came too." He ducked out and disappeared.

Nikki slid the card from the envelope. On the front, a woman dressed in safari style hung suspended by a rope off the side of a mountain. Inside, *She'd be proud of you, baby sister. Hang in there. Love, James.* Nikki pinned the card to the corkboard beside her desk and glanced at the antique mantel clock. Her phone chimed. She checked text messages. Yeah. Sheri and Sam were on their way. Nikki couldn't wait.

****

Perched on a stool behind the front desk, Nikki spotted Sheri and Sam climbing the front steps. She raced to the front door and yanked it open, opening her arms for a hug. "You made it! Welcome to The Palace." Embracing Sheri, Nikki tousled Sam's brown hair, breathing in the familiar scents of Sheri's favorite perfume and Sam's little boy smell. "It seems like forever since I've seen you, Sam. I swear you've grown at least a foot."

"Aunt Nikki, you always say that. Is Georgie here, I missed her."

"Just Georgie, not me? Well I missed you, little man. Come on, Sheri. Let's get you both settled in my apartment."

Wagging her tail and carrying a soft tug rope in her mouth, Georgie greeted them at the door. "Look, she remembers me. She's ready to play."

"Everything looks familiar; it's almost like walking into your mom's house. Does it comfort you?" Sheri asked.

"Sometimes, I almost expect her to call from the other room or be sitting at the window when I come in."

Sheri took Nikki's hand and squeezed gently. "We miss her too. Every time we walk by the old house, Sam asks if we can stop in and visit. I don't know how we would have managed without you two when Sam was born."

"Mom and I loved your visits. Even when her memory was fuzzy, she recognized Sam as a child she loved. It's great you're here." Nikki wrapped Sheri in a hug. "I need to return to the desk. Your bedroom's through that door, and there's stuff in the little fridge for snacks."

The warm scent of baking pizza greeted them when Nikki, Sheri, and Sam entered Willie's for dinner. Sam, ensconced in his booster chair, colored a cowboy hat purple in the book Sheri handed him the moment they sat down. "I've missed this," Nikki admitted. "Missed pizza with friends, time away from work."

"But it was still a good move, right?"

"Yeah. Have you been out much?"

"Some. I saw Andrea and Laurence the other night at Postino for happy hour."

Nikki frowned, "Postino happy hour doesn't sound like a Laurence type place."

Sheri raised an eyebrow. "Is there a Laurence type place? They were with other couples. I'd bet money someone else picked the restaurant. He looked a little out of place in his Armani suit."

"How's Andrea look? Did you talk to her?"

"Just for a second. She stopped at our table. As always, she looked perfect." Sheri shook her head. "What is she doing with that jerk?"

"Can't answer that. He's a subject we don't discuss even though we talk almost every week. I miss Andrea like mad, but Laurence? Not at all." Nikki paused and sipped her wine. "Speaking of missing, have you heard anything from Max?"

"Yes, finally. Still don't know where he is or what he's doing, but he claims he's okay."

"Your strength amazes me. If one of my brothers disappeared for months at a time on a mission he couldn't talk about, they'd probably have to lock me up somewhere. Otherwise, I'd be haunting the military wanting to know what was going on."

Sheri chuckled. "I can see you harassing the Department of Defense."

****

Sunday dawned a clear, cool, perfect spring day complete with chirping birds and tiny green leaves just showing up on the trees. Perfect, except way too soon. Too soon for a last breakfast together, too soon for final hugs. Tossing Sheri's suitcase in the trunk and slamming the lid, Nikki wrapped her arms around Sheri and Sam in a group hug and breathed deeply of their familiar scents. Sam escaped to his car seat and buckled himself in. A new skill since Nikki moved away. After a quick check of his work, Sheri climbed in the driver's seat, fastened her seat belt, and with a final wave drove away. Too soon.

When their car disappeared from sight, Nikki gazed up at room 15. There, partially hidden behind the lace curtain, Victoria stood, her hand resting on the glass as though she could call them back.

Night fell. Nikki closed Victoria's, grabbed Georgie, and slipped out the back door. Chief Stark joined them on the sidewalk in front of The Palace.

"Evening, Nikki. How was your weekend?" He strode beside her on the outside of the sidewalk, shortening his stride to match hers. Good manners.

"Excellent," she responded. "My godson visited."

"Ahh. Little boy with brown hair."

"Yeah. Great to have them, sorry to see them leave. How was your weekend?"

"Quiet. Just the way I like it." He nodded, turned away, and disappeared around the corner.

Nice guy, attractive, great voice, but getting involved with another man, especially someone she couldn't avoid when the relationship ended, not a good idea. She shook her head. Too bad. When his arm brushed hers even through layers of clothes, Nikki felt a spark. *Not going anywhere with that, though.* Georgie and Nikki retraced their steps.

Yanking open the heavy back door, Nikki stepped inside, Georgie plastered to her leg. Georgie whined. They stopped. The Palace lay utterly silent. Victoria stood at the door of room 11, her arm raised, hand fisted to knock. She dropped her arm and glided through the closed door. The scent of lavender lingered in the hallway. The Palace's usual sounds of creaking floorboards and muted conversations returned. Nikki pulled her master key out and approached vacant room 11. The lock clicked, and she pushed open the door. Shadows filled the room, only a soft glow from outside lights giving definition to the furniture. She flipped the light switch, chasing the shadows away. An empty room was the only thing there. Nikki turned off the lights, slipped from the room, and carefully closed the door. Local legend claimed Victoria haunted room 15, yet she appeared outside room 11 and disappeared through the closed door. In the dimension where spirits dwelled, who waited in room 11? Whom did Victoria visit?

Nikki slipped across the hall and entered her suite. Lights off, surrounded by quiet broken only by Georgie's familiar, quiet snore, Nikki slid between cool sheets into sleep. In her dream, she wore a long, yellow prom dress and slow-danced with Aaron. Their arms were around each other. She felt again the warmth of his body against hers. The scent of his Burberry cologne surrounded her, and his breath tickled her ear. "I love you; marry me."

The tinkling sound of a music box woke Nikki. In a shadowy corner, Victoria waltzed in the arms of a tall man. At the music's last strains, they disappeared, leaving behind the scent of lavender.

Chapter Three

"In 1920, two events impacted life at The Palace Hotel: women gained the right to vote and prohibition came to Creekside. Although Arizona gave women the right to vote in 1912, Mrs. Wyatt celebrated the national right to vote with a ladies-only tea party on the veranda of The Palace. The very next day liquor disappeared from the lobby bar and was replaced with an afternoon tea which, according to an advertisement in the Creekside Reporter, included three kinds of tea, finger sandwiches, and fairy cakes."
~A Brief History of The Palace by Arthur Welles

Thursday before Memorial Day arrived and so did Scott. Nikki met him at the Phoenix airport. His suitcases loaded in the truck, they drove through the city, caught the freeway, and climbed toward Creekside.

"Are you excited about spending the summer earning money?" Nikki asked as they drove through the city.

"Yeah. I was afraid Dad would change his mind about sending me here." Scott pushed the preset button, and the sounds of classic rock filled the cab.

"Why?"

"Lately, we battle over everything. He worries."

Of course he did—worry was Patrick's favorite

pastime.

"Focus on the positive. It means he loves you," Nikki pointed out.

"I know. It also means I can't do all the stuff my friends do."

"But you *can* spend the summer with me."

Scott grinned. "Yeah. That's cool. Maybe when I come home in one piece he'll chill."

"Maybe," Nikki answered. She didn't say not likely, but she thought it. "I'm sure The Palace will keep you busy. What did you do last summer?"

"Visited Mom and hated it. By the time summer ended, I was ready to go back to school."

"Ahh. So not interested in a repeat."

"Yesterday, Dad emailed her and said I would be with you for the summer. If she wants to see me, she can contact either you or me."

Nikki frowned and contemplated an unpleasant conversation with Amy. After the divorce, Nikki had little use for an ex-sister-in-law who placed her child at the bottom of her priority list. "Scott, you working with me is going to be a big help, but I understand if you want time off to see your mom."

"Don't worry about it, Aunt Nikki. My mom and her latest husband are traveling this summer. Brandon left his kids with their mother. Doubt he'd want me along." He switched the station and Lee Brice admitted, "I Don't Dance."

Sun glinted on the truck's windows as they drove Black Canyon Freeway North toward the Creekside turn off. Scott described humorous anecdotes involving learning to drive and obtaining his license. Listening to the description of his life with Patrick, Nikki flashed back to the first time she'd held Scott as a newborn. Fourteen at Scott's birth, Nikki remembered how tiny he was, how soft his skin, and the little blond fuzz on his head. Sometimes it was difficult to reconcile the tiny baby, mischievous toddler, and little boy full of enthusiasm with this six-foot-tall young man. Amy moved on to her new life and cut herself off from the past. That Amy could leave behind her six-year-old son shocked Nikki.

Nikki glided her black truck into her reserved parking spot. Scott hopped out, grabbed his bag, and followed Nikki through the hotel's back door. Nikki pulled Scott out to the front desk. "Wow. The sign's new, right?" he asked, staring at the drawing of Victoria hanging behind the bar.

Exactly the reaction she wanted. "Yeah. Hung it just last week."

"Where'd the drawing come from?"

"Local artist. Local sign shop. What do you think?"

"It's awesome." Scott turned toward his aunt. "Is that how she looks to you?"

"Yeah. How about you?"

Scott nodded. "Exactly."

After dinner, Nikki handed Scott a stack of polo shirts with *The Palace* embroidered on the left side. "Tomorrow, after breakfast in the lobby you start. This will be the longest you and I have lived together. Let's hope it's a fun experience."

"I remember living with you and Grandma the summer I turned five."

"The summer before college for me." Nikki shook her head. "My friends thought you were the cutest thing ever, and we took you everywhere."

"Fun for me. You girls knew how to have fun."

"Best nanny job I ever had. Swimming, movies, the zoo, all the stuff we wanted to do and a paycheck."

"Best summer for me. Three girls carting me all over town to do fun stuff during the day, and Grandma playing games and watching movies with me at night."

Warmth surrounded Nikki at the memory of coming home at night and finding Scott asleep on his grandma's lap, the TV turned low. "After we survive the holiday weekend craziness, we can talk about ways you can meet other teenagers. Can't work all the time."

"Do you have a life beyond The Palace, Aunt Nikki? I didn't notice you doing much besides working the last time I visited."

"Yes, I do have a life. I bet you're surprised by that." She raised her eyebrows in question. "Patrick's probably been complaining I do nothing but work!"

"You're right. Dad claims you're trapped inside The Palace with no outside interests."

She shook her head. "Not likely. Lots of entertainment in Creekside."

Memorial weekend rushed by. Since he had the youngest legs, Nikki sent Scott running up and down the stairs, showing guests to their rooms, sending their bags up and down the dumbwaiter, and running errands.

****

In the afternoon, Scott took Georgie to the square, playing with her on the grass. A beautiful, dark-haired girl walked up to him. "Is that Georgie from The Palace?"

Wagging her tail, Georgie greeted her.

"Right, this is Georgie." Scott held out his hand. "Scott Benton, Nikki's nephew."

Brown eyes gazed into his. "Casey Edgeware." Her smaller hand disappeared inside his.

He attached Georgie's leash. "Georgie and I are taking a break from the hotel business. How do you know Aunt Nikki?"

"My dad made the sign for Victoria's. Your aunt is my first paid commission."

"You're the local artist."

Casey nodded. "You're staying for the summer and working at the hotel, right?"

"Right. I should probably get back." Scott tugged gently on her leash, and Georgie moved forward. "I hope I see you again."

"Oh, you will. Creekside is so small you run into the same people all the time." Casey strolled beside him. "Friends and I are meeting tonight at Willie's Pizza at eight to celebrate the end of the school year. You should come. You'll get to meet some people from around town."

"That would be awesome! I'll come if I can. Nice meeting you. Thanks for the invitation."

With a wave, Casey turned away and Scott started Georgie down the path leading them back to the hotel.

After returning Georgie to the suite and checking her water, Scott searched the hotel for his aunt and found her in the basement folding towels. "What time am I off work tonight, Aunt Nikki? I was invited to join a group for pizza at Willie's."

"Who invited you?" Nikki grimaced at the blunt question. "I know that probably sounds like a personal question, but I'm trying to act like your parent since Patrick isn't here."

"Casey introduced herself while I played with

Georgie at the square. She invited me to join a group of her friends at Willie's. Casey said she's the artist."

"Willie's is only open until eleven on Friday so that would be fine. You can walk there. By eleven, some of the tourists have already had too much to drink, so don't get caught up in their craziness."

"Thanks, Aunt Nikki." Scott dashed up the basement stairs.

When his shift ended, Scott found Nikki in the kitchen loading the dishwasher. He gave his aunt a hug and, thinking about a tall, pretty girl with dark hair, he whistled quietly and looped toward Willie's.

****

"You made it! I'm so glad," Casey said as she made room for Scott on her right. Teenagers, including Casey, took up a large table in the back of Willie's. She introduced the others. "Pizza's on its way. Help yourself to the sodas."

They all talked at once, telling him about some of the ways they spent their limited free time in the summer. Casey and her friends kayaked on the lake, hiked through the National forest, went to movies, out for pizza or tacos, and attended anything happening on the town square. Several kids volunteered at different venues in town, including the Opera House and Welles Hall.

A girl named Lynne asked, "Has Victoria's spirit visited you yet?"

Conversation at the table stopped.

"Victoria the ghost? I've only been in the hotel since Thursday. We haven't hung out yet." Not exactly an answer, but maybe he would be labeled "weird" because Victoria appeared to him? "Have any of you seen Victoria?"

Scott's question sparked a discussion about Victoria's ghost and other ghosts supposedly haunting Creekside. Victoria was not alone in her haunting. Many of the buildings surrounding the square claimed a resident ghost, as did the Opera House and Welles Hall.

The party broke up, and Scott headed toward The Palace. Dodging tourists clustered on the sidewalk surrounding the square, Scott grinned. Maybe Creekside did have more to offer than a summer job with Aunt Nikki.

****

On Memorial Day, Nikki finally sent Scott and Georgie to the town square to enjoy the day and a big band concert. Smells from the food vendors reminded him of his skipped lunch. Walking across the lawn, Scott recognized many of the teens sprawled on the grass from his visit to Willies. He plopped on Casey's blanket and settled down with Georgie to enjoy the band. "I'm guessing this isn't your favorite style of music, yet you're all here?"

"Oh, it's not our favorite, but the concert's free." She shrugged. "The day's nice, and it gives us a place to hang out together. My dad claims exposure to all kinds of music is worthwhile, so we attend most of the concerts." A couple of young boys raced across the grass in front of them. "It's nice to be old enough I don't have to sit with my parents."

The unfamiliar music was upbeat, and Scott enjoyed the concert. Casey was certainly right about a place to hang out. By the time the music ended at six, almost all the teenagers from Willie's, plus Casey's parents and her twin younger brothers had stopped by.

Matt, Casey's dad, asked Scott what his plans were for the summer.

"Whatever my Aunt Nikki says they are."

The setting sun turned the sky shades of yellow and orange as Scott let himself and Georgie in the back door of The Palace. He returned Georgie to the suite, filled her bowls, and found Aunt Nikki tending bar in the lobby while Tim McGraw praised "My Old Friend."

"Hey, Scott, how was the concert?"

"Different, but cool."

"Scott, this is Henry Acton, the author. My nephew, Scott."

Scott greeted a distinguished-looking man sitting at the bar.

"Henry stayed here for a few weeks in spring until his condo was ready." The men shook hands. "Supper's in the Crock-Pot in the kitchen, Scott." Nikki nodded in that direction.

"All I did was eat at the concert. I'll wait until you close. Okay if I just go back to my room? Do you need me for anything, Aunt Nikki?"

"Please move the load of towels from washer to dryer. Then you can go," answered Nikki.

****

By the time Nikki closed Victoria's and the hotel, plus folded the load of towels from the dryer, it was nearly ten. She knocked on Scott's door. As they ate, Nikki asked, "What do you usually do for fun?"

"Baseball practice, surfing, hanging at the beach." He shrugged. "Dad bought a small truck I drive to school."

Remembering Patrick's ridiculous attachment to his first car, Nikki teased, "Do you miss your truck?"

"Other than school or running his errands, Dad doesn't let me drive much."

"Do the teenagers you've met in Creekside have cars?"

"Some. Mostly their parents' car. It sounds like they have more freedom than I do at home." He frowned. "Did Dad give you any idea what he expected this summer?"

"Not a word. For now, we'll just go with what I expect."

"Sounds good." He nodded.

"Beyond being a perfect hotel employee?" Nikki raised an eyebrow. "It's really just a courtesy. Ask before you borrow the car. Let me know where you're going if you go out. Please return to the hotel by Creekside's midnight curfew. If you're picked up for a curfew violation, your dad, the lawyer, will have my head. Does that sound like too many rules?"

"Nope." He shook his head. "Not at all. Dad made me promise to be no trouble and work hard."

"Even a perfect employee doesn't work all the time. I want you to enjoy the summer, too."

"Just being in Arizona in a town that advertises resident ghosts has to be fun. Add to that living in a haunted hotel, guaranteed fun."

Scott living in The Palace was a good thing. Embarrassing though, that her sixteen-year-old nephew in a single weekend enjoyed more social life than she had in her five months in town. As she prepared for bed, Nikki considered Henry's offer of dinner one evening next week. She'd no desire to fall in love again, too painful. But a return to dating, it was time. Why not begin with an author for her first date? Not like a blind date or someone she met at a bar. While Henry stayed at The Palace, they'd become friends, or at least familiar acquaintances. Any relationship with Henry had a six-month expiration date, since he rented a condo on a short-term lease, so no harm. Or at the very least any drama would end at six months.

Nikki checked the veranda, picking up empty glasses. After walking down the front steps to pick up a piece of paper stuck in the flowerpot, she glanced down Beatrice Street. A tall man wearing a bowler hat turned the corner and disappeared. Nikki gazed up at the second story veranda, glancing at the window for room 15. Framed by a lace curtain, Victoria looked out at the street, her hand against the glass. Nikki blinked. Victoria dissolved, leaving only a gently fluttering curtain behind.

Chapter Four

"On New Year's Eve, 1921, The Palace underwent another major change. The Creekside Reporter published the following announcement: 'Born 11 PM, December 31, 1921, a boy, Robert James Wellington Wyatt, to Victoria Jane Wyatt.' Although a popular overnight hotel, The Palace now housed three permanent residents, Victoria, RJ, and their dog Smokey."

~A Brief History of The Palace by Arthur Welles

What to wear on a date in Creekside? Silly to worry. Nikki perused her wardrobe one last time, hoping unrealistically that a bright new top would appear to pair with her white jeans. Tonight wouldn't be the first meal they shared. When Henry lived at The Palace for the weeks before his condo was ready, they'd shared a table for breakfast, or at least a cup of coffee frequently. On the nights she'd tended bar, Henry often plopped on a bar stool and entertained her with the hazards of researching murders. Though she didn't recall any physical spark, she found him a witty, intelligent companion. She'd read a few of his books.

Unfortunately, nothing had changed since she'd examined the contents of her closet earlier. Skinny jeans, black slacks, and casual skirts paired with colorful Palace polo shirts hung in a neat row. Dinner with Henry at Creekside Station required a different look. Her first dinner in Creekside with a single man not her relative deserved a bit of primping. Digging deeper into the back of her closet, Nikki located a pale green sheath and white sandals. Thinking of her friend Kassie, she wondered how Kassie's new husband was adjusting to living with someone who owned ninety-seven pairs of shoes. Nikki grabbed every opportunity to tease Kassie about her shoes, but she missed being able to borrow a pair for a special occasion since they wore the same size. Slipping out of her jeans, Nikki slid the green dress over her head, zipped it up, and donned her sandals. Standing before the bathroom mirror, she brushed on mascara, splashed on a little scent, added lip gloss, gathered up her clutch, and knocked on Scott's door.

"Aunt Nikki, you look great!" he said after opening to her knock.

"Thank you. Please take Georgie out for her walk tonight. Are you staying in?"

"I have some summer reading for my IB English class," Scott answered, shaking his head. "Have a great time. I'll be sure to tell Dad he's wrong about your social life." He took her hand. "And, Aunt Nikki, be sure to return by curfew."

Nikki rolled her eyes and strolled toward the lobby to the beat of Aretha Franklin's demand for "Respect." She snickered at the coincidence. With a wave to Eric, she walked through Victoria's and stepped onto the veranda. Henry pushed himself away from the veranda railing, a slow smile lighting his face. He took Nikki's hand, and suddenly Nikki was glad she chose a dress for this first date. As the sun began its descent, edging the sky with pink, they strolled three blocks to the Station through the cool evening air. Conversation and laughter surrounded them as they dodged groups of tourists. Originally a stage stop, after surviving dozens of owners, five years ago Creekside Station became a restaurant. The platform transformed into an elegant patio, and the counter a bar. Seated at a table in the corner, Henry and Nikki ordered wine.

Nikki glanced over the menu. *This has all the hallmarks of a first date, neither one of us knows how to start the conversation.* "How is your book coming, Henry? Are you finding it easier to work living in your apartment rather than The Palace?"

"Some things are better, some not. I miss the conversations with the hotel staff and guests. And breakfast. I miss breakfast. Lately it's coffee in the morning and very little the rest of the day, if the writing is going well. Otherwise, I'm grazing in the kitchen constantly!"

Nikki thought of her friend Jayne who used writing retreats to finish her books. "Do you usually stay away from home when you write?"

"No, but I'm temporarily without a permanent residence. My house in Tucson was on the market for two years when it sold a few months ago. The buyers wanted to move in quickly."

The waiter reappeared and took their orders.

Nikki sipped her wine. "I'm surprised you didn't stay in Tucson. Wouldn't that have been easiest?"

"Since I was in the middle of this book with a deadline looming, there was no time to look for a new house. My agent suggested I rent something until I could find what I wanted. Thus, the move way up here, with a stop at The Palace." Henry thanked the waiter when he placed salads on the table. "How is Scott adjusting to living in a hotel in a small town? He's from San Diego, right?"

"Scott's doing well. He already has friends his own age. So far, he hasn't expressed too much pain at being away from the ocean, I know at home he spends most of his free time surfing." Nikki slipped salad into her mouth and crunched on the fresh lettuce. "Do you have nieces and nephews, Henry?"

"No, just some cousins. Neither of my siblings have children, although my sister is expecting in a few months."

"Really? Congratulations to her. Does your family live in Tucson?"

He shook his head. "Clark went to college in California and established himself there. Jamie and her husband live in Colorado." Henry admitted, "I finally gave up on either of them returning home and that prompted my selling the house."

"I'm guessing you're the oldest, am I right?"

"How did you know?" Henry's eyes widened.

"Just like my oldest brother, you sounded completely confused about why they wouldn't move back with you." Nikki shook her head. "Patrick's biggest hesitation about joining James in investing in The Palace was accepting that it would tie me to Arizona."

"Are you originally from Arizona?"

Nikki nodded. "A native." She sipped the wine. "Will you stay in Arizona since your house sold?"

"Nothing's keeping me here, but I don't have a burning need to go somewhere else either. I travel some, researching for my books, but I haven't found anywhere that felt more like home than Tucson. How did you end up in Creekside?"

"I visited here a few years ago, actually stayed in The Palace." Nikki pictured her first sight of Victoria on the stairs. "When I figured out that I wanted to own a hotel, I started looking for opportunities and discovered The Palace for sale."

"But why such a small town?"

"The years I spent trying to figure out what I really wanted taught me I needed a sense of community in order to be happy, and small towns can provide that. How did you end up in Creekside? There are quite a few places you could have moved closer to Tucson."

After a moment's hesitation, Henry replied, "I needed a small town as one of the locations in my book. My agent remembered Creekside and, since I had neither family nor friends here, he figured focusing would be easier. Sometimes in Tucson, calls from friends and acquaintances plus invitations to events I felt I should attend distracted me. The hazard of living in the same place for too many years."

Conversation continued easily through dinner, and the earlier hesitations disappeared. Between appetizers and dessert, several local residents stopped by the table to chat, expressing pleasure in Nikki's success at The Palace, Victoria's sign, and mentioning meeting Scott. Nikki noticed she and Scott had become part of the community, as had Henry.

Under a black velvet sky sprinkled with stars, they strolled toward the hotel, holding hands. Clumps of tourists crowded the sidewalks. Music spilled from the bars surrounding the square. Glancing at the lobby when they passed The Palace, Nikki discovered Victoria's closed and only the low night-lights provided a yellow glow in the lobby. At the hotel's back door, Nikki turned to wish Henry good night and thank him for a lovely evening. Before the words formed, he leaned in, placed his hands on her cheeks, and brought his mouth to hers. Nikki relaxed into a gentle kiss, a light meeting of lips.

Henry stepped back. "Good night, Nikki."

"Thank you for a lovely evening, Henry." She turned, unlocked the door, and slipped inside.

As she passed her suite on the way to the kitchen, Nikki noticed a note on her door: *I walked Georgie. Scott.* Nikki entered the kitchen, checked on the preparations for breakfast, strolled into the lobby to check the locked front door, climbed the stairs to the veranda and checked that lock, and returned to her room. Glancing in the corner, Nikki found Georgie asleep in her dog bed. For the moment, all was right with her world. Nikki prepared for bed, crawled between the cool sheets, and fell instantly asleep.

Just before dawn, she woke to the mumble of voices. Glancing around her room, she found Georgie asleep but dreaming, her paws moving as though running. Sitting up, Nikki faced the window. Victoria stood facing Nikki, her arms around a tall man dressed in a long overcoat, her eyes peeking over his shoulder. A moment later the man stepped back, and Victoria dropped her hands to her sides. She lifted one hand and tenderly touched his cheek. They disappeared, leaving the scent of lavender in the air.

****

During the days that followed, Scott found himself

invited to join friends for pizza, tacos, or hamburgers, concerts at the square, a picnic at North Lake, and a movie at a theatre in the next town, thirty miles away. Either he walked or one of the group offered him a ride. A couple of times he offered to pay for gas, a cost he frequently split with his friends in San Diego when they shared a ride. His Creekside friends always refused, claiming their parents handled the gas bills since the cars belonged to their parents. Casey did most of the driving, claiming she exchanged babysitting her twin brothers for use of the car.

On Wednesday, the third week in June, Scott received a text from Casey.

—Call me if you're off this afternoon I have a fun job for us.—

Scott called immediately. "Hey, Casey, what job would you consider fun?"

"Ever ridden a horse, Scott?"

"Yeah, but it's been a while. Dad sent me to a horse camp for part of the summer after middle school. I've only ridden a few times since."

"Becca Stark called my dad this morning and asked me to gather a few friends and come out to Windsong Stables to exercise and groom the horses and clean up the stalls. Two of her staff are down with flu. She has a couple of trail rides and a few lessons scheduled, and she and her brother Alexander can't be everywhere at the same time," Casey explained. "Would you like to help out? Are you working this afternoon?"

"I'm off today. Let me ask Aunt Nikki and call you back."

Finding Nikki in the laundry room, Scott gained permission to visit Windsong with Casey, returned

Casey's call, and arranged to meet everyone at the square.

Ten teenagers arrived at Windsong Stables just after noon. Becca Stark greeted them with obvious relief and handed Casey a list of jobs. The group decided to work together rather than split the work up. First, they exercised the horses not going on the trail rides or involved in the lessons, groomed all the horses, mucked out the stalls, fed the animals, and gave them water. Scott knew although time riding the horses was brief, he was going to be sore tomorrow. As the sun set, Becca grilled hamburgers, turkey burgers, and hot dogs; the scent of smoke and grilling meat made Scott's stomach grumble. Becca set out fixings plus a couple of salads and chips, and the kids spread out over the porch and inhaled dinner. Dessert was ice cream and brownies. Exhausted, dirty, and sated, the group piled into vehicles and headed for Creekside.

"Have you worked for Windsong before, Casey?" Scott asked as they drove toward town.

"Of course, I learned to ride at Windsong when I was really small, and I spend quite a bit of time there riding and helping out. The year Becca decided to add trail rides, I helped out in exchange for lessons and chances to ride."

"But your family doesn't have a horse?"

"No. My dad claims there's no reason to buy a horse since Becca always lets me ride. All I have to do is drive out there, ask, and offer to help when needed." They entered Creekside and turned toward the hotel. "You're gonna be really sore tomorrow. Riding horses and mucking stalls uses very different muscles than hauling suitcases or surfing."

"You're right. It was worth it though. I really enjoyed today. Thanks for thinking of me," Scott said as he opened the car door. "Maybe I'll see you tomorrow."

"Maybe." Casey grinned. "Take care of your sore muscles."

Scott entered The Palace through the rear door and searched for Nikki. He found her in the kitchen. "Aunt Nikki, I'm back."

"Perfect timing. Would you mind moving the towels to the dryer?" Nikki turned toward Scott and chuckled. "Forget the towels. Looks like you need cleaning more than they do."

"I knew I wouldn't have to hike the basement stairs once you took a look at me. I can't remember when I've been this dirty." Scott looked down at his jeans covered in dirt. A mixture of sweat and dust darkened the fair skin on his forearms.

Thirty minutes later, Scott and Nikki settled in her sitting room. "What did you think of working at Windsong?"

"It was fun. Everyone else rides often, so I'm just glad I didn't fall off."

Nikki grinned. "How sore are you? Is it going to be hard climbing the stairs carrying luggage tomorrow?"

"Not bad yet. Mucking stalls is tough. Makes hauling luggage up the stairs look easy."

"And hauling luggage is cleaner." Nikki chortled. "I wish I'd gotten a picture of you for your dad. Did you get enough for dinner?"

"Dinner was awesome, and Chief Stark helped with the grilling and serving."

"So payment in food." Nikki shrugged. "Not a bad

currency."

"That part was a little weird. I can't imagine being served a hamburger by the Chief of Police in San Diego." He shook his head. "I'm on the schedule tomorrow, right?"

"Noon to five. You can sleep in if you like, but the plan is you will be sorting towels and helping guests with luggage. We've a nearly full house on the weekend and lots of check-ins tomorrow."

Expressing his desire to stretch his legs since he was starting to feel the effects of his day's work, Scott offered to take Georgie out for her last walk of the day. Nikki pictured Alexander Stark leading trail rides at Windsong, imagined the tall, dark chief of police on a horse. Well over six feet, broad shouldered, and dark haired, on foot Alexander was intimidating. Add the height of a horse, and he probably had no trouble keeping the guests in line.

Middle of the night she woke to whispered voices. In the shadows a tall man, a leather bag at his feet, wrapped Victoria in his arms. His words were indistinct, his tone tender, his deep voice whispered. Victoria rose onto her toes, her hands on his shoulders. She stopped his voice with a kiss. They disappeared. The scent of lavender lingered. Nikki drifted back to sleep.

Chapter Five

"The Palace became the first commercial establishment in town to offer homemade ice cream for consumption on the premises in 1924, coinciding with the opening of Creekside Movie Theatre on Center Street. Mrs. Wyatt opened her ice cream sales after movie matinees, providing a variety of flavors with movie-related names including Wild Orange, Picked Peach, Sherlock's Strawberry, and White Vanilla. According to The Creekside Reporter, 'On movie days Mrs. Wyatt may be found serving ice cream on the veranda of The Palace, RJ sitting at table enjoying the company of other children and strawberry ice cream.'"
~A Brief History of The Palace by Arthur Welles

A gentle breeze cooled the summer air, and stars filled the night sky. Live music played in the surrounding bars, creating a cacophony of sound. Alexander dodged the visitors crowding the sidewalks. They bounced from venue to venue, laughing, talking, and sometimes tripping their way along. Turning right, he moved into an alley and let his eyes adjust to the shadows. The parking lot lights flipped on then off as he passed under them. A yellow glow marked the back door of The Palace. Since Vanessa's death, he rarely dated, and never someone local. At thirty-eight, women his age usually heard the tick of a biological clock or they already had children. The thought of adding more children to his family and causing upheaval to his boys kept him away from anyone wanting a future. He didn't know what Nikki wanted other than success for The Palace.

As though conjured by his wandering thoughts, Nikki appeared, coming out the door, Georgie in her arms. She greeted him, and they strolled the sidewalk. Gossip claimed she was dating Henry Acton, but no sign of the author tonight. Georgie's white, plumed tail waved in welcome.

"It's nice to know you're checking on our neighborhood. There are so many people in town it feels like an invasion rather than a holiday!" Nikki commented as they wove their way around groups of tourists.

"So far, well behaved invaders." The sound of her voice and the dimple in her cheek raised Alexander's spirits. "Is the hotel full?"

"I could have rented out Scott's room and mine if I were willing. Do you think the guests will see the fireworks from the veranda?"

"Should have a good view." Tempted to ask her about Acton, Alex said nothing. At least the author found time to take her out to dinner. All he'd managed was "accidental" meetings when she walked her dog.

They merged with the tourists heading toward the entertainment around the square. He could ask her out now. Hearing the dispatcher's call through his headset, Alex loped off, leaving Nikki and Georgie on the sidewalk.

Picking Georgie up, Nikki reversed direction. Short

walk tonight, too many people for Georgie. A little creepy surrounded by so many strangers in the dark.

****

Scott, stretched out on the sitting room sofa, waited for her. He raised an eyebrow, and his lips tipped up in a grin. "How was your walk?"

She shrugged. "Short. Really crowded out there."

"Aunt Nikki, would it be okay if some friends and I rent movies one night this week and watch them here? The TV's not very big, but it feels like I should be returning all the invitations. They always include me in their plans."

He sounded just like Patrick, keeping it even, never taking advantage. "Sure. Pick up snacks, soda, pizza, and sandwiches. My treat. Might as well make it a party."

"Thanks, good idea. Would one day be better than another?"

"Try for a weeknight. In return, would you be willing to babysit Sam Larsen when he and Sheri visit next weekend?"

"Of course. I remember Sam from visiting Grandma. They lived a few houses away, right?"

"Right. When they came in March, we just took Sam with us, but if you don't mind watching him one evening it would give us an adult night out."

"No problem. Just remember not to schedule me to work. Don't want to be double booked."

After exchanging good nights, Nikki made her nightly rounds in the hotel. Sunday night would be the fireworks. Georgie didn't like fireworks, so her little dog would spend the holiday locked in the bedroom.

Nikki set her alarm, climbed into bed, slipped into

sleep, and dreamed. She ran through the night, dodging people on a crowded sidewalk. Alex loped ahead of her. No breath, she couldn't find the breath to shout, her heart pounded. She stopped, bent over, sucking in air.

Emma and Aaron stood in front of her. "He's gone. Just like me. Just like our baby. Just like your father. Gone."

Nikki felt a wet tongue on her face. She woke to Georgie's whine and another sunny day. Ridiculous dream. Alex didn't leave her. He wasn't hers to lose.

****

At noon, his shift over, Scott walked Georgie to the town square. He spotted Casey and several friends sitting on the grass sharing a pizza. Grabbing a slice when Casey offered, Scott joined them on the blanket.

"Are you going to the parade tomorrow, Scott?" Casey asked.

"What time does it start? Are you planning to watch it?"

"Actually, I'm in it, riding a horse from Windsong," Casey answered. "Starting time is ten."

Scott walked Georgie back to the hotel. No one he knew from San Diego rode in parades. He remembered the Rose Bowl Parade when he was eight. Squashed between his dad and Uncle James on the stadium seating, he'd envied the kids running along the parade route. When he'd decided to stay with Aunt Nikki for the summer, Scott thought he might be bored, at least when he wasn't working. He figured there would be plenty of time to complete all the reading assignments for his IB English class with time left over to explore the area. He never expected a busier social life in Creekside than the one he'd left behind in San Diego,

44

and he'd expected to miss the beach. Somehow, the beach wasn't nearly as important when he was busy with other things.

Leaving Georgie behind Sunday morning, Scott, weaving in and out through groups of tourists, headed to Center Street to watch the parade. Locals and visitors crowded both sides of Center. His height an advantage, he leaned against the Opera House just as the first strains of the William Tell Overture drifted on the wind. Creekside's mayor, riding in a blue 1956 Corvette convertible, started the parade. Historic cars, an antique fire truck, a marching band, and groups of kids on decorated bicycles wove their way along Center. Interspersed were small groups of horses. Casey, dressed in a red shirt, blue jeans, and a white hat, rode a large black horse, the small flag she carried identifying Windsong Stables. He caught her eye and winked. She winked in return and danced her horse in a circle.

As soon as the parade ended, Scott headed to Willie's to pick up sandwiches for lunch. Standing in line, he noticed a tall blond man leaving the restaurant, his hand on a woman's lower back, guiding her out the door. For a moment, Scott thought the man was his Uncle Aaron, but it couldn't be. Why would Aaron be in Creekside?

****

Darkness arrived, and many of the hotel's guests returned to either the upstairs or the downstairs veranda to watch the show. Scott dashed upstairs with snacks for the guests on the veranda, and Nikki served downstairs. Nikki remembered the fireworks of her childhood, sitting on the roof first with her older brothers assigned to keep her from falling off, and eventually sitting in a car with Aaron and friends. Now, she stood on her own veranda located not so many miles from her hometown, but very different from the city, serving snacks to friends and hotel guests as the night sky lit with an elaborate display of color. This holiday was very different and yet the same. The display ended with a final burst of color lighting the night sky, and guests drifted off the veranda.

"Did you enjoy the fireworks?" asked Nikki while she and Scott loaded the dishwasher.

"Great view from the veranda, Aunt Nikki." He shook his head. "Different seeing them over land instead of water."

****

Monday morning, another sunny July day, Nikki plopped the laptop on the front desk and calculated the receipts from Victoria's over the holiday, humming along with The Turtles' "Happy Together." She delighted in the bar's weekend success, largest holiday receipts so far. The front bell tinkling disturbed her gloating, and she gazed into the familiar gray eyes of her ex-husband.

"Hello, Aaron, welcome to The Palace Hotel. What brings you to Creekside?"

"Emma's family reunion in Freemont. Heard you bought The Palace. I wanted to tell you how sorry I was to hear about your mom."

"Thank you." Silence. As a young couple, friends labeled Aaron and Nikki chatterboxes. Now there was nothing left to say.

"Please forgive me, Nikki. I miss our friendship. We were friends before we married. You were always my best friend."

"I forgave you long ago." Nikki suddenly knew she spoke the truth. The all-consuming grief, anger, and pain of loss was replaced by acceptance and a dull ache.

"Could we be friends, Nikki?" A familiar crease appeared between his dark brows.

"Maybe friendly acquaintances." She gazed into his clear gray eyes, the corners bracketed with fine lines. A few gray hairs threaded through his sandy brown hair now. "We're not the same people."

"True. We were so young. I couldn't handle my own grief, much less yours."

"You couldn't have helped me." She shook her head. "It took my family, friends, and a therapist to get me beyond the pain."

"Are you happy being an innkeeper, Nikki? I don't remember this as one of your dreams." Sly humor lit his eyes, "Although you always did enjoy managing everything."

"Managing The Palace is perfect for me." Acknowledging his direct hit, she nodded. "How are Emma and your new baby?" She felt a pinch. He'd replaced her with Emma, and their lost child with a baby girl.

"They're good." Aaron took her hand and stared into her eyes. "Nikki, you've no idea how seeing you relieves my mind."

She accepted his sincerity. So much of her personal history was tied to this beautiful man, best friends, and first lovers. So much love and, at the end, so many tears. The Zombies sang it's the "Time of the Season" when love runs high, and she watched Aaron walk out The Palace door. The old pain and anger of watching him walk out their door surfaced. He walked away from her, their dreams, their shared grief. Before the final stamp sealed their divorce, Emma entered his life, bringing new dreams.

In the darkest hours of the night, Nikki dreamed. The twenty-one-year-old Nikki rocked slowly in her rocking chair, holding in her arms a yellow baby quilt embroidered with little animals. Tears filled her eyes. Victoria appeared, taking solid form as though walking out of a mist. Nikki suddenly felt encompassed in a comforting warmth. She woke to tears on her pillow and a warm feeling of comfort. Hints of dawn danced through the lace curtain, and her digital clock read four thirty. Too early. Eyes closing, she drifted into a dreamless sleep.

Lunching with Maggie, Mary Beth, and Shelby at the Station, Nikki debated bringing Victoria into the conversation.

"Have you met Victoria yet?" Mary Beth asked, startling Nikki from her internal dialog.

"We haven't been introduced." Not a lie, just not answering the question. "Have you seen her? You've lived in Creekside a long time, haven't you?"

"Except for going away to college, I've always lived here. But I only stayed in The Palace one time."

"Your honeymoon?"

Mary Beth shook her head. "Not likely. In a small town the only way to have privacy on your honeymoon is to leave town." She sipped her tea. "When I was small, my great grandmother visited, and I spent one night with her at The Palace. I considered it a big treat to have a sleepover in a hotel. Since Granny T died the following year, I would be more likely to find The Palace haunted by good memories rather than

Victoria's ghost."

"Mary Beth, living in Creekside your whole life, you can't claim you've never seen a ghost," Maggie teased. "That's disloyal to all of us who depend on tourists for our livelihood."

Mary Beth rolled her eyes. "I didn't say I'd never seen a ghost. Victoria's not the only spirit in town."

"Hey, even the *Reporter* claims a resident spirit," Shelby pointed out. "Victoria's probably Creekside's most famous spirit because there's a lot of information available about her life."

"True," agreed Maggie. "Almost all the historic buildings in Creekside claim at least one spirit."

"After the Hansens left and before you arrived to reopen the hotel, I thought I saw someone at one of the upstairs windows," admitted Mary Beth. "In fact, I was so sure someone was inside the hotel I called Jackson and Chief Stark and asked them to come over and make sure no one had broken in. By the time they arrived, the person in the window had disappeared. They searched the hotel from attic to basement and found no sign of anyone."

Of course, comments about the various businesses going out of business or changing ownership followed the discussion of the hotel's brief vacancy. The biggest concern was the Creekside Reporter and Michael Stone's decision to retire. Nikki wondered aloud if the employees involved in the buyout would be open to help from James and Patrick since the only local attorney was representing Mr. Stone. The others commented the employees would probably appreciate any help they could get.

Strolling toward The Palace, Nikki thought about

Mary Beth's vision in the window. Was the vision Victoria? Was Victoria lonely when the hotel was vacant? After all, she spent her adult life living at The Palace, surrounded by people. When Judge Welles inherited The Palace from Victoria, what did he do with her personal effects? Was Arthur Welles a relative of Judge Welles, was that relationship the reason Arthur wrote the history? Someday, maybe during the quieter winter season, Nikki planned to research Victoria and her relationship to Judge Welles. Aaron's sudden appearance explained Nikki's dream but provided no explanation of the other times Nikki saw Victoria. Entering The Palace through the rear door, Nikki immediately forgot Victoria and Judge Welles as she encountered the chaos of living in a hotel filled with strangers.

Georgie's excited barks were the first clue things had changed sometime during Nikki's lunch. A trained service dog, Georgie barked only when she or her person were threatened. Pounding on the door of room 10 was a young boy dressed in jeans and a red T-shirt. As the hotel's rear door slammed shut, he stopped pounding long enough to glance at Nikki. Calmly, Nikki gave the command "Stop," and Georgie immediately became silent, only a faint whimper indicating her disgust at the situation. Before the boy could begin pounding again, Nikki stared him in the eye and said, "Stop now." Suddenly, there was quiet. "Why are you pounding on the door?"

"Because I want the dog to bark," replied the boy.

"Why are you in my hotel?"

"We're staying here."

"Go to the lobby now and introduce me to your

family." Nikki herded the boy toward the front desk. She found Scott standing on the first step of the stairs, discouraging a toddling baby from climbing them. Eric was behind the desk talking to an obviously frustrated man. Young children climbed on the furniture, and adults, doing their best to ignore the children, filled the lobby. "Eric, what's happening?"

"Stupid here needs to give us rooms," replied the man.

"Does this gentleman have a reservation, Eric?"

"No, Ms. Benton." Eric shook his head. "No reservations for any of Mr. Walters' group."

Turning to face Mr. Walters and looking him directly in the eye, Nikki stated, "There are no rooms available for your group, Mr. Walters. I suggest you try St. George Hotel, as they are a much larger facility. If you will tell Eric how many rooms you need and how many adults and children in your group, he'll call St. George Hotel and ask if they have any vacancies."

"Who are you to tell me you have no rooms?" shouted Mr. Walters. "Dump like this can't possibly be full."

"Mr. Walters, I own The Palace. If you would like us to call St. George Hotel please provide your numbers to Eric," responded Nikki quietly. "Otherwise, please leave."

In the blink of an eye, Mr. Walters grabbed Nikki's arm and started shaking her. "How dare you talk to me like that, you bitch!"

Meanwhile, Scott yanked his cell phone out of his pocket and dialed 911, speaking quietly as he let the dispatcher know what was happening.

"Let go of this woman," Chief Stark demanded as

he entered the lobby. Approaching Mr. Walters from behind, he pulled Mr. Walters' hands behind his back and cuffed him. "Tell me what is happening, Ms. Benton, beyond what I could see."

Nikki watched Deputy Corbin pull the squad car in front of The Palace. He took the stairs two at a time, nodded toward Nikki, and after a brief conversation with Alexander, took Mr. Walters away, locking him in the back seat of the police car. Alex told the others to sit quietly until he released them. The women gathered their children, and the lobby was quiet. When Nikki, Eric, and Scott had given their statements and the others had provided names and IDs, Alex left and the group of women and children dispersed. Eric apologized for not being able to protect Nikki. She shook her head.

"You're not a bodyguard. Not your fault."

That night both James and Patrick called, asking for full details and wanting to know what Nikki intended to do to avoid this happening again. Nikki listened to their concerns, reassuring them the police department responded immediately and that she was fine, only an ugly bruise on her arm. Both brothers pushed Nikki to expand her staff so she would not be in the hotel alone. Nikki refused.

Comforted by her soft blanket, hot herbal tea, and her favorite quilt, Nikki drifted off to sleep. Just before dawn, she woke to the low rumble of a male voice in the shadows. "Take this." He reached out a hand toward Victoria. "Keep it in your pocket."

Victoria reached out, and a man wearing a long coat dropped a very small gun in her hand.

"A gambler's pocket pistol." Victoria laughed. "I'm not a gambler."

"It's a gamble, Vicky. Every time you offer a room, serve a drink, you're gambling."

She slid the pistol into her pocket. He took her hands and pulled her into his arms.

"Be safe, love."

They disappeared.

Chapter Six

"An advertisement copied from The Creekside Reporter: 'Join us Sunday May 29th at The Palace Hotel in celebration of Charles Lindbergh's solo transatlantic flight completed May 21, 1927, for a model-airplane-making party and contest. Contest is open to children ages 5 through 12; the party is open to everyone. Purchase models beforehand at Greene's General Store and complete them on The Palace veranda May 29. Food, drink, games, and the contest will begin at noon. Proceeds benefit Creekside High School Scholarship Fund.'"

~A Brief History of The Palace by Arthur Welles

"Everything okay in here?" Nikki asked, smiling at Scott when she opened the sitting room door looking for Georgie and found her on the sofa sleeping between Casey and Scott.

"Perfect. Don't worry, we'll clean up soon. The movie's almost over."

Teenagers lounged on the floor and four sat around the small dining table, focused on a game of Monopoly. Empty pizza boxes littered the coffee table. Scott glanced away from the TV and woke Georgie.

"Time to go out."

Georgie lifted her head, stretched, then bounced off the sofa heading for Nikki.

"No problem." Nikki and Georgie headed toward the back door. Strolling down the alley, through the parking lot to the front of the hotel, they headed down Beatrice Street toward Center. Warm summer air caressed her cheeks, scents of food cooking and music greeted her. How fast the weeks of Scott living in the hotel passed. Scott never appeared homesick or bored, even though he had arrived in town knowing no one but her. She hoped he returned next summer.

She turned the corner onto Center Street and gazed into familiar chocolate eyes. Chief Stark matched his stride to hers. "How are you, Nikki? Is the bruise gone?"

"Absolutely." Nikki rolled up a sleeve, revealing clear skin. "No lasting mark at all." They walked side by side around the square. "What became of Mr. Walters and his group?"

"When I arrested him, I ran a check on his finger prints and found he was wanted in New Mexico for aggravated assault and he'd failed to show up in court after being bailed out." Alexander shook his head. "New Mexico is coming for him. I don't know what happened to the rest of the group. After he was arrested, they just disappeared."

"I felt bad we couldn't handle an unhappy guest on our own, but I was certainly glad to see you walk through that door." Nikki shook her head as they dodged a group stopped in front of the Opera House. "It sounds like that wasn't the first trouble he caused that escalated to violence."

"Nikki, never hesitate to call the police if a guest gets out of control. This is a small town, and we realize sometimes you're alone in the hotel and might need back up, even if a crime hasn't been committed." Alexander paused. "Think of us as neighbors, not just cops, neighbors you can count on."

"I appreciate that, Chief. I lived alone for several years and then with my mom, and I don't remember being much concerned about safety even in Scottsdale." Nikki frowned. In Scottsdale, locking the doors at night and having a motion light at the front door seemed like enough precaution. "What's different is The Palace welcomes perfect strangers into my home, a rather disconcerting feeling. I wonder how Victoria handled living in the hotel for twenty years."

"Legend has it Victoria Wyatt carried a derringer in the pocket of her skirt and was a crack shot." Alexander chuckled. "While you could surely pass the background check for a concealed weapon in Arizona, I doubt that's a good option for you."

"No, somehow I don't see myself as armed and dangerous." Nikki shook her head.

****

Meanwhile, Casey and Scott discussed Scott's imminent return to California. "Will you return to The Palace for school holidays and next summer?"

"I hope so, at least next summer." Scott took her hand. "Dad and Aunt Nikki have the final say. Will you call and email me when I go home? I'm going to miss everyone, but you especially. I'd like to know what you're doing."

"Of course." Casey leaned against his shoulder. "And you promise to call me sometimes too."

"Everyone made me feel welcome in Creekside, and although I miss the ocean, I had fun. School, studying, and baseball practice are going to seem easy after working with my aunt. I worry about her being in the hotel at night without me."

Casey frowned. "Did your dad panic after the altercation with Mr. Walters?"

"He started to, but then he talked to Chief Stark and accepted he couldn't do anything about what happened. Aunt Nikki wants to take a few self-defense courses, though." He chuckled. "She told me the feeling of being helpless didn't agree with her."

Eventually, Nikki and Georgie returned to The Palace, and after dropping Georgie off in the sitting room with Scott and his friends, Nikki headed to her office to work on the accounts. While her laptop came alive, Nikki unlocked the safe, removing *A Brief History of The Palace Hotel*. Glancing through the chapters, Nikki found no mention of Victoria's gun; either Arthur Welles didn't know about it, it was just a legend, or it was knowledge he wasn't willing to share. The relationship between Victoria Wyatt, Arthur Welles, and Judge Welles was still a mystery. Just as Nikki returned the book to the safe, her cell phone rang with the ringtone "Friends in Low Places" Sheri Larsen had chosen years ago.

"Hi, Sheri, how are you?"

"I'm great, Nikki. And before you ask, so is Samuel," Sheri offered. "In fact, Samuel is the reason I called."

Nikki pictured three-year-old Samuel Nicolas Larsen, his tousled hair and stubborn chin. "Whatever you want for Sam just let me know. I'd do anything for my precious godson and you know it."

"This favor is for both Sam and I, Nikki. I'm working with a lawyer tomorrow about my will."

"How can I help, Sheri? You're not ill or anything, right?"

"Totally healthy. No worry about that. Nikki, are you okay with being Sam's guardian if something happens to me?"

"Of course. I adore Sam. Remember how Mom's eyes lit up every time you brought Sam to visit?" Nikki pointed out. "Even when her hold on the present started to fail, she remembered how to hold a baby."

"Oh, Nikki, I miss your mom." Nikki recognized the break in her voice. "I pray I can be as loving and compassionate as she was."

"Me too. In answer to your question, I'd love to be Sam's guardian. Just remember I plan on both of us watching him grow. But what about your brother?"

"Max is career army; that's not the life I want for Sam." Sheri had grown up on army bases all over the world. When she bought the house next door to Nikki's mom, she told Nikki that was it, her very last move no matter what.

Scott stuck his head in the office doorway, letting Nikki know his friends were on their way out and he was going to walk Casey home. Nikki waved him on and remembered those heady high school days of first love with Aaron as he walked her to her mom's front porch after a date. Fortunately, it appeared Scott and Casey were more friends than a couple; of course, that was how her relationship with Aaron had started. Scott and Casey were unlikely to see each other much over the coming year, and so many things could change in that length of time.

****

"We're here, Auntie Nikki," Sam announced as he

raced into the lobby, his mother a few steps behind pulling her wheeled suitcase.

"You are, and I'm so happy to see you." Nikki reached out and gathered Sam in her arms for a hug, enjoyed the feel of little boy wiggles and the scent of boy and soap. "I can hardly wait to show you who's visiting me."

"Can I see Georgie first? We brought her a new toy." Sam bounced from foot to foot in his excitement.

"Perfect. Let's go see Georgie." When they walked into the suite, Georgie raced to the door, her tail wagging. "Sheri, you remember my nephew, Scott."

Scott walked over to shake hands.

"Sam, looks like you brought Georgie a new toy." Scott kneeled down, and he and Sam took turns playing tug with Georgie.

Friday night, Scott settled on the floor of Nikki's sitting room with Sam. Chutes and Ladders was spread out before them, their game already in full swing. "Aunt Nikki, is it okay if I take Sam to the square tomorrow while you and Sheri are at the wine tasting? Casey's going to be there with her brothers."

"That's a good idea. Okay with you, Sheri?"

Sheri's brow crinkled in concern. "Fine. Are her brothers Sam's age?"

"A little older. It'll give Sam a couple of playmates."

After brief goodbyes to Sam, Nikki and Sheri walked out of the hotel into the warm night, joining clumps of tourists strolling around the square. "You're sure Sam will be okay with Scott at the square tomorrow?"

"Between Scott and Casey he should be fine. I

don't know how much babysitting Scott does, but Casey's responsible for her brothers a lot." Seated across from Sheri on the patio of the Highwayman, Nikki gazed into her friend's sad eyes. "Now, tell me what's going on. When you called to say you were coming, you sounded upset."

"Not upset exactly, just sad. After I talked to you about Sam's guardianship, I called Max to let him know what I decided."

"So your brother thought he should be Sam's guardian?"

Sheri shook her head, her lips turned down. "No. That's the sad part. Max says he'll probably never have a home or family. Or at least not until the army throws him out."

"So he understood exactly why he wasn't Sam's guardian."

"Yeah," Sheri agreed. "For Max, all that matters is the next assignment, the next training, the next war, the next promotion. He's so much like our father."

"You told me once that until college you felt rootless. That you had no home."

"It's true. I lived on campus four years, and that was the most secure I ever felt. When I found myself pregnant, I promised my baby he'd have roots."

After dinner, they walked back to the hotel. Approaching the front door, Nikki looked up and stopped. In the window stood Victoria, her hand against the glass. Nikki touched Sheri's hand to gain her attention, "Look up at the window," she whispered.

"Oh. I see her too." At Sheri's last word, Victoria vanished. They climbed the steps and entered the hotel. When they reached the suite, they opened the door and found Scott and Sam asleep on the floor. Their game was spread across the rug, Georgie standing guard.

They talked through Saturday's wine tasting. When they returned to the hotel, Scott and Sam waited, stretched out on the floor watching an animated movie. Through dinner, Sam regaled them with stories about his new friends, Justin and Jason. Exhausted, he fell asleep as soon as his head hit the pillow.

Nikki waved from the veranda as Sheri and Sam drove away on Sunday. In her quiet suite, she discovered an abandoned toy truck, a game piece from Chutes and Ladders, and one blue little boy sock. If her life had followed the original plan, the sound of childish giggles would fill her home. At twenty-one she'd had everything planned. A career, a husband, and at least two children by the time she was thirty. Instead, silence filled her suite in a haunted hotel, only the clicking of Georgie's toenails on the oak floor reminding her she wasn't alone. By ten thirty, exhaustion claimed her, and she slid gratefully between clean, white sheets. The drifting scent of lavender and angry voices pulled her from dreams. In a shaft of moonlight, Victoria faced a bearded man, his hands raised. "Come on, lady; you don't want to shoot me."

"I will, though. Get out." A small gun in Victoria's hand glinted in the moonlight. A low growl from the man, stomping boots, slamming door. Victoria slid the gun into her pocket and disappeared.

****

Ten thirty Thursday morning, Patrick arrived at The Palace. Eric was handling the checkouts, and as soon as Patrick placed his bag in Scott's room, he joined Nikki in the kitchen.

"How was your drive, Patrick? You must have left before dawn to be here already!"

"Definitely an early start, but I was ready to leave San Diego and my office." Patrick shook his head. "Sometimes the only thing I dislike about being a lawyer is the clients. I'm meeting with Mr. Stone's attorney today, and I needed to verify the employee group is clear on what's included in the contract of sale."

Hesitantly, Nikki inquired, "Have these clients been any particular trouble, Patrick?" *I hope not since this was my idea.*

"No. It's surprising how cooperative with each other and with me they've been." Patrick headed to Scott's room to shower and change. Nikki released a breath of relief that Patrick had no regrets about working with the Reporter's employees.

"Is my dad here?" Scott asked when he returned from walking Georgie.

Nikki nodded. "He's getting ready for a meeting this afternoon at the paper. Why are you carrying Georgie?"

"We came in the front way instead of the back today. It seemed a good idea to carry her through the lobby." Scott grinned and set the dog on the floor. "Anyway, Georgie gave it a good try but couldn't quite pull her backside up when her front paws were on the step above. What do you need me to do, or am I off until check in?"

"You can start today at two thirty. Be sure to fill in your hours on the time card."

After putting Georgie in her bed in the sitting room, Scott opened his door and found his dad tying a tie.

"There you are. I'm on my way to a meeting at the newspaper, but are you free for dinner tonight?" Patrick asked.

"Sure, Dad, where did you want to go? The Station has solid food according to Aunt Nikki." Scott caught his father's eye, and Patrick raised an eyebrow. "She went there on a date. It's close enough to walk and somewhere I haven't been."

"Works for me. Make a reservation for seven?"

Patrick headed toward his meeting. Long emails and phone negotiations filled the summer, and this should be the final meeting until the sale of the property cleared. Patrick's phone and email conversations with Shelby and the other employees spanned the summer. Today would be the first face-to-face in two months.

Shelby greeted Patrick as he entered the Creekside Reporter. Thirty minutes flew by as they discussed the final details. Then Mr. Stone and his attorney, Jason Henderson, arrived, everyone signed the final papers, and the Creekside Reporter officially belonged to an employee group. When the others had filed out of the conference room, Shelby and Patrick gathered the last of the papers and headed toward the door.

"May I take you out tomorrow night for a drink and dinner, Shelby, to celebrate the signing?"

"I would love that." Shelby shook her head. "But I really should be taking you out. Your help made all the difference in the buyout."

"It's what I do. Negotiate contracts," Patrick admitted and lifted his shoulder in a shrug. "Is there somewhere you would particularly like to go tomorrow? I'm taking Scott to the Station tonight."

"Let's have dinner at Wellington's." Shelby looked up from the papers as she plopped them on her desk. "It's within walking distance of The Palace but not in the square. Will a reservation for seven work?"

Patrick agreed. As he strolled toward the hotel, he yanked off his tie, stuffing it in his pocket. The midday summer sun warmed the back of his neck, and he covered his eyes with Oakley sunglasses. Weaving between clumps of tourists blocking the sidewalk, Patrick cut across the square. Looking around at Creekside, the square, the commercial buildings, all of them built in the styles of buildings a hundred years ago, and people out walking in the summer sun, suddenly Patrick understood what lured Nikki to Creekside. Rather than looking like a movie set, Creekside looked and felt like a place where people still knew their neighbors and cared what happened to them. A safe place to walk your dog and greet strangers. Although he and Scott talked almost daily, Scott said nothing about his attachment to Creekside. Would he want to return for school holidays and next summer? He hoped he could get a feel for what Scott wanted as well and find an opportunity to let Scott know what Amy said last week when she called. Patrick headed to his room to change.

"Hey, Dad, will you join us in the sitting room for lunch?" Scott poked his head in the door. "Aunt Nikki put chili in the Crock-Pot, and there are corn bread muffins."

The spicy scent of chili tantalized him when Patrick opened the door for Nikki. "Is this how you managed to feed Scott, Nikki?" Patrick took the tray and carried it to the table.

"Not always. It embarrasses me to admit the number of takeout lunches and dinners. Our schedules frequently conflicted, and he ate a substantial number of meals with his friends."

"Scott's old enough to fend for himself." Patrick shrugged. "You shouldn't be embarrassed about using takeout."

"Yeah," admitted Scott, "Dad and I are takeout pros, right?" He grabbed a corn bread muffin from the basket and slathered it with butter. "Of course, takeout can't compare to your cooking, Aunt Nikki."

Nikki and Scott entertained Patrick with anecdotes about the various guests they encountered over the summer, including the slightly drunk couple who kept punching in the wrong code for the front door until Nikki finally heard the racket and let them in. Then there was the occasional guest who wanted room service. Scott cleaned up the dishes. Patrick slipped into their room and changed into jeans and a golf shirt. Plopped in a comfortable chair in the lobby, he opened a mystery he'd brought. Before he could immerse himself in the twisted plot and tricky clues, he was distracted by the choreography of Nikki and Scott greeting guests, checking in, transporting luggage. Nikki handed a key to a young man checking in. The low rumble of his response reached Patrick, though the words were indistinct. Surprise lit Nikki's face, and she laughed aloud, the happy sound filling the lobby. Patrick smiled in response. Yeah, to hear Nikki's laugh was worth their investment in The Palace.

A world dressed in twilight greeted them when Patrick and Scott strolled toward the Station. Children raced across the grassy square, music poured from restaurants and bars, the enticing scents of cooking food combined with the subtle scents of perfume as they moved around groups of people in intense discussions of what to do next.

Walking down Beatrice Street, Patrick commented, "Looks like you and Nikki have an effective routine. Are you interested in working at the hotel again next summer?"

"Yeah. Aunt Nikki's a tough boss," Scott claimed with a grin. "But she says I'm a natural innkeeper."

"From what your mom told me a few days ago, she won't be demanding you visit her."

Scott frowned. "What did Mom say?" They turned toward the Station.

"She and her new husband are moving to England for Brandon's job. She invited you to spend your last two years of high school with them. Are you interested?"

"No way." Scott shook his head. "After going on vacation with them the one time I know what would happen. I'd be a convenient babysitter for his kids. His kids are little monsters, old enough to have some manners but spoiled rotten."

"Well, I promised I'd ask." Patrick shrugged. "So you'd rather spend summer in Creekside, Arizona, than London, England."

"Could I?"

At the Station, seated with menus, Patrick asked Scott if he finished the reading for his upcoming IB class and they discussed the books. Patrick paid attention to Scott's opinions and encouraged him to voice his reasons. He enjoyed Scott's younger take on some of the classic stories. Their views frequently diverged, but since they'd started discussing books as soon as Scott held his first picture book, their differences brought color without animosity to their discussions. Listening to Scott's intelligent, thoughtful opinions, Patrick thanked whatever quirk in her makeup pushed Amy to leave Scott behind when she deserted their marriage.

The golden glow of the Victoria's lights and the mellow sound of Frank Sinatra crooning "Summer Wind" welcomed them when Scott and Patrick returned to The Palace. Nikki nodded a greeting from behind the bar and returned her attention to a couple ensconced on barstools, wine glasses in hand and a local map spread before them. Plopping in a comfortable chair in the library, Patrick looked at Scott. "What are your plans tomorrow, Scott?"

Scott lounged on the sofa and pulled a paperback off the table. "If it's okay, after my shift a bunch of friends and I are meeting for tacos, then going to the concert on the square and a late movie."

"You're going to miss all your new friends when we return home." Patrick chuckled. "I never thought you'd create a whole new life for yourself in Creekside."

Scott shrugged. "It's an easy place to fit in. People go out of their way to include new people in everything going on," Scott admitted. "You should've been here at the Independence Day celebrations. The population tripled, and everyone was determined to have a good time."

"Do your new friends work during the summer?"

"Yeah, usually in a family business. Plus, most of my friends have known the adults in town all their lives, so even if they are not truly related, they act like they could be, helping out when needed and meeting on the square for events."

Patrick enjoyed his enthusiasm. "It sounds like you appreciate the small town lifestyle, Scott."

"Definitely. I was never bored and rarely alone. Not like at home where we waste a lot of time deciding what to do and how to get there; even going to the beach required strategy until I got my license. Here, I didn't even miss my car. The only time I drove was running errands for Aunt Nikki."

"Will coming home be difficult?"

"Maybe." Scott frowned. "I'm ready to see my friends and start school. I haven't had much time for baseball this summer, so I'm ready to play again." Patrick and Scott headed to their room and put a baseball game on TV.

****

Nikki watched her brother and nephew walk down the hall. Only a few days and Scott would be gone. Her life in the hotel would change when she and Georgie were the only residents.

Nikki prepared to lock the front door for the night. Her guest was still reading in the lobby, and Nikki verified she needed nothing from the bar, and then locked the front door. She knocked on the door of room 8, letting Patrick and Scott know she was taking Georgie out and, after declining their invitation to accompany her, Nikki entered the sitting room, woke Georgie from her nap, attached the leash, and headed out the back door for their nightly walk. The leaves in Creekside changed in late October, but fall was already in the air as families enjoyed this last long weekend before school started. A frenzy of activities for visitors of all ages filled the Labor Day Holiday.

Walking out of the parking lot and onto the sidewalk on Beatrice Street, Nikki noticed Alexander Stark walking toward her. Georgie waited patiently beside Nikki as Alexander approached.

"How are you and Georgie handling the holiday weekend?"

"So far things are great." They strolled down Beatrice Street. "The Palace will be full by tomorrow night, my second weekend of one hundred percent occupancy."

"And family visits for the weekend."

"Patrick's here. He and Scott will return to San Diego on Sunday. Monday will be my first major holiday checkout without Scott's help. How are the visitors behaving?"

"Traditionally, this is a family holiday." Alexander shrugged. "The activities are geared to a calmer crowd than the rodeo rowdies we host in July. The kayak race at North Lake and the mountain bike race on Juniper Trail both draw big crowds, but that group seem to be able to have a good time without getting out of control."

"Are Colin and Mitch ready to return to town?"

"Windsong is booked for the weekend with campouts and trail rides, and my boys are out there helping." He chuckled. "It's not going to be easy for them to return to school." He shook his head. "They'd rather spend their days with the horses."

"Does Becca offer lessons in the fall?" Nikki asked, and they walked around a clump of tourists standing in line at Willie's. "I'm thinking about taking a few. I haven't ridden in years, and I need to find ways to escape The Palace."

"What days do you have off? I'm guessing no weekends?"

"Not Friday or Saturday." Nikki shook her head. "But usually I can manage a Sunday afternoon."

"Come out to Windsong next Sunday afternoon," Alexander suggested. "I'll be out there with the boys, and we'll go for a ride. That way you can see what you remember before you sign up for lessons."

"Hey, I appreciate that." Surprise lifted her voice. Was this a date?

"Can you be there around three?"

After agreeing to meet Alexander at three next Sunday at Windsong, they walked toward The Palace. At the back door, Nikki turned to wish Alexander good night. He reached for her, pulling her gently into his arms. She looked up, reading desire in his chocolate brown eyes. She melted against him, comforted by the strength of his arms, the beating of his heart. The familiar male scent of aftershave and soap drifted on the air. Her own desire rose, a feeling she thought lost in the aftermath of her failed marriage. He stepped back, leaned in, and kissed her, first a brief meeting of lips, then a questing tongue. Ending the kiss, he placed his hand gently against her cheek.

"Sunday, Windsong. It can be our first date."

"Sunday. Good night, Alex." Nikki opened the door. Alex tipped his hat and walked away.

In the sitting room, Nikki bent down and released Georgie. When she straightened, in the corner of the room stood Victoria holding the hand of a small boy. At their feet lay a large, dark gray dog. Victoria and the boy smiled suddenly, a light flashed, and they disappeared.

Chapter Seven

"'Its veranda decorated with airplanes and its lovely proprietor dressed in clothing designed by Ms. Earhart, The Palace hosted a benefit luncheon on May 22, 1932. Celebrating the first solo transatlantic flight completed by a woman aviator; proceeds from the event will be donated to the Creekside High School Scholarship Fund,' reported Andrew Stone, editor, the Creekside Reporter."

~A Brief History of The Palace by Arthur Welles

"What's up with your brother and my sister-in-law?" Eric stared out the lobby window, a clean wine glass in one hand, a polish towel in the other.

Nikki filled a bowl with snack mix and shook her head at his worried frown. The veranda's lights glinted on Patrick's blond hair as he stood and walked toward Shelby, meeting her at the bottom of the steps. Shelby, wearing a flowy peach dress and heeled sandals, looked up and took his hand. Two blond heads passed beneath the veranda's twinkling lights. "As far as I know, just a celebratory dinner. Yesterday the deal for the Reporter finalized."

"Isn't he a little old for Shelby? How old is Patrick?" Eric glared as Shelby looped her arm through Patrick's.

"Shelby's over twenty-one, right?" Nikki set the

filled bowl on a table. "I think she's the only one who can decide if Patrick's too old. After I ranted and raved about James and Patrick interfering in my social life, no way do I want to interfere in Patrick's."

Eric glared at the couple now disappearing in the crowd on the sidewalk. "When I married Charlotte, I felt I inherited older brother duties since Charlotte is the oldest. I'll ask Charlotte what she thinks."

"Fair enough." Nikki patted his shoulder. "Just don't think to get me involved."

****

His hand on the small of her back, Patrick guided Shelby around clumps of tourists. "Do you feel any different about your job, Shelby, now you're the owner?"

"Yeah. Instead of worrying about losing my job because the paper closed, now I'm worrying about managing the paper so we all have a job." Shelby shook her head, the action setting her delicate earrings dancing.

Amused at her disgruntled attitude, Patrick commented, "I gather running your own newspaper wasn't your long-range plan."

"Long-range plan included working my way up to editor, not suddenly owning the newspaper." Shelby shook her head and shrugged. "Now I'm a reporter-owner, whoever heard of such a thing?" She frowned. "I don't think any of us were prepared for leading by committee. How do you make major decisions with James and Nikki about Sweet Dreams?"

Patrick remembered the heated sibling negotiations involved in creating Sweet Dreams. "Our situation's a little different. All three of us have an equal financial investment, but Nikki makes the decisions. James and I suggest, but Nikki is always the deciding vote."

"Wow, good for Nikki. How'd she manage to arrange veto power?"

"Nikki approached James and I about helping her arrange financing to purchase a hotel." Patrick remembered their surprise. They didn't even realize she wanted to be an innkeeper. "James and I decided to combine our portion of the inheritance with Nikki's and create Sweet Dreams. Nikki accepted our money only with an agreement that she alone made final decisions about operating The Palace." Oh, the battles that raged. Nikki wanted complete control. Her brothers as partners sounded like no control to her.

"Very clever of Nikki." Shelby frowned. "I can't picture my family trusting me to make all the decisions involving their money."

"Of course, James and I still give her advice," Patrick admitted. "Sometimes when she'd rather we didn't and certainly about subjects that are none of our business. But that would've been the case even if we hadn't been financial partners. I guess it's just part of being older brothers."

"Has Nikki always been in the hotel business?"

"No." Patrick shook his head. "She was a commercial insurance underwriter. A very successful one who started right out of college as a trainee with a large company. She rose to a senior underwriter position by the time she was twenty-six."

"That's a big change, insurance to innkeeper."

"We were shocked when Nikki asked our help financing the purchase of a hotel."

Patrick and Shelby reached Wellington's on

Charles Street and entered the restaurant through ornate double doors. Greeted by a smiling host dressed in classic black and white, they followed their host to a table by the window.

"When you're not running a newspaper, what do you do with your free time?"

The waiter arrived and poured the wine.

"Hiking, yoga, college classes on-line. Plus, Creekside has something going on at the square nearly every weekend." Shelby sipped the wine. "How do you spend your time?"

"Running on the beach, working out, surfing." Patrick shrugged. "The ocean was the big attraction when I moved from Arizona. Sixteen years later, it's still a draw." The waiter placed ravioli appetizers on the table. "Have you lived in Creekside long?"

"About fifteen years. We moved here when I started high school." Shelby lifted a crispy ravioli from the plate. "Charlotte and I both fought the move."

"Where are you from originally?"

"San Diego, and yes, we missed the ocean every day. Creekside grows on you, though. At least it did for us."

Walking back to The Palace, they continued their conversation, comments now interspersed with a comfortable silence. Patrick gazed at this beautiful young woman, surprised they found so much to talk about. "Would you like to go somewhere else for a drink, or should I drive you home?"

Shelby shook her head. "That's so sweet. No need, I parked my car in the hotel lot. I need to get home since I'm working early tomorrow morning. Will you be at the concert on the grass tomorrow afternoon? If so, I'll look for you."

"I'll be there. Probably with Nikki and maybe Scott. Although, Scott's spending as much time with his friends as possible."

They reached Shelby's blue SUV, and she unlocked the door. Patrick wrapped his arms around her, pulling her close, and putting his lips to hers. Shelby melted into the kiss. Patrick pulled back slowly, "Thank you for joining me for dinner, Shelby; drive safe."

Thanking Patrick for dinner, Shelby slid into the driver's seat, placed the key in the ignition, and drove away. Patrick watched her go. Awesome kiss, but way too young. He sighed.

****

"How was dinner at Wellington's, Patrick?" Nikki asked as he walked into the kitchen. "I've never eaten there. Is it as good as the reviews claim?"

"The food's excellent. It's a beautiful night, and the view from the patio was fantastic. Was Victoria's busy?"

"Victoria's did very well. When the weather's good, our veranda is a popular place for a pre-dinner drink."

"Is Scott back?"

"No, not yet." Nikki shook her head. "They were going to Manuel's, then a movie. Knowing how controlling you were with James and I, providing boundaries for Scott and letting him have fun wasn't easy. He worked as hard as any adult, so it was easy to forget he's only sixteen."

"Scott had a great time this summer." Patrick accepted sometimes single parenting meant he drew the boundaries and enforced them without back up. "He may find it difficult to adjust to San Diego. Unfortunately, there are way too many opportunities to get into trouble at home. I wish I could be around more to see what he gets into."

"I can understand the problem." Nikki pulled a cutting board out and started slicing bread for french toast. "Since he lived with me and worked for me, it was easy to keep track of what was going on."

"Thank you for taking him on." Patrick shook his head, a frown between his eyes. "Amy had no wish to have him visit. After last summer's experience, he probably would have objected to being with her anyway," he admitted. "Actually, I wanted to let you know Amy and her new husband are moving to England for a year."

Nikki stopped slicing and gazed into her brother's concerned eyes. "How is that going to affect Scott?"

"Other than reinforcing his low opinion of her?" Nikki nodded. "Probably not much. Amy offered to have Scott join her there, which he refused to consider. No mention of the holidays, but I doubt Scott will want to visit her then either."

Nikki took her brother's hand. "You know Amy's relationship with Scott is not your problem, right? He's a great kid, so you're doing a great job."

Patrick sighed. "Yeah, it's not that. Sometimes I feel guilty because I'm glad she's gone. It's only since he turned sixteen, I stopped worrying about her enticing him to move in with her." He shook his head and squeezed her hand. "What kind of person am I that I'm grateful she's not interested?"

Nikki wrapped Patrick in a hug. "The best kind of

dad. A dad who loves his son enough he wants him around, takes full responsibility without complaint. She made her choice, and it wasn't to be a mother." Nikki's warmth comforted him, and he hugged her back. "Anytime Scott wants to work at The Palace, I'll be more than happy to have him." She released him. "Since this year is our first holiday without Mom's house, let's plan on Thanksgiving and Christmas here. If Scott wants to work during his winter or spring break, that's great. I'll extend an invitation to James for the holidays as well."

Patrick headed to room 12 with the idea he would walk Georgie. Opening the door to the sitting room, he found Georgie playing doggie soccer with her ball, pushing the ball around the floor with alternating front paws. Attaching her leash, Patrick lifted her in his arms and headed back toward Nikki. Letting Nikki know he was taking Georgie out, Patrick exited the rear of The Palace and placed Georgie on the ground.

Walking around the building and through the parking lot, Shelby filled Patrick's thoughts. From outside it didn't appear they had much in common, but there were so many things to talk about. Their values were similar, including strong family loyalty. Amy walking out on the six-year-old Scott was a rude awakening. His mother held the family together after divorce, working full time and doing alterations to keep them in their home. Patrick grew up believing mothers always put their children first. Amy was his first experience with a mother who had no idea how to parent and no desire to learn. Once the divorce was final, Amy found a thousand reasons for not taking Scott on his assigned visitation days: no childcare while she worked, she would be on a business trip, an adult vacation already paid for. Eventually, Scott stopped asking when Amy would see him, and finally, when she called, he had nothing to say and was not interested in visiting. Patrick breathed a sigh of relief. He couldn't imagine losing Scott for even part of the year.

Returning to The Palace, Patrick was joined by Chief Stark.

"You're on dog duty tonight, Patrick. How did that happen?"

"I volunteered," Patrick admitted.

"You're taking Scott home with you this weekend, right? The whole town will miss him. He's a great kid; you should be proud."

"I am proud of Scott. But much of the credit for raising him belongs to my entire family," Patrick mused. "Until my stepfather died and my mom started showing signs of dementia, his grandparents played a huge role in Scott's life. Do your sons spend time with your family?"

"Oh yeah. Colin and Mitch would rather be at Windsong working with the animals and riding horses with my sister Becca than in town with me," he admitted. "Tuesday's going to be difficult since Monday night I'll bring them back to town."

The scents of cinnamon and nutmeg, the hum of conversation, and Louis Armstrong claiming, "It's a Wonderful World" greeted Patrick and Scott when they joined the guests for breakfast. Plates filled, they slid into chairs across from a young couple from New York. Scott grinned at his dad. "Don't suppose you're going to hire someone to make us breakfast during the week when we get home? Nikki's breakfast is so much better than cold cereal."

Taking a sip of Nikki's excellent coffee, Patrick shook his head. "Nope. But you're welcome to cook breakfast for us anytime." Patrick pictured the times he'd yanked the covers off Scott trying to get him moving in the morning. "Course you'd need to get up earlier and clean up the kitchen after."

After breakfast, Scott started toward the basement stairs, ready to face the laundry. Patrick gathered the remaining dishes from both verandas and carried them to the kitchen while Nikki cleared the bar. Soon the lobby and kitchen sparkled.

"Anything else I can do?" Patrick asked, realizing how accurate Scott's description of Nikki was; she worked too hard.

"Just check on Scott. He has laundry duty."

Patrick joined Scott at the laundry table in the basement, watched for a moment to figure out the towel system, and joined in the process.

"Thanks, Dad. This isn't my least favorite job around here, but it takes the most time, especially when the hotel is full. Aunt Nikki runs down here as often as possible and washes and dries a load of towels, piling them on the folding table, and rarely having time to actually fold them."

"So does that mean you're willing to take on laundry duty at home in addition to making our breakfast?" Patrick chuckled at Scott's horrified expression. "If not laundry, what's your least favorite job?"

"I'm surprised you have to ask. Hauling the trash to the dumpster, just like at home. I hate taking the trash out. Here I can't put it off with promises until you shout at me to get it done."

Scott's shift over, Patrick and Scott returned to their room to change, then headed out the front door of the hotel, walking toward the square.

****

Nikki watched them go, two of the most important men in her life, their identical blond heads shining in the afternoon sun.

Nikki headed for the sitting room, rousing Georgie from a nap when Eric arrived at three. A pale blue sky trimmed with fluffy white clouds greeted her as she strolled toward the square. Weaving expertly among the clumps of visitors gathered at corners and in front of restaurants and shops, they finally reached the edge of the square. Nikki waved to Casey and Scott, who lounged among a group spread across a bright red blanket. After a dozen stops and starts greeting both locals and guests, Nikki spotted Patrick sitting on a blanket. Shelby leaned against his shoulder. While she debated walking over or going back, Shelby glanced up and made eye contact, waving Nikki over.

Lifting Georgie, who kept pulling toward a couple of children rather than continuing her walk, Nikki joined them. "Wow, I knew The Palace was full, but I couldn't imagine so many people on the grass for a free concert."

Music filled the air for the next hour. Familiar songs blended with music new to Nikki. Old songs and the crowd sang along, new songs and they quieted, completely focused on the music. Old or new, claps and whistles from the crowd punctuated each number. At the end of Windjammer's set, Nikki left Shelby and Patrick on the grass and headed back to the hotel. The scent of food surrounded her, conversation, and children's squeals, blended with music. Just as the sun set, lighting the summer sky orange and red, Nikki pulled open the back door to The Palace. From the lobby she heard the low rumble of Eric's voice counterpoint to "Rhapsody in Blue." Home. Eight months and Creekside already felt like home.

Leaving Georgie in the suite chomping kibble, Nikki entered the kitchen, heated the oven, and pulled the lasagna out of the refrigerator. Sliced Italian bread, buttered and wrapped in foil, waited ready to heat, and the salad only needed tossing. Table set, Nikki returned to the kitchen, placing the lasagna in the oven. The timer rang, and Patrick entered.

"Where's Scott?"

"Walking Casey home for a last goodbye." He frowned. "Do you think I should be worried about that relationship?"

"Did you ask Scott? As far as I know their dates have been big groups or they had Casey's twin brothers along."

"I just flashed back to being sixteen and how intense summer love could seem."

"Ask Scott. He seems happy about going home. Plus, they can stay in touch easily enough, and he'll be back in a few months for the holiday." She watched Patrick frown. "Talk to him, Patrick. They're friends, maybe a little more, but I haven't seen anything to worry about."

Scott walked in the kitchen. "Dinner about ready?"

"In a few minutes, go wash up; by the time you return, we can carry dinner to the sitting room."

During dinner, Nikki asked, "Scott, what was your

favorite part of spending the summer in Creekside?"

"Since I want to return next summer, I should say working for you, Aunt Nikki." He shrugged. "Because I'm honest I'll admit it was all the new friends I made and the fun we had."

Nikki patted his arm. "Your honesty wins you an offer to return anytime to work here."

Sunday morning sun glinted on the lobby windows, the scents of cinnamon bread pudding and fresh coffee blended, and The Righteous Brothers promised "You'll Never Walk Alone." Patrick and Scott grabbed Nikki in a group hug. With the toss of their bags in the trunk and the car doors' slam, they drove away.

From open until closing a stream of local residents stopped in the bar asking about Scott. Did he get away all right? Was he anxious to go home? Locking the doors at nine o'clock, Nikki cleaned up the bar and lobby and gathered Georgie for one last walk.

As she entered the sitting room, her cell phone rang with "The 59th Street Bridge Song." "Patrick, you and Scott are home?"

"Yeah, the drive was long, but we made it. Scott drove part of the way."

"Did you talk to him about Casey?"

"Tried, but it wasn't much of a conversation. He claims they're just friends."

"Then that's what they are. Now they're friends in different states. Stop worrying." She shook her head, Patrick always worried.

"I'll give it a try. As you say, they are in different states."

"Thanks for letting me know you made it home." Nikki hung up. She remembered all of Patrick's worrying, and how much free advice he offered when she was young and dating Aaron. Now he could worry about Scott.

Monday morning, Nikki woke to the sound of Georgie whimpering. Nikki lifted her head from the pillow and forced tired eyes open. She glanced toward Georgie's bed. As usual, Georgie still slept, but this morning she whimpered in her sleep. Sliding out from under the covers, Nikki knelt beside Georgie, keeping her voice low and whispering soothing nothings in an effort not to startle her awake. As her fingers stroked Georgie's soft fur, Nikki searched the shadowy room. Under the window, a German shepherd sat, ears perked, tongue peeking from the side of his mouth. For just a moment, the stillness in the room tangible, the familiar sounds of a settling building disappeared. Georgie stopped whimpering. The German shepherd slowly dissolved, leaving first only what appeared to be smoke, and then nothing. Did Georgie sense the shepherd's presence? Did he appear in this room because of Georgie, a spirit dog attracted to a live one? Nikki padded back to bed, slid between the sheets, and slipped into sleep.

Nikki woke to the sound of whispering. She opened her eyes. In the shadowed corner of her room, Victoria stood facing a tall man, his face drenched in shadow. "We can fix this, Vic. We can," he pleaded, his voice gruff with emotion.

"Too late. It's okay. I'll manage," Victoria answered. "Go now. You'll be late. We'll talk another day." The man took one step back and disappeared. Victoria turned, her face a profile in the moonlight, a tear on her cheek. The vision dissolved, leaving a drifting scent of lavender and haunting sadness. Nikki closed her eyes and, as she slid into sleep, she pondered who was the man with Victoria? Was he the reason she visited in room 11?

Chapter Eight

"On December 10, 1933, The Palace Lobby Bar returned to its origins and began serving alcohol. By this time, the tea and ice cream offered on the veranda in the afternoon had become traditions in Creekside and both activities continued after the repeal of Prohibition. Mrs. Wyatt celebrated the return of alcohol with a grand opening. According to the Creekside Reporter, 'While not the first local establishment to serve alcohol after the repeal of prohibition, on the evening of December 10, The Palace Hotel served a celebratory punch with elegance and style. Dressed in an emerald gown of velvet and serving from a crystal punch bowl, Mrs. Victoria Wyatt created an ambiance of celebration with flair.' "
~A Brief History of The Palace by Arthur Welles

The breeze through the open car window tickled her cheek and tangled her curly hair as Nikki drove out of Creekside. Beside the two-lane road, fields of grass and stands of trees were interspersed with small enclaves of houses. Grape vines at White Cloud Winery, the final landmark before the Windsong turn off, glowed bright green in the sun. Turning right onto a dirt driveway, Nikki spotted a blue two-story house surrounded by a railed veranda. By the time she turned off her engine, barking dogs with wagging tails circled her truck.

Alexander stepped onto the front porch, "Quiet!" Suddenly, silence.

Nikki pushed open the door. How different he looked in scuffed boots, worn jeans, and a blue T-shirt. Dogs following, Alexander met Nikki halfway.

"Impressive. Does everyone immediately obey your commands?"

He shook his head. "I wish. The command only works with the dogs."

Accompanied by Becca, Colin, and Mitch, they strolled toward five horses tied at the railing. The boys and Becca swung into their saddles and walked their mounts away from the corral. Alex stood beside Nikki's horse and watched her mount. After he adjusted her stirrups, he climbed into his saddle and they followed the others away from the corral.

Riding beside Alexander, Nikki relished the quiet as they entered the woods on horseback. The clop, clop of horseshoes on dry ground, birds twittering, insects buzzing, the soft sigh of a gentle breeze through the trees, and the far off sound of water on rocks created a peaceful backdrop. No music from the hotel sound system, no slamming doors, ringing phones, or hum of conversation. Quiet. Colin shouted, "Race you!" Becca and the boys barreled across a meadow, Alexander increased his pace slightly, and Nikki's horse followed.

When she pulled up beside him, Nikki asked, "Should we speed up to catch them?"

Alex shook his head. "No. They'll slow down in a minute where the trail crosses the stream and heads up the mountain. How long has it been since your last ride?"

"Six years, I think," Nikki admitted. "You could tell, huh?"

He shrugged. "You're doing okay."

The sounds of rushing water drowned out the scrape of horseshoes on rocks and the creak of leather saddles. Sunlight danced on running water, creating tiny rainbows as the creek rushed over rocks scattered randomly through the creek bed. In the distance, Colin, Mitch, and Becca slowly moved up the narrow trail toward the top of the mountain, their horses walking in single file. Following Alex, Nikki's horse stepped carefully over slippery rocks, crossed the creek, and started up the mountain. Nikki concentrated on keeping her seat and watching the horse's cautious steps. The boys' laughter and Becca's answering calm tones became background noise.

"Nikki." Alex's deep voice brought her head up, and her horse stopped.

Stretched before her was a valley, its center jewel an emerald lake. Tall trees cast random shadows across the edges of the lake; a few boats drifted across the water, so distant they appeared toys.

"It's beautiful. How do you live in town when something this beautiful waits for you?"

Alex leaned over and kissed her cheek. "Well, Creekside has its charms."

"Oh?"

"Yep. My job, the boys' school, and an innkeeper who walks with me at night."

Nikki felt warmth and color infuse her face. Alex turned his horse to follow the ridge. The boys' voices drifted on the air, the sound of the boys' happy screams competed with the sound of rushing water when they reached the creek. Becca, Mitch, and Colin, their horses tied to a tree, splashed each other in the creek.

Becca, her smile knowing, offered, "We'll be home in a bit." She splashed Mitch. "I'm drowning these two first." She aimed a splash at Colin who retaliated immediately.

Reaching the corral, Alex lifted Nikki from the saddle, his big hands at her waist. Her feet hit the ground. Her legs a little shaky, she held Alex's shoulders for a moment.

"You okay?"

She gazed into his chocolate eyes and dropped her hands from his shoulders. "I'll probably be sore tomorrow, but the ride was worth it."

Alexander removed the saddles and tack. As he tossed the saddles on their stands, he offered, "I'd be happy to give you a few pointers if you'll ride with me again." They started brushing down the two horses.

"I'd love that," Nikki confessed. "I'm sure you were tempted to correct my seat, and I was impressed you stayed silent." She'd noticed him grimace every time she bounced in the saddle.

"You noticed I changed the stirrup length. I hoped that'd be enough to give you a better ride without the bounce."

"Thanks for that. It took me a while to remember what I learned."

Becca, Colin, and Mitch returned, and declining an offer of dinner, Nikki climbed into her truck for the trip home.

****

Alexander watched Nikki's truck kick up dust as she headed down the driveway. Thinking about his hands on her waist, he'd wanted to pull her body against his. Soothe and massage her sore muscles. Each time she bounced in the saddle, he watched her face. She frowned in concentration and attempted to correct her seat. Between his sons, his job, and Windsong, he sometimes felt twenty-four hours in a day were not enough. Yet, occasionally, especially when he crawled into his empty bed, loneliness haunted him. In the darkest hours of the night, he remembered coming home to another adult, sharing plans, and conversation, whispering shared dreams. Maybe this would be a good time to find companionship and eventually a lover. He'd never marry again. Colin and Mitch stood on the edge of young manhood. No way would he begin again with a wife and possibly another child. But a lover, a smiling, happy, intelligent, beautiful lover—yeah, he was ready. Becca's warm hand on his shoulder pulled him into the moment.

"It's about time," she commented.

He turned his head and gazed into eyes identical to his own. "Time for what?"

She shook her head. "Time you brought a woman riding at Windsong." She tipped his hat off his head. "Time you got a life, big brother." She strolled toward the house, her laughter a bright sound floating on the air.

****

Nikki's legs ached, bottom hurt, knees felt raw when she jumped out of her truck and entered The Palace. The shower's pulsing hot water relieved the tension in her neck and her black leggings felt soft against raw skin. Denim against tender skin rubbing against the leather saddle, ouch. Dressed in a bright yellow tunic over black leggings, Nikki grabbed Georgie for their evening walk. They walked toward the square, easily dodging the few clusters of tourists on the sidewalk. No sounds of nature here, instead the usual Creekside sounds of conversation and music. After the afternoon ride with Alex, the city sounds seemed louder. First date, no goodnight kiss. Ahh, but the sparks. When Alex lifted her from the horse, slung his arm around her shoulder, and walked her to the truck, sparks. Nice being reminded that part of her wasn't dead, just sleeping, waiting. But waiting for what? A lover, a friend, a partner?

Nikki drifted into a dreamless sleep and woke abruptly to the scent of lavender. Victoria stood in a shadowy corner, her arms outstretched toward a man wearing a long black coat. Their hands met and a sense of joy filled the room. Victoria beamed, and the corners of her lips lifted. The man wrapped his arms around her waist. They disappeared. The scent of lavender remained; Nikki drifted back to sleep, her last conscious thought that Victoria found her partner, her heart open to love.

Within a few days, the leaves began their journey from green to orange, yellow, gold, and brown. Occupancy at The Palace increased as residents of the Valley visited on weekends to drive through the forests and admire the changing scene.

A ringing phone woke Nikki. Unfortunately, Charlotte, her mother, and the twins were sick. Eric didn't feel comfortable leaving them, so Nikki was on her own for the entire day. After feeding Georgie and dressing in black jeans and a sky-blue Palace polo shirt, she headed for the lobby and unlocked the front door.

Before she could reach the kitchen, the bell on the front door chimed, and Shelby walked in. "Good morning, Nikki. Eric asked me to check with you to see if I could help this morning, at least with the breakfast set up."

"Thank you!" With Shelby's help, by eight thirty, the scent of coffee filled the lobby and the first guests piled their plates and filled their mugs to the accompaniment of James Taylor's promise "You've Got A Friend." Outside, a few leaves drifted from the trees, floating on a cool fall breeze. Inside the lobby, the hum of conversation competed with a cover of "I Want to Be Loved by You." Nikki handed Shelby a coffee mug and a plate. "Least I can do is feed you."

"Hey, what are friends for?" Shelby shrugged, filling her mug and plate. "Anything else I can do to help?"

Carrying her coffee mug, Nikki moved to the front desk. Tablet in hand, she verified only two checkouts today and eight check-ins. By the end of the day, occupancy would be ninety percent. "Looks like I should be okay. Stop by Victoria's tonight, and I'll buy you a drink. This will be the first time I have worked alone the whole day when the hotel's been full."

Dark replaced the colors of sunset, and the yellow glow from low lights warmed Victoria's. Bing Crosby crooned "You Must Have Been a Beautiful Baby" from the hotel's playlist, and Nikki perched on a stool behind Victoria's bar. Shelby strolled through the front door. Her blonde hair picked up the low light turning gold, her smile lit the room. *Yep, must have been a beautiful baby.*

Shelby plopped on a stool at the bar. "You look happy. Must have been a good day even by yourself."

Grabbing a glass and Shelby's favorite white wine from the cooler, Nikki shook her head. "Good day, true, but I was grinning at the coincidence." Handing Shelby the glass of wine, Nikki chuckled at Shelby's confused expression. "Did you notice the song when you opened the door?"

"Nope. Sounded like Bing Crosby, but I didn't notice the song."

Nikki shook her head. "I must be tired because you opened the door and Bing started singing 'You Must Have Been a Beautiful Baby.' " She shrugged. "Appropriate, huh?"

"No good way to answer that one. If I say yes, I sound conceited. If I say no, I'm insulting you and Bing." She sipped her wine and shrugged. "Sounds like you might be a little punchy?"

"Maybe, but it still seemed an appropriate song for your entrance." Nikki turned away, pouring a glass of wine for a young man standing at the bar. He chuckled. Nikki returned to Shelby.

"You had a busy day? Does it look like you'll have time for sleep tonight?"

"Definitely. How are Eric, Charlotte, and the twins?"

"Better, but I don't think Charlotte will be here tomorrow since now Eric is sick and the twins are not quite well." Shelby frowned. "Should I come tomorrow morning and help out again? I'm happy to help."

"If you could come about the same time tomorrow, that would be great. Keeping the breakfast buffet filled with a full house is easier with two." Noticing the couples on the veranda were gone, Nikki gathered their wine glasses, the empty bottle, and all the used dishes and pushed the bus cart to the kitchen.

Loading the dishwasher, Nikki glanced at the calendar above the counter. Tomorrow afternoon at three, Alexander expected her at Windsong for a riding lesson. She grabbed Georgie from the suite. At the click of the back door's lock, Nikki startled as Alex stepped out of a shadow nearby and appeared beside her, taking her free hand. She gazed into his eyes, now the darkest chocolate color in the low light. "Evening, Chief."

He nodded, "Evening, Innkeeper." The yellow glow of the motion lights marked their path through the parking lot.

"I have to cancel our date tomorrow. Looks like I'll be innkeeping alone," Nikki confessed as they dodged a group of tourists near the square.

"Are you exhausted, Nikki?"

Nikki glanced up into his concerned eyes. Nice to know he cared. "Tired, but actually today went well." Nikki snickered, thinking of Shelby and Bing's song. "It helped that Shelby arrived early this morning. I feel extremely lucky in my friends."

In a shadow beside the hotel's back door, Alex wrapped her in his arms. She leaned against his shoulder, closed her eyes, and inhaled his familiar scent. A potent mixture of warmth, comfort, and arousal pulsed through Nikki.

His deep voice rumbled, "I'm disappointed our ride's cancelled. Another time?" She nodded. With one long finger, he lifted her chin and placed his lips against hers, his kiss gentle. He stepped back. "Good night, Nikki."

Nikki gazed into his eyes. "Good night, Chief Alex." She picked up Georgie and slipped inside the hotel. The door lock clicked, the only sound in the silent hallway. At the door to room 11, Victoria stood with her hand poised to knock. She dropped her hand and glided through the closed door. Nikki pictured Victoria wrapped in the arms of the tall man in the long coat and trusted his embrace brought Victoria the comfort and warmth Nikki found in Alex's arms. Though not in the market for love herself, Nikki hoped Victoria found love.

****

Giving the lobby tables a final wipe down after breakfast, Nikki noticed a young woman reaching for the front door, holding the hand of a little girl and pushing a sleeping toddler in a stroller. Rushing over to hold open the front door, Nikki greeted the very damp, curly-haired Catherine Jessup. "Welcome to The Palace Catherine, Lily, and Hope."

Catherine stepped over the threshold. "Thank you. James said you had room for us?"

"Of course. Even if James hadn't asked, I'd have room for you." Nikki reached for the stroller, parking it near the front desk and crouched with a smile for sleeping Hope Jessup. "According to James, you don't know how long your stay will be?"

Peeling off Lilly's damp jacket and hanging it on the stroller, Catherine whispered to her daughter and then stood facing Nikki. "Not really."

"Rooms 3 and 5, with a shared bath, are yours as long as you need them."

"Thank you, Nikki, for making an exception for us. James told me the rooms aren't really set up for small children."

Nikki shook her head at James' warning to

95

Catherine. True, upstairs wasn't best for children. The rooms were small, no room for a crib, and rails on the upstairs veranda were far enough apart a small child could slip through. "Catherine, James is Hope and Lily's godfather. You're family." She shrugged. "Your rooms are on the first floor. If you think of anything we can do to keep your children safe during their stay, please let me know." She hugged Catherine. "I'm glad you're here."

Nikki and Catherine unloaded Catherine's late model Lexus SUV. In Hope's stubborn chin and Lily's twinkling eyes, Nikki could see traces of Craig as a boy. Friends with James since middle school, Craig hung out with James through middle school, high school, and college. When Craig married Catherine, James was best man. When Hope and Lily were born, James frequently asked Mom and Nikki what gifts he should buy for birthdays and holidays. James took his godfather responsibilities seriously. Now Craig was dead, killed in a hit-and-run car accident, and Catherine, according to James, needed a safe place. From day one, The Palace surrounded Nikki with feelings of warmth and safety. Hopefully, Catherine, Hope, and Lily felt the hotel's comforting welcome.

That night Nikki secured the doors and closed Victoria's, and The Palace settled around her like a familiar blanket. The sounds of low-voiced conversations from the guest rooms and the quiet creaking of old wood as the building settled created a sense of safety. Georgie whining in her arms, Nikki walked toward the back door. The scent of lavender drifted in the still air, and Victoria stood at room 11, her hand raised to knock. She dropped her arm and glided through the closed door. Georgie stopped whining. Nikki set her on the floor and opened the back door. Outside, the threatening clouds had disappeared, leaving a black velvet sky dotted with tiny stars and a half moon.

Chapter Nine

"August of 1939 The Palace hosted a celebration for all Creekside young people heading off to college. According to The Creekside Reporter, 'Victoria Wyatt hosted an afternoon celebration on the hotel veranda, providing an appropriate and joyful send-off for Creekside young people. Included in their number was RJ Wyatt, Victoria Wyatt's son, who will be attending Arizona State Teacher's College.' "
~A Brief History of The Palace by Arthur Welles

A tall lean shadow pulled away from the building as Georgie and Nikki stepped into the alley a few nights later. The shadow materialized into Chief Alex dressed in worn jeans, boots, and jacket. First time he'd joined their walk in nearly a week. His deep voice rumbled, "Evening, Ms. Innkeeper." He slipped the leash from her hand and placed his arm across her shoulder.

Nikki wrapped her arm around his waist and squeezed gently. "Evening, Chief." They walked through the parking lot, the motion lights blinking on then off as they passed.

At the sidewalk, he took his arm away, twining their hands together. Familiar sounds of music and conversation surrounded them. They wove their way through groups of tourists. "How are your long-term guests working out?"

"Great." Nikki pictured Catherine's disbelief at Lily's story about seeing a lady who walked through doors. "They fit right in with the other guests."

"So, you're happy with the arrangement."

"Of course." She shrugged. "It's a hotel. Guests are what we do. Anyway, getting a chance to know Catherine better is a plus. I've known them a long time, just not very well since Craig was James' friend."

"I know."

They walked beneath a streetlight, and Nikki gazed in his chocolate eyes and raised an eyebrow. "Yes, but how do you know? I don't think I mentioned it."

"Creekside's a small town. Everyone knows everything." Alex shrugged. They started the return walk.

"Hmm. Maybe, or maybe James called you." Nikki remembered the urgency in Catherine's voice, the flash of fear in her eyes when Catherine entered the lobby bar filled with guests. "Catherine's afraid of something, but I'm not sure what."

"What makes you think she's afraid?" Alex frowned.

Nikki decided on logic rather than on her intuition. "No other reason I can think of that she packed up her girls and drove away from her home the day after Craig's funeral. I'm guessing James or Catherine talked to you."

"No comment. Georgie seems to enjoy their visit. I see her every morning walking with them."

"Not a very smooth subject change, Alex, but I get the hint. Yes, Georgie loves accompanying them to preschool."

At The Palace's back door, Alex handed Nikki the

leash and drew her into his arms. His warmth surrounded her, his scent a mixture of aftershave, laundry soap, and masculinity. Nikki hummed.

"Some days, this is the best part of my day," Alex whispered as he kissed her gently on the lips. He tasted of mint and coffee. Her lips softened in welcome, enjoying the gentle friction of lips meeting. Alex ended the kiss. His chocolate eyes met hers.

Nikki caressed his scratchy five o'clock shadow with her fingertips. "Good night, Chief."

She opened the door and walked down the hallway toward the shadowed, empty lobby; only the rainbow diffused light of the front desk Tiffany lamp illuminated the bar. At the window, Victoria watched the street. A man in a bowler hat walked away, his long coat fluttering behind him as he turned the corner. Victoria turned toward Nikki, a tear drifting down her cheek. Their eyes met, and Victoria slowly dissolved, leaving only a whisper of lavender and the essence of sadness in her wake.

October first, Catherine found Nikki in the office surrounded by open boxes. Outside, autumn leaves danced across the hotel's veranda. Inside the office, a ghost lay spread out across the chair, orange pumpkin lights tangled in a clump on top of the desk, a witch's black hat peeked out of a plastic cauldron, and Nikki sat cross-legged on the floor sorting through large black spiders, random plastic bones, and a disconnected arm attached to a bloody hand. "Nikki. Want some help?"

"How do you feel about decorating for Halloween?" Nikki tossed a second ghost toward the chair where he managed to knock the first one off. Nikki frowned at Catherine's attempt to hold back a laugh. "I thought I carefully packed up the decorations after my last Halloween party."

Catherine picked the ghosts up and hung them on the back of the door. Then she grabbed the orange lights and started untangling. "But somehow they messed themselves up?"

"Well, remembering that last party and my girlfriends helping me pack the boxes after a night of fun, games, and drinking, I should be grateful the decorations ended up in boxes," Nikki confessed.

With help from Hope and Lily, by evening, tiny orange lights rimmed the verandas. Spider webs hung from the rafters. Giant black spiders with glittering eyes waited for their next victim. Ghosts glided on the breeze across the veranda. A witch crashed into a pole, her broom at her feet, her hat crushed. Beside the front step, a tombstone identified the dearly departed while a disembodied arm with a bloody hand attempted to escape from the grave. Hope in her mother's arms, Lily holding Nikki's hand, they crossed the street in front of The Palace just as the sun disappeared. Tiny pumpkin lights cast an orange glow, lighting the white spider webs and making the spiders' eyes glitter. Ghosts fluttered in the evening breeze. Catherine and Nikki looked at each other and nodded in unison. "We do good work."

At the window of room 15, the lace curtain moved. Victoria appeared. "Catherine, do you see her?" Nikki nudged Catherine's arm. "Second floor room on the right."

"There's that lady, Mommy." Lily's piping voice broke the silence. Victoria disappeared.

****

Brittle fallen leaves drifted across the parking lot, the night an unbroken expanse of black velvet. Georgie whined and tugged gently on her leash when they reached the sidewalk. Nikki stilled. Alex's deep voice came from a shadow next to the veranda. "Evening, Innkeeper." He took the leash and looped her arm through his.

"Evening, Chief." Nikki noticed his cowboy boots, worn jeans, and leather jacket. "Or are you just Alex tonight?

He chuckled, the sound a low rumble next to her ear. "Ahh, Innkeeper, never 'just' anything. Got off duty a couple of hours ago." They dodged a clump of tourists arguing about which direction to Willie's Grill.

"Not going to stop and offer directions?" Nikki raised an eyebrow. "Tonight you are 'off duty.' "

"Hey. It's not like they'll get lost. The town's too small." He guided them around another group staring at the menu on the Lone Star. "So is that Georgie's Halloween costume?"

Georgie's white plumed tail wagged slowly at the sound of her name. "Almost. Just missing her cape and witch's hat." Nikki admired Georgie's bright white fur against the black sweatshirt and boots.

"From a distance, she looks like a floating head and tail. Is she channeling a horror movie character?"

"Not exactly," Nikki mused, and they dodged a group of teens throwing a Frisbee on the square. "She looked fashionable in black and white during the day." Nikki frowned. "Didn't think about a floating head and tail in the dark."

Alex smirked. "So, will she play the part of disconnected floating head and tail when the haunted tour visits The Palace?"

"So, you know about that, huh." A disgruntled sigh escaped Nikki.

"Hey, it's a small town. I'm the police chief; I know everything." He shrugged. "You're letting them in The Palace?" They reversed direction. Now the night sounds included music combined with conversation. Nikki already regretted giving in to Karen's entreaty and allowing her group inside the hotel.

"We've compromised. Only the Saturday night before Halloween and only in the lobby."

"It'll be the first time in a long time the tour's been inside The Palace."

"Karen Transome claimed The Palace always welcomed the ghost tour, but I checked with Brenda, Mary Beth, Eric, Charlotte, and Shelby and they disagreed."

Alex nodded. "About five years ago, after several pre-tour drinks, one tour guest managed to enter the lobby and break several of the glass decorations."

"This story doesn't sound like it's going to end well." Nikki couldn't remember if Mary Beth mentioned a particular problem or just a falling out between Karen and the prior managers.

"After he dashed up the stairs, he ended up hanging over the balcony railing shouting obscenities and threatening pedestrians on the sidewalk."

"Great, I hope I don't regret giving in to Karen." Nikki frowned, wondering how she was going to protect the hotel and guests if Karen's group rowdy.

In the shadow beside the hotel's back door, Alex handed Nikki the leash and pulled her into his arms.

Through layers of clothes, Nikki felt his warmth, the strength in his arms. She inhaled his familiar scent of aftershave and laundry soap. Laying her cheek against his shoulder, the puff of his breath pushed her curls around, tickling her cheek.

"Would you join me for dinner either Wednesday or Thursday this week? Those are my two nights off."

Nikki pulled back slightly, looking into his brown eyes. "Why, Chief, is this date number two?"

"Date two. No kids, no dogs, no horses. Are you free?"

"Date two, Thursday," she agreed.

He placed his lips near hers and whispered, "Seven o'clock." Their lips met, first gently, then with more pressure. In the chilly night air, Nikki's blood heated, running a warmth under her skin. She felt his smile, tasted his minty breath. Alex gentled the kiss, pulled back. Nikki's fingers caressed his scratchy five o'clock scruff. He tapped a finger to the end of her nose. "Thursday, seven, date two." Nikki slipped inside.

Jacket hung on a coatrack beside the sitting room door, Nikki tossed Georgie's sweatshirt and boots in the drawer, and her cell phone chimed "Wasted Time." "Hi James, how's my big brother?"

"Great, Nikki. How are you and Georgie? Are you ready for Halloween?"

"Ready. We decorated The Palace today. Occupancy is above last year. It's all good."

James chuckled. "You and Georgie decorated The Palace? Wish I could have seen that."

Nikki's laughter rang through the phone. "You're ridiculous. Catherine, Hope, and Lily helped me decorate. Georgie helped by staying inside."

"I can still hardly wait to see it. Do you have room for me this weekend?" James asked.

"Of course there's room. You're welcome to my second bedroom." Nikki shook her head. He wasn't traveling to Creekside to admire the decorations. He wanted to see Catherine. After a few minutes of general conversation, the siblings exchanged goodbyes. During the last two weeks, Nikki and Catherine had discussed the hotel, the girls, the preschool, and Catherine's plans for Halloween. Never discussed Catherine's reason for the move to Creekside or the fear in Catherine's eyes the first day. Sometimes, after the little girls slept soundly, Catherine brought her monitor to Victoria's and sipped a glass of wine at the bar. After a few sips, tears glistened in Catherine's eyes. Standing on the other side of the bar, Nikki touched Catherine's hand sometimes or simply stood nearby, offering silent comfort. Catherine had lost her young husband and her home in one fell swoop. What could Nikki possibly do to ease the pain?

Catherine leaned against the doorway to the office the next morning. "Do you know anyone trustworthy who might watch Lily and Hope on Saturday night while I have dinner with James?"

Today, Catherine wore jeans, flannel shirt, and running shoes. Not quite the local cowboy look or the young executive look Nikki remembered from seeing Catherine in James' office. "Let me call Casey Edgeware. If she's not responsible for her brothers that night, she'd be great with the girls."

Wrapped in a white terry robe bearing her initials monogramed in neon blue on the pocket, Nikki knelt and pulled out the dresser's bottom drawer. Yep,

Stella Jayne Phillips

nothing different from the last time she looked. Carefully folded jeans filled the drawer. Dark jeans, black jeans, light washed jeans, ankle length jeans, boot cut jeans, each pair different but the same. Regretting she'd neglected getting details about date two, Nikki yanked out skinny black jeans, dressy enough even at Wellingtons. No channeling witches tonight, she slid her favorite sky blue sweater over her head, clasped a gold chain bearing the initial N around her neck, added small diamond studs, a quick brush of mascara, and pulled her leather jacket from the closet, dropping it on the sitting room sofa. Just as she finished zipping up her boots, a knock sounded at the door. Hand on the doorknob, Nikki took a deep breath, steadying her nerves. Nerves for a date with Alex? Alex, who she walked with several times a week, saw around Creekside all the time. Kissed. Yeah, the kisses changed things.

Nikki pulled open the door. "Hi. I'll get my jacket." She stepped back. He followed her inside. She heard the door latch and suddenly felt his arms wrap around her from behind. He turned her gently in his arms, and their lips met. She inhaled his familiar scent, her blood warming at the feel of his lips on hers, his rough tongue licking along the seam of her lips. Lifting onto her toes, she wrapped her arms around his neck.

Alex slowly ended the kiss. Nuzzling her neck, he whispered, "I've waited all day for that." He stepped back, reached down, and lifted her leather jacket, settling it on her shoulders.

Fingers entwined, they walked through the cold night air toward Wellingtons, dodging the clumps of tourists on the sidewalk. "One excellent thing about

Creekside is walking everywhere," Nikki commented.

"You don't like to drive?"

"It's not that. A second date in Scottsdale, and I wouldn't be ready to get in a car with you or let you know where I lived."

Alex shook his head. "But I already know where you live."

"Yeah, and so does everyone else. But if I don't like this date, I can always walk home." She pictured walking out on Creekside's police chief. Gossip would fly. They climbed the stone steps to Wellingtons. The host greeted them by name, so different from white tablecloth restaurants in Scottsdale. "I already know I'm going to enjoy this date."

They were seated, and their drinks poured and food ordered. "Did that happen much, you uncomfortable enough to walk out on a date?"

Nikki shook her head. "Not to me. But I rescued a few of my girlfriends, especially if they'd taken a shared ride and were spooked about getting a ride."

"So, what did you do?"

She shrugged. "Drove over and picked them up. Once I texted James." Nikki shook her head. "Ruined his evening since he claimed he was moving on a beautiful woman."

"But he rode to the rescue?" Alex lifted an eyebrow.

"Yeah, he said sometimes being my brother wasn't easy."

"Do you miss living in Scottsdale near your family and friends?"

Nikki slid a bite of her salad between her lips, considering his question. She swallowed. "I miss James and my girlfriends. Don't miss Scottsdale, though." She took a sip of wine. "Guess I'm a small town girl after all. Do you miss working in the city?"

"No. I thought I would, when we moved back to Creekside. Now I'm glad we moved. The boys are happy and surrounded by family."

Nikki sipped her wine. "And you get to live with your mom."

His eyes lit with humor. "Yeah, she's great, but it's a little embarrassing living with Mom at forty."

"Hey, I'm the last person to judge. I moved home to Mom too."

Stepping through the door into the clear night, Alex took her hand. "So, how am I doing so far with Date Two?"

"Well, I won't be calling James to rescue me, so it's all good." She squeezed his hand. They strolled around groups of tourists waiting outside the clubs and bars surrounding the square.

"Good. Let's check out the new band at Lone Star. Who knows, I might get brave and take you out on the dance floor." Alex nodded at the bouncer blocking entrance to the Lone Star. The bouncer nodded, winked at Nikki, and led them around the group waiting to get in.

Glancing back at the people waiting Nikki chuckled. "Hey, do all residents get VIP treatment or just the police chief?"

"Neither. That's a Stark cousin, and in Creekside, family rules." He tugged her toward a table near the front where Jackson, Maggie, Matt, and Lissa sat, half-empty drinks in front of them and a decimated plate of nachos filling the round table's center.

As they greeted the others and slid into the wooden chairs, the server appeared. "Hi, Chief, what can I get you to drink?"

"Hi, Caitlin. When did you get back in town?"

"Just a week ago." Caitlin took their orders. "I'll be right back with your drinks."

As Caitlin moved away, Lissa looked at Alexander. "Are you surprised she came home?"

"Definitely. She was seriously angry when she left town."

Conversation changed to general topics. Sometimes living in a small town resembled entering a theatre in the middle of a movie. Things happened, and everyone knew the context except Nikki. Their drinks came. The band played a cover of Josh Turner's "Your Man," and they danced. Breathing in Alex's familiar scent, Nikki laid her head on his shoulder. His strong arm wrapped around her waist. His other hand, clasping hers, lay against his chest. She heard his deep voice rumble against her ear, and he hummed the song.

"So you dance; do you sing?"

He chuckled, the sound a baritone rumble. "Nope. At least not on a second date." He pulled her closer; they slowly drifted around the dance floor. His warmth surrounded her.

Walking back to The Palace, Nikki's curiosity got the better of her. "What's Caitlin's story? Why were you surprised to see her?"

"Caitlin was engaged to her high school sweetheart." Alex frowned. "Unfortunately, during the wedding planning, Jack suddenly ended the engagement, left town for a week, and returned married to someone else. Within a couple of weeks, Caitlin accepted a job in Phoenix and left town. That was two years ago."

"Ouch. Bad enough her fiancé ended the engagement, but having him marry someone else immediately must have really hurt."

"Not only did Jack marry, but five months later his wife gave birth to their daughter."

Nikki empathized.

After they grabbed Georgie for her evening walk and returned to The Palace, Alexander drew Nikki into his arms. "So, what did you think of date two?"

Nikki gazed into his chocolate eyes. "Hum. Dinner at Wellingtons, drinks and dancing at Lone Star, both excellent. Plus, I learned you dance and sing." She frowned. "As promised, no kids, no horses, but Alex, we did take Georgie."

"True. But not to dinner so it doesn't count." He pulled her closer, and their lips met. Nikki's eyes drifted shut, blocking out the yellow light above the back door and the star-filled night. She returned his kiss, inviting his tongue into play. Warmth surrounded her along with Alex's scent, a mixture of man and aftershave. Pressed against Alexander, Nikki felt melting sexual attraction. Alexander drew back slowly, releasing her, and finally placed his callused fingers against her cheek. He stepped back and wished her good night.

Falling into an exhausted sleep, Nikki woke to the sound of a music box playing "Someone to Watch Over Me." Hints of dawn filtered through the lace curtains, and in the shadows, Victoria danced with a tall man wearing suspenders over his white shirt. They swayed to the music. As the music drifted to a close, he wrapped both arms around her waist, her sigh audible in the silent room. Their lips met and the vision dissolved, leaving only an elusive scent of lavender and silence. Nikki hummed the old song under her breath and slipped back into sleep.

From her perch behind the front desk, Nikki watched James yank his black leather bag from the back of his SUV and slam the door. His black suit blended with his black car and his black bag, his white dress shirt a jarring contrast. Knowing he must have worked this Friday morning, she'd bet a conservative tie lay crumpled on the passenger seat. James hated wearing a tie, but he always wore one with his black suit. He dashed across the street, took the steps two at a time, and yanked open the front door, good humor lighting his face. He dropped the bag, and Nikki ran around the front desk and flew into his arms. The familiar softness of the expensive wool coat caressed her cheek and a whisper of his aftershave surrounded her. "Welcome, big brother. You worked this morning."

"Yep, and I still made it here before two."

Nikki raised an eyebrow as he dropped his arms and she stepped back. "Was it a contest with the clock?"

He frowned. "Nope. Just a Friday morning client who wanted to talk. And talk. And talk," he explained. "Wish I could charge them by the hour just for conversation. Like Patrick."

She shook her head. They teased Patrick about making money every time he opened his mouth. "Go settle in. Catherine should be back soon. She and Hope left a few minutes ago to pick up Lily." Nikki shook her head as he started stripping out of the suit coat. "And you might want to ditch the funeral suit."

He ruffled her hair. "I'll do that."

****

A gentle breeze drifted by, conversation provided background noise, and James chuckled at Lily's giggles as they strolled toward the town square, weaving around clumps of tourists. Catherine pushed Hope in the stroller. Lily rode on James' shoulder, her fingers grasping his hair with a constant tug. "Hey. At this rate I won't worry about losing my hair; you're pulling it out."

Catherine laughed, and Lily giggled harder. "Craig claimed they'd either turn his hair gray or pull it all out before he was forty." They stopped at a food vendor for chicken nuggets with fries for Hope and cheese pizza for Lily. While Catherine blew on the nuggets, James ordered hamburgers from another vendor, and they moved onto the grass. Spreading a blanket on the grass, they watched the girls play. Lily found a friend from preschool, and the children giggled excitedly during a game of Duck, Duck, Goose. "Are you happy living at The Palace, Catherine?"

"Content might be a better word. At least I feel safe." She frowned. "Happiness still seems pretty far away, but it's getting better and the girls are happy."

Grasping her little sister's hand, Lily ran toward them. She stopped in front of Catherine and touched her arm. "The other kids had to go, so can we have our dinner now?"

Catherine pulled out a baby wipe and cleaned both girls' hands. "Here you go." She handed out their food and bottles of water. Then she pulled out the hamburgers, handing one to James.

"Moving to Creekside feels like a good decision then?"

"Both girls have learned to relax with strangers at breakfast. Sometimes I miss my privacy, but I feel safer surrounded by people than I did living alone with the girls." She grabbed Hope's water bottle before it spilled, replacing the cap.

James looked in her sad eyes, noticing tears threatening to fall. "Did you tell Chief Stark why you're living in The Palace?"

"Yes. He's actually a very nice man. Did you know he is dating Nikki?"

James grimaced. "After all the harassment Patrick and I gave Nikki about dating when she was young, it doesn't surprise me she doesn't share that kind of information. What about you, what do you do with your time now you don't come into the office?"

"You know I work for you quite a few hours a day. You pay my bills." Catherine shrugged. "I take care of my children, walk Georgie, and visit with hotel guests at breakfast. I've also managed a few coffee dates with other preschool mothers." She paused. "I'm seeing a grief counselor through the church."

"I'm glad. I miss him too. Whatever helps you deal with the loss, I'm all for it."

Lily crawled on his lap, her sweet little girl smell bringing back memories of picnics, birthday parties, and walks to the neighborhood park with Catherine, Craig, and the girls.

"Do you think the vandalism at my home was personal?" Catherine wiped Lily's hands and face, picked up a nearly sleeping Hope, and wiped her off too. "Was Craig involved with someone he should have avoided?"

"Since we cleaned up the house and installed the alarm, there haven't been any problems." James frowned. "Unfortunately, the detective still believes Craig being run off the road and the house being vandalized are related."

Catherine hugged Hope a little tighter. "It's the timing, having the vandalism happen almost immediately after the accident."

James kissed the top of Lily's head and heard her gentle snore. "Catherine, Craig knew trouble was coming the last time we spoke. He asked me to watch out for you."

Catherine's eyes widened. "So I should be afraid?"

"Cautious. Be cautious. All I really know is something worried Craig."

Catherine frowned. "Something worried him before the accident, but he didn't say what."

"Until there are answers, it makes sense for you to stay in The Palace. This was the only way I could figure out to avoid creating a paper trail."

"Are we safe then?"

"So far no one's inquired about you at the office, so I don't think anyone made a connection between us." James turned the conversation to the people Catherine met since moving to Creekside and what she thought of small town living. While he paid attention to Catherine's words, he made a note to discuss the situation with Chief Alexander. James hoped Catherine and her children were safe and he hadn't put Nikki in danger.

****

Nikki greeted them from behind the bar. Catherine

carried sleeping Hope. Lily, her arms wrapped tightly around James' neck, rode piggyback. The empty folded stroller hung like an umbrella on James' arm. "Looks like everyone had fun! Did you enjoy the band?"

"We did." Catherine shook her head at their reflection in the mirror over the bar. "In fact, we had so much fun we ran out of diapers and both girls are covered with grass and dirt. I'm going to take them back for baths now before they crash."

"Would you like a glass of wine to take with you before I close the bar?"

"The Pinot Noir would be awesome. I'll save it until the girls are sleeping."

Nikki handed Catherine the glass of wine, and the Jessup family headed to their rooms with a chorus of goodnights.

When James returned to the bar, his arms now empty, Nikki pointed at the fingerprint smudges on his cheek and grass stained knees. "Wine, James?" He nodded. "Keep me company while I close up." He sat on the barstool and picked up his glass.

He saluted his sister with the glass and took a sip. "Have you had any questions about Catherine, Nikki?"

Nikki frowned. "Not really." She replaced a clean glass on the shelf. "Creekside's an unusual small town. They gossip about each other but respect newcomers' privacy."

"Not what you expected?"

"Nope." She shook her head. "Small towns have such a reputation for being nosy. Creekside doesn't fit the mold."

"Yeah. Well, it might be the ghosts. Gives them something more interesting to talk about than the new people in town."

"Hmm. Maybe, or could be that tourists are big business here, so the residents respect their privacy."

"Well, if someone you don't know asks about Catherine, let her or Chief Stark know, okay?" James frowned. "We think she's safe here, but better to be careful. You might mention it to Eric and Charlotte as well."

Promising to pay attention, Nikki allowed James to move the direction of the conversation to other topics.

"I ran into Andrea Hamilton and Laurence the other day at Houston's. Has she visited you yet?"

"No. From what I know of Laurence, Creekside wouldn't interest him." Nikki pictured Laurence, Armani suit, power tie, shiny loafers, and his reaction to laid-back Creekside. His Rolex watch and silver Jag would stand out in a town filled with SUV's, trucks, jeans, and boots. "Had you met him before?"

"Yeah. He's a member at Orange Tree. We've played golf a few times." James smirked. "He was severely disappointed when I won."

"I think I knew that. In fact, Andrea mentioned she tried playing with him and another couple, but they were all so much better than her, everyone ended up frustrated." Nikki refilled his glass.

James sipped the wine and sighed in appreciation. "But you and Andrea are still in touch, right? She calls?"

"Yeah, pretty frequently. Living in Creekside it's easier since I no longer need to see Laurence but can still visit with Andrea by phone." Nikki dried the last of the wine glasses, replacing it on the rack.

James raised his eyebrows, a twinkle in his eyes.

"Not your favorite guy?"

"No, not so much." Nikki picked up James' now empty glass. "But as long as Andrea likes him, I won't say anything." Bar closed up, lobby lights dimmed, Nikki started toward her suite.

At the door to room 11, Victoria waited, poised to knock. The air around her shimmered, and she glided through the closed door. Nikki stopped, listening for sounds of distress or surprise from the guests in room 11. Silence, only the usual sounds of footsteps overhead and the old building settling for the night.

****

Dressed in identical leather jackets, Nikki and Georgie stepped outside the back door. Cold air chilled her cheeks. The half-moon lit a black sky punctured with stars. The door latched with a click, and Nikki admired Alexander loitering under the lamppost in the parking lot. He strode to her side, took the leash from her hand, and leaned down, brushing her lips in a fleeting kiss. Too quickly, he pulled away.

"Evening, Chief."

He nodded his head in return. "Evening, Ms. Innkeeper." In the quiet alley, their boot heels clicked on the asphalt. The motion lights in the parking lot flicked on and off as they passed. They strolled toward the square; the sounds of merriment grew louder. Conversations punctuated with sudden laughter, music drifting beyond the doors of a dozen bars and clubs. The scents of autumn surrounded them—wood-burning fireplaces, meat cooking on a grill overlaid with pine. Weaving through the groups of tourists, their silence comfortable, they cut across the square, their boots crunching on the dry grass.

Stepping onto the sidewalk along First Street, they started back. "You're quiet tonight, Alex. Everything okay?"

He squeezed her hand, "Yep. Just trying to come up with a plan for date three."

"Does your plan involve kids, dogs, and horses?" she asked. "Or food, music, and friends?"

"My preference?" She nodded. "You, me, food, wine, music, and a soft place to land."

"On the third date?" She raised her eyebrows. "Isn't that a little quick, cowboy?"

He pulled her into the shadow under a tree and wrapped his arms around her. "Can't we count all the kisses at your back door dates?" He leaned in and placed tiny kisses at the edges of her lips. "That has to be fifty dates, maybe a hundred." Their lips met, gently at first. His tongue touched her lips at the seam; she opened for him. She breathed him in, the scent of aftershave, soap, and Alex. He gentled the kiss, slowly lifting his head.

"But we live in a small town, and you live with your mom and two sons. I live with about forty strangers and a dog," Nikki pointed out.

He took her hand again and they walked on. "Your predecessor managed it at least once. I promise I'll find a way, Nik, and no one in this small town needs to know."

In the shadow beside the hotel's back door, Alex handed Nikki the leash and wrapped her in his arms. Nikki's mind ceased running in circles and paused in relief, her only thought how comforted she felt held in Alexander's arms.

Pulling back slowly, Alexander looked into Nikki's

eyes and raised a single eyebrow. "Date fifty-one? A hundred and one?" He winked, turned, and sauntered into the night, disappearing around the corner of the hotel. Not since Aaron had Nikki felt that particular warmth, comfort melded with desire.

****

The scratchy sound of a gramophone playing "The Charleston" woke Nikki from a dreamless sleep. Dawn's subdued light slipped through the lace curtains. In a shadowy corner, Victoria and a tall man stood side by side, their heads down, focusing on their feet. Victoria moved a foot forward to the music, he followed, she stepped back, and he copied her move, she kicked, he kicked and tripped, catching himself by wrapping his arms around Victoria. The room filled with the sound of laughter. The dancers disappeared.

The scents of fresh coffee and cinnamon filled the lobby. Nikki flipped the lock and yanked open the front door for Eric.

"What's for breakfast? Do I have time for coffee?"

Nikki stepped back. Ears and nose red from cold and his hands shoved in the pockets of a heavy puffer jacket, he breathed in the scent of coffee with an "Ahh, my favorite thing about morning, coffee."

"Grab a cup and oatmeal too if you want," Nikki offered. "How's the family?"

Warming his big hand around a mug, he took his first sip. "Fine, except the twins were in a mood this morning and by the time they were dressed and fed, I was late." He saluted her with his cup. "My first cup today. Now I'm likely to survive."

The clatter of feet on the hotel's wooden stairs and the hum of conversation filled the lobby by the time

Nikki and Georgie, dressed in an orange sweater, escaped out the back door for a quick pass through the parking lot. Walking through the alley, Nikki felt the cool fall air caress her cheeks. She probably could have talked James into walking Georgie this morning, but she loved crisp fall mornings in Creekside. Returned to the lobby, Nikki spotted Catherine and her children with James on the veranda, the remains of breakfast spread before them. Lily spotted her first.

Sliding off her chair, landing solidly on her feet, Lily rushed to Nikki just as she opened the door. "Nikki, Nikki, Uncle James brought me a new book."

Lily hung on tight to her treasure but turned the front toward Nikki. "*Berenstain Bears and the Truth.* Hmm. I remember this one. I think Patrick gave me a copy when I was your age." Oh yes, she remembered this book and Patrick's giving. She'd just been sent to her room for some whopper of a story. Patrick, always trying to be the man in the family, the adult to his younger siblings. She didn't remember her father, but Patrick acting like a father when he was barely twelve, that she remembered. She took Lily's hand, leading her back to Catherine. She answered James' grin with a smile. "You remembered the book."

"Yep. Patrick always determined to be the adult, the man of the house, the leader."

"And we fought him every step of the way," she admitted. "Hey, we gave him great practice for being Scott's parent."

Yanking open the basement door, heading toward laundry duty, Nikki chuckled at her memories. Miss Effie had stayed with her during the day while James and Patrick, six and eight years older than her, went to school. But the minute Patrick got home, he acted like the boss, telling them what to do, sitting them down for serious talks when they misbehaved. By the time she reached high school, Nikki understood Patrick better. He just wanted to fill in for their father, to prove they didn't need a father. She was barely two when their father stopped showing up to visit the boys. Her parents divorced six weeks after her birth. As hard as she tried, she couldn't picture him, couldn't pinpoint a single memory he was in.

As she folded the last of the dry towels on the long table, the monitor connecting the lobby to the basement laundry cackled to life, startling her. "Nikki, please come to the lobby."

The basement door clanged shut behind her just as she reached the lobby. Face turning red with anger, his stance intimidating, James stood toe to toe with Keith Johnson on the veranda. Walking onto the veranda, Nikki stepped next to James and both men became silent. "Hello, Keith, what are you doing here?"

"Looking for you, Nikki. Except James stopped me before I could even verify this was the right place." His usually mellow voice boiled with anger and frustration, his handsome face marred by an angry frown.

"What do you want? I can't believe you came all this way just to say hello." Not Keith. She'd learned early in their relationship it was all about Keith's needs, his wants.

"We need to talk. I tried calling, but you blocked my number."

Nikki nodded in satisfaction. "Yep. Blocked. I had nothing to say to you and nothing I wanted to hear." He looked exactly the same. Styled black hair, pressed dress shirt, subtle blue sport jacket, navy trousers on a six-foot frame. Handsome but plastic. A Ken doll with carefully studied expressions and a deep voice.

His frown softened, replaced with a pleading look. "Please, Nikki. It's important. Can we go somewhere so I can explain?"

Nikki recognized the stubborn look on his face. "If it's the only way I can get rid of you. We'll go in my office. James, if you don't mind, you can join us." James nodded, and followed them inside.

Settled behind her desk, Nikki looked at Keith's arrogant expression. Yep, he thinks I'm going to give him whatever he wants. "What is it, Keith? I need to get back to work."

"I have an opportunity to join a general agency. In fact, I would be a partner. It's a great opportunity and all I need to close the deal is a promise from you to consult."

Ah, an opportunity. No doubt an opportunity he couldn't afford. "What does my consulting have to do with you becoming a partner?"

"When you sold the condo, establishing myself in a new place put a hole in my savings. I'm a little short on cash to buy into the agency. They asked what I could give them instead. I said you, as a consultant." He reached across the desk toward her hand. She pulled her hands out of reach.

Nikki shook her head. No surprise Keith still used her name to get ahead. Not hard work, not creative ideas. Just whoever and whatever he could use to make his life better, easier, flashier. "I tossed you out three years ago. Why would I help you now?"

"I knew you weren't at the company anymore.

They all recognized your name. Apparently, you handled getting them started with the company years ago and made a lasting impression."

She shook her head. "Not interested. Why would you think I would be?"

"Because it's great money, and you owe me." His voice rose. "We were lovers once. You owe me."

Nikki stared Keith in the eye, shaking her head. "I owe you nothing." She stood. "This conversation is over. James will walk you out."

"Nikki, you can't mean that. This is important and we both win. You get money, and I get a great opportunity."

"Trust me on this, I do mean it. Goodbye, Keith." Nikki stood behind the desk until James and Keith walked out the door.

Returning to the laundry, she mindlessly folded towels. Everything about their past relationship benefited him. He shared her condo, contributing as little as possible to the bills. He used her knowledge of insurance marketing and management to improve his position in the company where they both worked. Yet he offered nothing in return. Certainly no emotional support while her mom was ill. Every time Nikki approached Keith about contributing financially, he acted as if she was trying to steal from him. Keith believed his charm and good looks should be enough, his presence sufficient payment for room and board. If she hadn't been distracted by Mom's illness, Nikki would have tossed Keith from her life a lot sooner.

She pictured that last morning, the day she kicked him out. The day before was brutal. She started work at seven and ended at six thirty. She picked up dinner from Whole Foods, raced to Mom's. They ate in the kitchen. Nikki felt herself relax surrounded by the familiar, listening again to a story about Mom's brother and sister when they were all young. Mom settled for the night with her therapy dog, Georgie, on a blanket on the floor; Nikki grabbed the bread and eggs she'd bought at Whole Foods and drove home. The sound of Keith talking on his cell phone greeted her when she dragged herself into her condo. She fell, exhausted, into bed, the annoying sound of a television show Keith watched the last thing she heard.

In the morning, dressed for work, Nikki entered her kitchen to the scent of coffee. Toast crumbs covered the counter. The fresh bread left drying out on the cutting board, dirty dishes, and a coffee cup rested on the table. Keith was gone, already on his way to work. No more, last straw. James helped her pack Keith's stuff in boxes, his only comment, "Remind me not to mess up your kitchen or leave the bread out." Nikki cancelled Keith's electronic key. She visited her mom for the afternoon. James waited for Keith. She'd blocked his number. Nikki could see how her focus on career and the signs of her mother's illness allowed Keith to slide deeper into her life without contributing anything.

Pulling herself back to the present, Nikki headed outside. She discovered James and Catherine gone.

Cold, damp air bit into her cheeks when Nikki pushed open the hotel's back door with one hand, Georgie's leash held in the other. The door shut, and she listened for the click. A shadow straightened from the wall beside her, and Alex appeared in the glary yellow light. He leaned in and placed a soft kiss on her lips. "Evening, Lady Innkeeper."

"Evening, Chief." She looped her arm through his, noticed tonight he wore his uniform. As they walked Georgie through the parking lot and dodged tourists on the sidewalk, Alex brought Nikki's thoughts back to Keith.

"It looked like James was about to hit someone on your veranda this morning, Nikki."

Nikki admitted her mild-mannered accountant brother did look at Keith with fire in his eyes. "Yeah. James is a protective older brother." Nikki shook her head. Keith was an idiot to think she'd do anything for him after three years of silence.

"Did a guest get out of hand?" Alex asked, his shoulder bumping hers.

Not surprised Alex heard about James' confrontation with Keith, Nikki knew she'd get questions from her friends about James and Keith. "That wasn't a guest, just an old roommate. He was definitely a mistake I won't make again."

"Looked pretty upset for an old roommate issue." He paused. "Was he more than a roommate?"

"Keith was an unpleasant learning experience. Shows how little attention I was paying to my personal life." Never again would she ignore her personal life. From here on in invited guests only.

"Having a roommate didn't work for you?"

"Being anywhere near Keith didn't work for me. Now I have lots of roommates, but at least they pay their own way." They wove their way around the strolling tourists.

At the back door of The Palace, Alex pulled Nikki into his arms. He gazed into her eyes and whispered, "I promise, Nikki, I'll give more than I take." Lips touching, then pressing, mouths slightly open and tongues gently exploring, Nikki felt her heart race, her skin warm. Alex pulled back slightly and slowly ended the kiss. Nikki realized her arms were wrapped around Alex's waist.

When they separated, Alex gently stroked Nikki's cheek, and quietly said, "Goodnight, Nikki. Dream of me?"

Nikki drifted to sleep. At midnight, she woke to the tinny sound of a slow waltz played on a Victrola resting on a table in a corner. Victoria danced in the arms of a man wearing a long coat. She felt Victoria's sadness as the music ended. The dancers separated, then disappeared, leaving the distant echo of romantic music and the drifting scent of lavender. Hours remained until dawn; she closed her eyes and focused her thoughts on Sara and Kassie, longtime friends and soon to be guests of The Palace. Would Victoria appear for Kassie who believed in spirits, zodiac signs, and the power of good karma? What would they think of Alex? Both attempted matchmaking after her divorce. Both were married and only wanted Nikki happy. She pictured Kassie's husband Neil faced with his new wife's ninety-seven pairs of shoes and chuckled. Nikki drifted back to sleep with a smile on her face.

Chapter Ten

"December 8, 1941, Editor Andrew Stone of the Creekside Reporter wrote, 'Dressed in both patriotic red, white, and blue plus funeral black, homes and businesses in Creekside honor the fallen at Pearl Harbor and the entry of our great country into a second World War. On the veranda of The Palace Hotel, Mrs. Wyatt offered an open bar plus tea, coffee, and lemonade, providing a welcoming place for Creekside residents and visitors to comfort each other. Emanuel Lutheran Church, Saint Mary Catholic Church, and First Baptist Church are holding candlelight vigils tonight at six o'clock. As a community, Creekside joins all the American people in mourning the loss of life at Pearl Harbor, and we pray for those who fight in our name.' "

~A Brief History of The Palace by Arthur Welles

Butterflies danced in Nikki's stomach, anticipation warmed her heart. Two long years since their last girls' trip, a combined girls' trip and bachelorette party for Kassie. Last time they'd been together was Mom's funeral less than a month after Kassie's wedding. So many big events in such a short time—Kassie's wedding, Mom's funeral, birth of Sara's first child. Friends since middle school, celebrating each other's milestones, lifting each other up when things went wrong. From her perch behind the front desk, Nikki watched the spider webs dance in the breeze and the ghost travel across the veranda on his wire. Any minute now, Kassie and Sara would breeze through the front door. Yes, they talked all the time, phoned and texted. Nikki even followed Kassie on social media. Still, nothing could replace being together. The double doors of The Palace banged open; Kassie and Sara burst into the lobby. "Nikki, we're here!"

Nikki dashed around the front desk and flung herself into a group hug. Their familiar scents surrounded her: Sara's light and flowery, Kassie's deeper and slightly exotic, like a subtle orchid. This was what she'd missed. The company of true friends. "Welcome to The Palace. I'm so happy you could make it." By the time husbands Neil and Kevin entered with the luggage, conversation filled the lobby, competing with James Taylor's promise "You've Got a Friend." The two couples grabbed keys and bags, climbed the stairs, and disappeared around the first landing.

Footsteps on wooden stairs and laughter announced their return to the lobby. Nikki watched from her perch behind the bar. Seated at the bar, the couples looked like bookends. Neil and Kevin on the outside, Sara and Kassie the books boasting colorful covers between them. "Hey, Nikki, awesome wine in the welcome basket. Is that local?"

Nikki nodded at Neil, California lawyer, Texas raised. "Yep. Did you drink it all, or are you ready for another glass?" She placed a wine glass in front of him and raised her eyebrows.

"Well, get Kassie and Sara something first, but I'd like another glass."

Taking orders and pouring wine, Nikki smirked at Kevin's description of their flight from Texas. While the others sipped and chatted, she moved among the guests in the lobby, taking orders, pouring wine, making dinner suggestions. Returning to the bar, she offered Neil another glass. "Neil, what do you think of Creekside?"

"Reminds me a little of Temecula, lots of green, a vineyard, some scattered ranches." He frowned and took a sip of wine, chasing it with a handful of the bar's snack mix. "But Nikki, why are we in the ghost room?"

Shrugging, Nikki answered, "Kassie asked."

"You couldn't tell her it was taken?" Neil asked, raising one eyebrow.

"Come on, Neil. You know how hard it is to tell Kassie no." He grimaced. He was famous for not telling Kassie no, for doing whatever she needed, finding whatever she wanted.

"Yeah, but I'm married to her. You're the innkeeper. You needed to say it was already taken."

Nikki shook her head. "And we're friends, so I couldn't lie. You'll like Victoria."

Neil gave her his fierce attorney frown. "I don't plan to see Victoria."

"Quit it, Neil. Stop complaining. I'll protect you from the ghost," Kassie admonished, kissing Neil on the cheek. He moved his wine to his left hand and placed his arm around Kassie's shoulder.

"Nikki's lived here since January and never seen Victoria inside room 15. Unlikely a nonbeliever like you is going to," piped Sara.

"Well, I've seen her at the door of your room, Neil. And Sheri and I saw her at the window from the street."

She didn't mention the other times, or the other spirits who glided through the hotel.

"Oh, big brother, you're such a disappointment." Kevin frowned. "You scared of a little ghost?"

"Not," grumbled Neil.

Waving to Nikki on their way out, Sara and Kassie left in search of dinner. The love between the couples was palpable. The husbands, brothers; the wives, best friends. With an Arizona map spread between them on the game table, the only remaining occupants of the bar were an elderly couple from New Mexico in a heated discussion about where they were going next.

By eight, Nikki hummed along to Sinatra's "Summer Wind" as she set the sparkling wine glasses on the shelf behind the bar. The low squeak of a bar stool sliding across the lobby's old wood floor announced another customer. Nikki turned to Catherine seated at the bar. Catherine propped her elbow on the bar and held her chin in her hand. "Girls asleep, Catherine?"

"Finally. They had a long day." She set a small black box on the counter. "I've brought the monitor just in case, but I think they're both down for the count. Glass of red wine?"

"Of course, Pinot Noir?" At Catherine's nod, Nikki poured the wine, and the music changed to The Platters' "Smoke Gets in Your Eyes." The older couple brought their glasses to the bar and headed down the hallway, wishing a general good evening. Outside, an autumn breeze blew the ghost across the veranda, made spider webs dance, and the tiny pumpkin lights sway. Nikki finished putting the glasses away, and the music changed again, Cole Porter's "I've Got You Under My

Skin."

"Nikki, where do you find your music?" Catherine closed her eyes, sipped her wine, and hummed along to the music.

"Most of it comes from a playlist I created for Mom." Nikki warmed to the memory of Mom tapping her feet to music and humming along to tunes from her youth. "James and Patrick helped me find songs popular when Victoria owned The Palace, so the music's a mix of style and time."

The Beach Boys sang "Good Vibrations," and Catherine commented, "Must be quite a list. I haven't heard the same song twice since I moved in."

Nikki shrugged. "Well, Patrick and James really got into adding songs. Even Scott snuck in a few of his favorites. James added a few more while he was here last weekend. He can be a very useful brother sometimes."

"Definitely a useful friend." Catherine sipped her wine. "I'm not sure what I would have done without him. Lucky break for me, meeting James in college."

"I didn't realize you met in college."

Catherine sipped her wine. "In an international management class. James introduced Craig and me."

"Then you married Craig and instantly became a member of the Benton extended family." Nikki held up the bottle, and at Catherine's nod, poured more wine. The Benton extended family grew every year, adding friends, their spouses, significant others, and children. The other Bentons, Nikki's father's other family, she wondered what became of them. The Beatles sang "Yesterday," and Nikki let the thought go.

"Exactly. I miss Craig, but when I needed him

James stepped up." Catherine's eyes shone with tears, Nikki yanked a tissue from beneath the bar and handed it to her. She wiped her eyes and gave Nikki a tired smile.

"I miss him too. As a fellow member of the Benton family, is there anything I can do to make your stay more comfortable?"

"We're very comfortable. When we move out, it's going to be difficult to give up having breakfast cooked for us," Catherine quipped. "And if Georgie disappears, look first in Lily's suitcase."

"Well, Georgie would probably sneak herself in your car given half a chance. She really loves the girls." She pushed a bowl of snack mix in front of Catherine. "Are you planning to move soon?"

Catherine shook her head. "No, James convinced me to hold off leaving The Palace." She frowned. "When I do leave, I'm thinking about renting something in Creekside. Don't plan on going back to Scottsdale."

"Excellent. Bad enough you'd leave The Palace. At least I'll keep you in Creekside."

"Small town life has definite blessings," Catherine acknowledged. "Friendly people. Walk everywhere so no juggling car seats. Excellent preschool. Lots of blessings."

"And don't forget the community events. The Halloween Party is just around the corner. Do Hope and Lily have their Halloween costumes picked out yet?"

"Lily and I can hardly wait for the party." Catherine took a handful of snack mix. "Hope has no idea what's going on. She gets excited every time Lily gets excited, but I don't think she knows why. Another great thing about living at The Palace, I don't have to worry about how I am going to hand out candy and take the girls out too."

Catherine picked up her monitor and slid off the barstool. "One more excellent advantage is having an adult to talk to at the end of a long day spent with two little ones." She placed her empty glass on the bar. "And an endless variety of wine. Thanks for the wine and the conversation." She disappeared down the hallway to the mellow sound of Frank Sinatra singing "Young at Heart."

****

Cold wind and a black sky greeted Nikki when she stepped through the back door. Clouds covered most of the crescent moon, the only light artificial yellow back door light, and white streetlight. Georgie's fluffy white ears blew up like tiny kites. Nikki laughed. "Oh, are you channeling the flying nun tonight, Georgie?" With a short bark, Georgie pulled Nikki toward the light post and a man-sized shadow. Alex leaned against the pole. The click of his boot heels on asphalt, the jingle of Georgie's tags, and they met in the alley. He leaned in and placed a fleeting kiss on her lips. "Evening, Ms. Innkeeper."

Placing her hands on his shoulders, Nikki lifted to her toes and returned the kiss. "Chief." She nodded at his jeans and flannel shirt. "You off tonight or undercover?"

He took Georgie's leash and placed his arm around Nikki's shoulder. "Off. It'd be really difficult to be undercover in a town the size of Creekside." They dodged the few clumps of tourists on the sidewalk. The wind picked up, restaurants and bars closed their doors against the cold, the sound of music escaped only when someone entered or left.

Under the yellow light at the hotel's back door, Alex pulled Nikki against him, wrapping both arms around her, his chin on the top of her head. Nikki turned toward Alex. She laid her head against his chest, breathing in the scent of his aftershave, accepting his comfort, feeling his heartbeat. Alex kissed her cheek, then her ear, nuzzling her neck. "You're the best part of my day." He placed his lips gently against hers, licking the seam. Nikki sighed, and his tongue slid in. Alex groaned softly. "Someday soon, Nikki." He stepped back, ending the embrace.

Nikki stepped out of his arms. "Perhaps Date Three?" Nikki yanked open the door. Georgie pranced through and stopped. Victoria stood at the door to room 11, her hand raised to knock. Complete silence filled the hallway. Victoria lowered her hand and glided through the closed door. Nikki waited. No sounds of surprise, no screams. Victoria managed to enter the room without disturbing the guests. From the lobby, the slow sounds of the Everly Brothers singing "All I Have to Do is Dream" drifted down the hallway. Perhaps tonight she'd close her eyes and dream of Alex.

Startled awake from a dream involving flying ghosts, dancing trees, and black clouds, Nikki opened her eyes to faint light peeking between the curtain panels and Georgie making whimpering sounds in her sleep. Pulling aside the curtain, Nikki watched the gathering storm. Within the hour the scent of coffee, the hum of conversation, and the joyous sounds of The Fifth Dimension's "Aquarius—Let the Sunshine In" filled the lobby. Nikki kept the coffee pot filled, the breakfast bar full, and found time to greet all her guests moving about the tables. She joined Kassie and Sara for a quick cup and admired Kassie's emerald green raincoat hanging on the coat rack. "Boy, I miss borrowing your clothes and your shoes."

"Show up in California anytime, and I'll share." Kassie's eyes twinkled. "I told Neil the reason I have ninety-seven pairs of shoes is so my friends can borrow." Breakfast ended and the clouds moved on, leaving a cold mist behind and Bill Withers singing "Ain't No Sunshine When She's Gone."

From behind the front desk, Nikki watched Eric bounce up the steps at four o'clock. "Oh, I love late days. Charlotte and the twins let me sleep this morning, and I'm ready to work." He tossed his jacket on the coatrack and stuck out both hands.

"Good." Nikki handed him the laptop. "It's all yours."

Neil pulled open the front door, and the lobby filled with the sound of Kassie and Sara's laughter. Kassie grabbed Nikki's hand. "Half hour on the veranda, right?"

Nikki nodded. The sound of their animated conversation drifted down the stairs.

"You gonna change too? Or are you wearing a Palace shirt to White Cloud?"

Startled out of her distraction, Nikki looked at Eric's raised eyebrow. "Guard The Palace, Eric. Don't wait up." His chuckles followed her down the hallway.

Outside the windows of the White Cloud van, fields of grass marched beside rows of grape vines. Kassie turned from the window and asked Nikki, "So, beside vineyards, what else is out here?"

"Other than National Forest, there are a few family owned ranches, a large commercial farm, and I'm not sure what else. I'm embarrassed I haven't had time to look around much."

"What about horseback riding?" Kassie suggested. "I know you ride. Surely there's a stable around here."

Nikki felt hot color warm her cheeks. "I've taken a couple of rides at Windsong. It's just past the winery."

Kassie winked. "Oh, Windsong…right. Where the police chief lives." They burst into giggles. "So, when do we meet the cowboy chief?"

Before Nikki could answer, the van stopped. The driver opened the door, offering his hand for the long step down. "Welcome to White Cloud Winery Tasting room." A meticulously restored Craftsman home stood before them. "The tasting room building was built in 1910 by Brian Andrews, who homesteaded the one hundred and sixty acres that are now White Cloud."

They climbed the few steps to the old-fashioned porch where a pair of wooden rockers glided in the fall breeze. He grinned as though he knew a secret and pulled open the front door, indicating they should enter. They stepped over the threshold into a large room, one long wall filled with wine bottles and a long bar stretched the length of the wall. A young woman dressed in black and white came from behind the bar, leading them to a table under the front window. For the next four hours they sipped, ate, and learned about wine, food, and the history of White Cloud Winery and the original homesteader.

Sated and completely relaxed, they climbed into the van. Kassie collapsed against Neil's shoulder. "Ugh. Between the alcohol and the food, I'm exhausted. Only one thing was missing."

Kevin wrapped his arm around Sara, pulled her close, and closed his eyes. "What?"

Giggling, Sara nuzzled against him. "No ghost story. Is White Cloud the only old building in Creekside without a ghost?"

"Maybe they just don't advertise their ghost. Probably want your focus totally on the wine," Nikki suggested. During dessert, she'd caught a glimpse of a man dressed in overalls and flannel shirt, his elbow on the bar. A smirk on his face, he'd winked at her. Before she could comment, he'd disappeared.

Kevin frowned. "But a ghost is good for business in a hotel?"

"Victoria's great for business. Lots of guests book rooms hoping to see a ghost." Nikki nodded. "Plus, I can't see the winery admitting someone died in their tasting room. Doesn't go well with food and drink."

Kassie opened her eyes. "Is that the reason The Palace is haunted? Did Victoria die in her room?"

"Legend has it she did, but I don't imagine she was the first or last person to die in a hotel room. My personal theory is she haunts the hotel because she was happy there with her son and her dog. Even though her son died on the battlefield during World War II, for Victoria, his memory lives in The Palace where he grew up."

"That's pretty comforting when you think about it, being able to surround yourself with good memories for eternity. Have you been visited by Victoria?"

"Visited by? Not really, but I've seen her. Sometimes she's alone, but mostly there's someone else involved. It's why I think she may have chosen to remain in the hotel. She didn't want to leave everyone she loved behind."

Kassie's eyes widened, and Neil groaned. "Who else do you see?"

"Her son, her dog, and a man. You may think I'm nuts, but sometimes when she disappears, she leaves a whisper of intense emotion behind and the scent of lavender."

"We're sleeping in her room." Kassie frowned. "We haven't seen her. Sometimes I turn around and think someone is standing there. Neil keeps telling me it's my imagination."

"Victoria may be visiting you." Nikki shrugged. "Many of the town's people tell me they saw her in your window while the hotel was vacant. In fact, my neighbor at Cuppa Joes called the Realtor asking him to check on the property because she saw something in the window and thought someone had broken in. They couldn't find anything, and the only explanation for what she saw was a ghost."

"Nikki, please don't encourage Kassie," Neil groused. "I can accept she's more sensitive to things the rest of us can't see, but it still drives me nuts. Besides, we have happier things to discuss. Tell them Kassie."

"A birth mother chose us." Kassie's face lit up. "We're adopting her baby as soon as she's born, only three months from now. It's crazy; we never thought we'd start our family so soon." Congratulations filled the van as it cruised to a stop in front of The Palace. Nikki climbed out last, sliding the van door closed behind her. Standing quiet at the bottom of the veranda steps, she noticed the shadow of a woman at the lobby window. Nikki blinked. The woman disappeared.

Warmed by Victoria's version of a welcome home, Nikki followed her friends inside, listening to the bantering interspersed with laughter as they climbed the stairs. Watching them go, Nikki felt a pang of envy pinch her heart. A baby. Kassie a mother. Someday, maybe she'd adopt. She didn't need a partner to be a parent. After all, a single mom raised her, and she turned out okay.

Dressed in a flannel nightgown, her feet encased in fuzzy socks, Nikki curled up on the sitting room sofa. Georgie hopped up beside her, laid her head on her paws, and closed her eyes. Nikki tried focusing on the romance novel. Tonight, the book couldn't hold her interest. Her mind wandered away from the story. Instead, she pictured Kassie and Neil with their new baby. Her friends were moving on, chasing their dreams, and building families. She put the novel back on the table, reached over, and scratched behind Georgie's ears. Closing her eyes, she imagined a child running through the sitting room, doing homework in the library, eating breakfast in the lobby. Yeah, she could do this.

Just before dawn, Nikki walked out the front door to the veranda. She looked up. In the window of room 15 stood Victoria. Nikki turned toward the street; a man wearing a long coat and bowler walked away, disappearing into the shadows.

Chapter Eleven

"Arriving in a black Ford coupé with several young men from college, RJ returned to The Palace in May of 1942 prior to entering the army. For two weeks, the young men enjoyed the hospitality of The Palace and the encouragement of their neighbors. According to the Creekside Reporter, 'Victoria Wyatt hosted a festive celebration on June first, providing a cheerful send-off for the group.' According to Victoria's letter, found among Judge Welles' personal effects, the very next day all the young men piled into the Ford Roadster heading to Fort Huachuca."

~A Brief History of The Palace by Arthur Welles

The scent of coffee lingered in the lobby, sunlight through the front windows warmed the room, and Nikki leaned against the front desk. The tap of shoes on the wooden stair, the hum of conversation from the stairwell, and Kassie and Sara reached the desk, grabbing Nikki in a hug.

"Oh, Nikki, this was so much fun," exclaimed Kassie as she and Sara checked out. "I can't swear I saw a ghost, but maybe."

Enjoying their familiar banter, Nikki returned the hugs. "Haunted hotels can't guarantee ghost sightings. I'm so glad you came for the weekend. Maybe next time I can take more time off."

"Next time you visit us. I can't promise a ghost, but you won't have to work at all."

"Yes, next time you come to us," the others chorused.

"Oh, I'll find a way even without a ghost, especially when Kassie's baby comes home." Nikki grabbed Kassie for another hug. "I'm so excited for you."

Kassie looked at Nikki, then at Neil. "Home, that's right, our baby's coming home." She reached for Neil, and he pulled her close, wrapping his arm around her shoulder. "Nikki, please do come, anytime, before the baby comes home or after."

Nikki watched her friends walk outside and down the steps to their car. Neil carried a suitcase, his other arm around Kassie's shoulder. Sara's blond ponytail danced in the sun as she laughed at something Kevin said. Love surrounded them, so strong it was almost tangible.

****

Conversation and loud music coming from the Highwayman muffled the sound of the latching back door as Nikki walked through the parking lot. Cold air struck her cheeks, making her grateful for warm boots and a leather jacket. Georgie wagged her curly white tail as she passed under the motion light, each one offering a white circle shining on the asphalt. Nikki merged onto the sidewalk; just like the freeway, they paused at the edge until she spotted a break and slipped between groups out for a good time. Turning left onto Beatrice, Nikki then turned onto Center, heading toward the square. Georgie went from prancing slightly ahead to plastering herself against Nikki's leg.

"What is it, little girl, too many people in too small a space?" Nikki whispered as she lifted Georgie into her arms. Removing Georgie's hat and sliding it into the pocket of her leather jacket, Nikki placed Georgie against her shoulder and reversed direction, returning to the back door of The Palace with Georgie in her arms. Alex waited in the shadow beside the door.

Straightening from his slouch against the wall, he leaned in and brushed her lips with a soft kiss. "Mind if I come in?"

Nikki answered, "Of course not, Chief. I'm surprised to see you though."

"I'm surprised to be here," he admitted.

The click of the key in the sitting room door seemed loud. She pushed open the door and looked around quickly, hoping she'd straightened up before her walk. "Georgie and I attempted a walk, but once beyond the parking lot, she didn't like all the people and noise." Nikki grabbed the throw from the sofa and folded it along the back while Alex hung his jacket on the coat rack beside the door. "Have a seat. Something to drink?"

Alex collapsed on the sofa. "I'd love a glass of water. I'm still working but needed a break."

Nikki poured water from a pitcher into two glasses, pulled off Georgie's coat and boots, and curled up on the sofa's other end.

Nikki watched him down the water, and his eyes drifted shut. "Tough night?"

"Yeah, I've been on about eighteen hours, filling in for a sick officer. The sidewalks are full of tourists, excellent for the economy but a stretch for our small department." His eyes opened. "Promise me if you have a problem beyond the usual with any of your guests, rather than handle it alone, you'll call for back-up."

Alex set the glass on the coffee table and stood. His big hands reached for Nikki, drawing her into his arms. He placed his lips on hers. On a sigh, Nikki parted her lips, touched his lips with the tip of her tongue, and wrapped her arms around him. Comforted by the strength in his arms, the sound of his heartbeat, and the familiar scent of his aftershave, she relaxed against his hard chest. Nikki felt rather than heard him moan. He gentled the kiss, drawing away.

Placing his callused hands on her cheeks, he focused his beautiful eyes on hers. "Ah, Nikki. Sometimes this is the best and worst part of my day." Dropping his hands, he stepped back and grabbed his coat. "Good night, Innkeeper." The click of the latch and he was gone.

Nikki washed their glasses and wondered at his comment, best and worst. His body told her he wanted her physically. Then what? An end or a beginning? If a beginning, a beginning of what? Feeling restless at the questions without answers, Nikki slid her feet back into shoes, grabbed her key, and slipped out the door toward the lobby and a glass of wine. Shadows filled the lobby, the night-lights shining only on the front desk and the base of the stairs. A shadow moved away from the front window. Victoria faced Nikki. The spirit lifted her eyebrows and turned her head slightly to the side. Nikki heard a scratching sound. Victoria disappeared and Nikki realized the sound came from the upstairs veranda. Nikki climbed the stairs and used her code to open the door. "Thank God you're here," said a voice from the shadows. "We're freezing."

Nikki turned toward the sound and faced two teenage girls. "You're from room 23?" They nodded. "What are you doing out here?"

"We were just telling ghost stories and someone locked the door," answered the taller girl.

Nikki held the door open. "Be sure to lock your room door." Nikki listened for the sound of the dead bolt sliding into place. Hmm. Shaking her head at Victoria's attempt to help the two girls, Nikki climbed the attic stairs. The sound of children's giggles echoed in the stairwell. Yanking the door open, she stopped. Three young boys in stocking feet slid across the polished wood floor. Playing a game that involved a great deal of falling and laughing, the boys ignored the rain sheeting down the attic windows as they slid. A large dog bounded into the fray, knocked one boy down then licked his face, and Nikki suddenly knew the boy was RJ and the dog Smokey. Nikki blinked, and the vision disappeared.

After sipping a glass of red wine, Nikki finally crawled in bed. She awoke with a start. Rain sheeted the window. At the side of her bed stood Georgie, whining quietly, her warning whine. Focusing on the sound for a moment, Nikki heard someone at the front door; grabbing her sweatshirt and slipping into a pair of loafers, Nikki slipped the leash on Georgie, put her keys and phone in the sweatshirt pocket, and headed for the front door.

On the other side of the glass doors, four couples dripped onto the veranda. "After ten, only registered guests are allowed in the hotel. Which rooms are you in?" The tallest of the young women held up one key, a tiny blond held up the other. "Welcome home, Ms.

Andrews, Ms. Romero, Ms. Holden, and Ms. Rice. Gentlemen, have a safe journey home. Please let me know if I should call you a cab."

A tall, dark-haired man shook his head. "No thanks. We're staying at the St. George. Goodnight."

The young men turned toward the street, walking quickly in the rain, and her guests headed up the stairs. Nikki waited in the lobby until she heard the doors close upstairs. Leaving only very dim light in the lobby, she returned to her suite. She couldn't remember when she was young enough that drinking a little too much and walking in a cold rain just before dawn was fun. Her sweatshirt back on the coatrack, the loafers relegated to a basket beside the door, Nikki watched Georgie trot through the doorway into the bedroom and curl up in her bed. Alex probably wouldn't consider Georgie much back up. Nikki slid into bed, closed her eyes, and drifted immediately back to sleep.

****

Morning arrived, and with it clear skies. Last night's rain left puddles on the sidewalk and wet grass in the square, but not a single cloud in the sky. Eric and Nikki worked together, keeping the bar supplied with breakfast items and fresh coffee and loading the dishwasher. When Nikki returned to the lobby from the kitchen, she found the four young women waiting.

"Good morning, ladies. I hope you slept well."

"We did, Ms. Benton; we wanted to apologize for waking you last night," said a blushing Ms. Rice. "The second we saw you headed toward the front door we knew we were making too much noise."

"Apology accepted. I hope you enjoy the balance of your stay at The Palace." Nikki watched the young women gather breakfast from the bar and head out to the veranda. Four young men carrying coffee cups from Cuppa Joe's joined them. Nikki chuckled; at least the young men remembered them in the morning.

Walking through the bar to the front desk, Nikki saw Karen fidgeting at the desk. "Hi, Karen, how may I help you today?"

"Hi, Nikki, I want to rent Victoria's room for tonight. I know you said the tour couldn't go upstairs, but I figure if I pay for the room you wouldn't keep me out."

"The room's taken. The hotel's completely full for the weekend." Nikki frowned. "The tour members couldn't go up there anyway, since they're not registered guests."

Karen's voice rose. "You're not being reasonable."

"Your tour is welcome to enter the lobby and that's all. If you choose not to stop at The Palace, that's fine."

Karen turned on her heel and stomped out the door. Deciding acting was better than reacting, Nikki called Eric and asked him to return at seven thirty and stay until closing.

When Victoria's opened at five, a mixture of hotel guests and local people filled the bar. By the time the tour arrived in the lobby at eight o'clock, only a few patrons remained in the bar, including Mary Beth and Clinton Wright and Shelby. Nikki stood behind the bar and Eric behind the front desk as Karen began her ghost story. Five minutes into the story, Nikki heard mumbling from Karen's audience, shuffling of feet. "Thought we were going upstairs," a young man mumbled. Karen gathered her group and headed out the front door, and Nikki wished the group a good evening as the last person exited.

Eric turned to Nikki. "Did it sound to you like she promised them a visit to Victoria's room and the upstairs veranda?"

"Yes, which explains her visit this afternoon. Thank you all for hanging out until she left. The last drink's on me." She headed up the stairs to lock the veranda. The guests from room 27 sat at a table, glasses of wine in front of them. "Good evening. It's time to lock the veranda. You're welcome to take your drinks to your room, the lobby, the library, or the downstairs veranda."

"We'll take our drinks downstairs," Mrs. Cove commented. "When we checked earlier, the lobby was busy with a group."

"The group's gone." Probably not a coincidence her friends visited Victoria's tonight and stayed until Karen's group left. How lucky she was in her friends.

The sound of squealing children and the clanks of a miniature amusement park drifted on the cold night air of Halloween. Ghosts, goblins, cowboys, pirates, witches, and super heroes visited The Palace, threatening trick or treat, thanking Nikki for the treats. The party ended, and Nikki began removing Halloween decorations, leaving in place the uncarved pumpkins in honor of fall.

Balancing boxed Halloween decorations in her arms, Nikki climbed the steep stairs to the attic. At the threshold, she paused at the sound of laughter. She unlocked the door and stopped. There, in the shadows, four boys sat on the floor playing a board game. Smokey lay next to RJ, his focus on the action. Victoria stood in the shadows, a smile lighting her face. Nikki flipped on the light. Boys, dog, and Victoria disappeared, leaving only an echo of laughter. Nikki stacked the boxes next to the wall, and her eyes swept the attic. No wonder guests returned to The Palace. Who could resist the sense of fun and echoes of laughter lingering in the rooms?

Chapter Twelve

"On July 1, 1942, a white star appeared in the front window of The Palace, announcing RJ was officially serving in the Armed Forces. In an editorial written by Cyrus Stone of the Reporter, he states, 'Ten family businesses in our small community proudly display the white star honoring a family member serving the United States, including Creekside Theatre, the Creekside Reporter, Maple's Grocery, Abel's Hardware, Gas and Go, the Birdcage Saloon, Wilton's Dry Goods, Grandma's Bakery, Emanuel Lutheran Church, and The Palace Hotel. War has come to our small town in a big way. We pray no star ever turns to gold.'"

~A Brief History of The Palace by Arthur Welles

Sunlight danced through the windows, turning the mellow wood floors to gold. Perched on the stool behind the front desk, her mind focused on the laptop and upcoming reservations, Nikki suddenly felt a warm presence beside her and inhaled the scent of lavender. Lips curved in a smile, Victoria stood beside Nikki. The click of the door latch and the doorbell chime pulled Nikki's attention to the front door. A leather duffle on his shoulder, a young man strode over the threshold, his teeth flashing in a smile, his blue eyes framed by wire glasses. "RJ Wyatt. I have a reservation." He dug into his pocket, pulling out ID and a credit card. Nikki checked RJ in, handing him the key to room 15. "The ghost room, right?" he asked as she dropped the key into his hand.

She nodded. "First room on the left at the top of the stairs."

He started climbing the stairs. Nikki felt Victoria dissolve, leaving the faint scent of lavender. The click of nails on the wood floor and Smokey appeared at the base of the stairs. With a leap, he took them two at a time and disappeared.

Five o'clock darkness crept across the sky and Nikki lit the front veranda's fire pit, enjoying the sudden whoosh of warmth from the gas flames. Tourists still congregated on the square and crowded the sidewalk, conversation punctuated by laughter drifting on the night air. She strolled down the stairs to the sidewalk, slipping between clumps of tourists. Across the street she turned back, examining The Palace from the outside, seeing what others saw when they noticed her. Light shone from the lobby, Eric visible behind the bar. Small lamps lit the upstairs veranda where a wine bottle rested between two glasses on a small table and a couple lounged in two Adirondack chairs. Nikki recognized RJ Wyatt sitting across from a young woman at a table in the window. In the shadow behind the front desk, Victoria appeared. She faced RJ. He threw back his head in laughter. Victoria disappeared.

At nine o'clock, bundled in heavy coats and boots, Georgie and Nikki slipped through the back door and listened for the latch clicking into place. A black velvet sky sprinkled with stars and a crescent moon greeted them. The motion lights' glow lit their way across the parking lot. Nikki's mind whirled with questions about the relationship between the living RJ Wyatt and the ghostly Victoria. She felt herself crash into a warm body wearing a familiar scent.

A deep rumbling voice asked, "Isn't this how we met?" Alex leaned down and kissed her cheek.

"Why, Officer, is that how you greet every woman who crashes into you?"

His arm around her, their sides pressed together, she felt rather than heard him chuckle. "Only innkeepers of haunted hotels."

They walked through the cold, quiet night, her arm around his waist, his across her shoulders. Music from the surrounding bars and restaurants seemed far away. As they returned to the hotel, he pulled her into his arms, and his lips met hers in a combination of cold softness and warm breath. Ending the kiss, he stepped back, wished her good night, and slipped away, disappearing in the shadows of the alley.

Leaving Georgie curled in her bed in the suite, Nikki climbed the stairs for a final check of the upstairs veranda. Cold air blasted her cheeks when she stepped outside. Across the street, a tall man wearing a bowler hat faced The Palace. He turned away, strode toward the shadows in the next block, his long coat flapping against his legs, and disappeared. Nikki slipped back inside, locking the veranda door. Her hand on the knob, Victoria stood facing room 15. She slipped through the closed door and disappeared.

The Sunday afternoon sun shone through the lobby windows, the autumn sky boasted only a few white clouds, and dry leaves danced across the veranda at the whim of a gentle breeze. Sitting at the front desk responding to emails on her laptop and humming along to Nat King Cole's "Autumn Leaves," Nikki glanced up to find RJ watching her.

"Hi, are you enjoying your weekend, Mr. Wyatt?"

"Please, call me RJ." He nodded. "For a small town, Creekside certainly believes in entertainment. Do you mind if I ask you questions about Victoria and the hotel?"

"Of course not." Nikki closed the laptop. "Stories about our famous ghost help me stay in business." Nikki handed him a copy of the hotel's brochure, folded to the section giving a brief history of The Palace. "It's one reason room 15 is popular."

Frowning, he took the brochure. "Did Victoria Wyatt actually die in room 15?"

Nikki shrugged. "Legend claims she did, although there are multiple versions of her passing." Knowing RJ specifically requested room 15, she continued, "You wouldn't think that would make the room particularly attractive, but it's our most popular room."

He slipped the brochure in his backpack. "But it wasn't a violent death or early death."

"Some claim she died quietly in her bed; others say the housekeeper found her in the rocking chair facing the window, waiting for RJ to return. Another story says she died on a settee in the lobby." Since Victoria appeared throughout the hotel, no way to guess where she died.

"So maybe the room's not really special."

Nikki shrugged. "Who knows? The Creekside Reporter ran an obituary at the time but stated only that there would be a graveside service for Victoria, no details of her passing."

RJ frowned. "Would the newspaper office have copies of the papers from that time?"

"I've no idea, but until a few months ago, the Reporter was owned by the same family for several generations." Nikki slid the laptop into the safe under the front desk. "Are you a history buff, RJ?"

"At the moment I'm focusing on my family's history," he admitted. "Victoria Wyatt was my great-grandmother, although my father never met her. I'm also trying to determine who my great-grandfather was."

Nikki realized Victoria recognized RJ Wyatt and so did Smokey. Victoria visited his room. Smokey followed him through the hotel. "I wish you luck in your quest."

Laptop bag thrown over his shoulder, RJ waved to Nikki and slipped out the front door into the early evening. Beside the lobby window, Victoria stood staring toward the sidewalk, Smokey, his ears pricked up, sat beside her. As Nikki watched, RJ slipped out of sight. Victoria and Smokey disappeared.

Wednesday morning, the lobby hummed with conversation and the scent of coffee lingered in the air. Doris Day sang "Sentimental Journey," accompanied by the Les Brown Band. Perched behind the front desk, Nikki handed a receipt to an elderly couple, felt a warm presence beside her, and caught the scent of lavender. Footsteps clattered on the wooden stairs, and RJ appeared at the front desk, his laptop bag slung over his shoulder. He dropped a leather duffle at his feet and handed her the room key. Nikki looked into his youthful face and realized he did not sense Victoria.

"Did you enjoy your stay, RJ?"

"Yep. Thanks for the tip about the newspaper. It helped a little." He dashed a signature across the tablet. "I know more than when I started. The Reporter has back copies of the paper. Most of the newspaper is still paper instead of digital."

Nikki pictured a hundred years of newspapers stacked in boxes. "Were they organized at least?" She printed his receipt and handed it to him.

"Filed in boxes by year and stored in various closets."

Nikki grimaced. "Oh, that must have been very slow research. Did you learn anything?"

He frowned, stuffing the receipt into his pocket. "The Reporter didn't delve much into Victoria's past when she arrived in Creekside; the community seems to have allowed Victoria to keep her secrets even when she gave birth to her son with no husband around."

"For that time, she should have been a scandal."

"Yeah. In a small town, I expected to find evidence of any scandals or secrets in the newspaper. What else do small town papers have to report?" RJ shook his head. "Today a child without a father is accepted. Almost normal, but in 1921?"

"Victoria built a hotel; she obviously had money, and perhaps that bought her privacy." Nikki decided to satisfy her curiosity. "What made you start researching her now?"

"I told my father I was taking some time off to see the country. He asked me to find what information I could about his father. Grandma Gracie never mentioned her first husband except to say he died during World War II. Judging by the newspaper, my father was born just before Robert died."

"Will you be back to continue your research?"

"For now I'm off to Phoenix looking for copies of Victoria's and RJ's birth and death certificates. I'm hoping those will give me a clue where to go next. I'm also going into Freemont to see what I can discover about the judge listed as beneficiary in Victoria's will."

"Good luck, RJ. I hope you find what you're looking for." Watching RJ stroll through the front door, Nikki felt Victoria's presence slip away, leaving only a faint scent of lavender.

Thanksgiving Day, Nikki woke to a cold nose and freezing toes. Pulling her feet under the blankets and curling her legs against her chest, she dreaded placing naked feet against the cold floor. No sound of the cycling heater greeted her. She wished she'd turned the heat on last night. Nikki forced herself out of bed. She dashed to the dresser and yanked out a pair of thick socks, flipping the heater on as she passed the thermostat. Peeking over the top of her dog bed, Georgie's gaze met Nikki's.

"Don't bother getting up till it's warmer," Nikki commented. The thermostat read forty-eight degrees, twenty cooler than yesterday's low. Shivering, Nikki threw on clothes, brushed her hair and teeth, and started for the kitchen. Moments later the scent of fresh coffee filled the lobby, breakfast crowded the bar, and Bing Crosby crooned "Deep Purple." The lobby filled with the hum of conversation. James and Patrick bused tables and kept the coffee pot full while Scott hauled dishes to the kitchen and loaded the dishwasher. Patrick, watching Nikki wash white potatoes and toss them in the Crock-Pot, asked, "Does this remind you of all our other Thanksgivings? You're washing potatoes, and the rest of us are fetching and carrying."

Nikki dropped the last tiny potato in and stuck the lid on. "Definitely, except this one is a little different."

Patrick rinsed a mug and piled it in the dishwasher. "How? Other than location and Mom not here."

"You know that expression 'It takes a village to raise a child'?" Patrick nodded. "Well, it took a town to make Thanksgiving dinner."

"Really?"

Nikki counted on her fingers, "Turkey from Wellingtons, green beans from Lone Star, ham from Creekside Station, rolls from Grandma's Bakery, and Catherine's bringing pies from there too. I'm making potatoes and Mom's dressing. Pretty much the whole town."

Patrick pulled her into a hug. "Then I won't feel guilty you did all the work since you had a whole town to help."

****

At one o'clock, Nikki slid into her chair at the table in the library. The table groaned under the weight of Thanksgiving dinner. Conversation and laughter filled the air. Lily climbed off her chair and settled on James' lap, Hope giggled at Scott's funny faces, and Vera Lynn sang "We'll Meet Again." Patrick rose and quiet reigned.

He lifted his glass. "To Nikki, Catherine, and the town of Creekside. Thank you for Thanksgiving dinner." He sat, taking her hand and Scott's. Soon all their hands were linked, and they gave thanks. Platters and bowls of food traveled around the table, and their voices filled the air.

A still, cold, clear night greeted the Bentons when they trooped out the back door at nine thirty. Bundled in heavy coats, they strolled through the parking lot, Georgie in the lead.

A tiny white cloud formed from Scott's breath. "Oh, this is cool. Something I've never seen in San Diego."

"Yeah. We don't have a beach, but wait a few weeks and we may have snow." She shivered, and James put his arm around her shoulder.

Scott asked, "Tomorrow we decorate, Aunt Nikki?"

"Right. The minute our business meeting's over, we decorate."

"Just like every Friday after Thanksgiving any of us can remember." James groaned.

"Bentons thrive on tradition," Patrick added. "Nikki, can we expect to see all our old favorites among the decorations?"

"Some old, some new. Are you getting anxious to get started?"

"More like anxious to be done," chorused Patrick and James. Every year they decorated their mom's house the day after Thanksgiving. Every year Patrick and James complained. She knew they secretly enjoyed the decorating. The moans and groans were for effect.

Friday morning after breakfast, the Bentons, carrying mugs, left the scent of coffee and the hum of conversation behind and trooped down the hallway to Nikki's sitting room. James lounged on one end of the sofa. Nikki set her coffee down and pulled a stack of papers off the small desk.

"Are you calling the meeting to order since you're

officially in charge?"

Nikki handed James and Patrick a packet. "You're just jealous because I'm managing partner."

Flipping through the cost estimates, James shook his head. "Oh no, never jealous. The managing partner gets all the problems and all the grief. Patrick and I just get the income."

Hands on her hips, Nikki frowned. "If that's true, why did you fight putting me totally in charge of the hotel?"

James blushed. "Hey, just trying to protect my baby sister from working too hard."

"Right." Nikki shook her head. "Let's get started."

James flipped through the pages. "Your occupancy is higher than we predicted. Are you regretting turning room 4 into a library and making your suite three rooms?"

"No regrets." Nikki shook her head. "The library is popular with guests, especially on rainy days or unusually cold nights. Plus, with the high occupancy, sometimes I need the library for breakfast."

Patrick turned the pages and pulled out the proposal for the attic remodel. "How will you use the attic rooms? If I remember, the steps are steep and hidden behind a panel door."

"The bid's for four baths and dividing the space into four large units and one storage area."

"Is there much stuff still stored up there?" James frowned. "I don't think I even climbed the stairs when we looked at the property."

"Very little," Nikki answered and shook her head. "You climbed the stairs, looked around, and immediately left." Nikki pulled out the occupancy figures and a comparison of rates with the other two hotels. "I'm sure we can support two additional rooms and the increase in price for the extras. I'm just not ready to commit the entire attic to guests."

James nodded. "Sounds good."

"Well, it's a good thing I agree since I don't have enough clout to veto," Patrick commented. "Who knows, maybe I'll take over the second half as a vacation apartment."

The Palace was dressed for Christmas when the weekend ended. Circled by a small electric train and decorated with lights and tiny toys, a living pine tree nestled in a red pot sat on the veranda. Solar fairy lights and ribbon garland wrapped around the railings, a wreath hung on the front desk, and on the backs of the bar stools, red felt covers with white pom-poms provided the illusion of giant Santa hats.

From her perch behind the front desk, Nikki watched James and Patrick drive away. As they turned the corner, disappearing out of sight, Victoria appeared behind the bar with a champagne glass in her hand. Their gazes caught. Victoria lifted her glass in a toast and slowly dissolved, leaving the scent of lavender drifting in the air. Nikki shook her head. Was Victoria approving the Christmas decorations? Nikki shrugged. Why not?

Smiling at memories of Patrick and James complaining about decorating the hotel, Nikki drifted off to sleep. In the darkest part of the night, she woke to the sound of laughter. On a nearly transparent table in the corner, Victoria sat across from RJ, a board game spread between them. Victoria moved a playing piece and whispered, "Got you. And I'm not sorry." Her laughter and RJ's giggles filled the room. Georgie whined. They disappeared.

****

Breathing in the scent of fresh coffee, Nikki hummed along to the Rascals singing "A Beautiful Morning." The patter of little tennis shoes on the wood floor announced Lily's arrival. "Aunt Nikki, today I'm decorating the church for Christmas." Lily turned in a circle and danced over to a table by the window.

"You are. Wow, that's a big job for one little girl."

Lily giggled. "My friends will help."

Catherine followed Lily, holding Hope's hand as she slowly followed her sister.

"Morning, Nikki." Catherine secured Hope in the booster chair and started filling plates. "Thanks again for including us in Thanksgiving."

"Thank you," Nikki responded. "It was so much fun having you and the girls." She poured herself another mug of coffee and rinsed the pot. "Plus, the girls helped a lot with the decorating."

Catherine rolled her eyes. "Oh yeah, a lot of help if you like having your train moved a dozen times and the ornaments hung mostly on one branch."

Nikki shrugged and refilled the coffee pot. "But having the girls meant James and Patrick couldn't complain as much."

Catherine started cutting up Hope's food. Soon the lobby filled with cheerful conversation. Nikki looked up from a final cleaning of the bar. Bundled in heavy winter coats, her tennis shoes replaced with boots, Lily wrapped her gloved hand around the stroller handle and helped Catherine push Hope down the sidewalk. Nikki pictured Lily decorating the sanctuary at Emanuel

Lutheran Church all by herself, surrounded by giant ornaments. Today a brisk wind pushed the nude branches of the Sweetgum tree planted at the edge veranda around, rattling the windows. Yeah, winter was here, and Christmas was right around the corner. She hummed along to Dean Martin crooning "Winter Wonderland" and sashayed down the hallway to her office.

****

Leaning her weight against the heavy back door, Nikki forced it open against the wind. Before she could grab the handle, it shut with a slam and she grimaced. Alex's form disconnected itself from the shadow beside the building.

"Trying to wake up your guests?" He took Georgie's leash, leaned in, and kissed her gently. "Evening, Innkeeper."

Nikki wrapped her arms around his neck and kissed him back, ending the kiss before he could respond. She shook her head. "Evening, Chief. I'm hoping the guests are all out having fun and not sleeping. Just hope I didn't wake Hope and Lily." She slipped her arm through his, and they strolled through the parking lot, Georgie stopping randomly to check out smells.

They walked in front of The Palace. "Hotel looks good. Ready for Christmas."

"Yeah, I had lots of help this year. Even Hope and Lily put in some time. How about your family? The ranch and Beth's house both decorated?" Nikki shivered.

Alex moved Georgie's leash to his other hand and wrapped his arm around Nikki, pulling her against his warmth. "Yeah, we're ready for Christmas. The whole weekend was filled with eating and decorating." He nodded toward Georgie. "Is Georgie channeling Santa with the red coat, hat, and black boots?"

Georgie stopped and turned her head over her shoulder, looking at Alex at the sound of her name.

Crossing the street, Nikki quipped, "That's just one of Georgie's Christmas outfits. Wait till you see the reindeer costume."

Alex shook his head as they turned the corner. "Where does a person buy a reindeer costume for a dog?" He pulled her tighter against him when they moved into the shadow behind the gazebo.

"Mom made most of the outfits." Nikki remembered the suitcase full of outfits she'd brought from Scottsdale. "She claimed sewing them was reminiscent of making doll clothes when I was little."

"You still miss her. I can hear it in your voice."

"It's difficult accepting she's gone, especially at the holidays." Nikki shook her head. "Mom loved Christmas, and hauling the boxes from the attic to the living room, then decorating every available space became a favorite tradition." Backing off from her sadness, Nikki changed the subject. "How was your Thanksgiving; did you have to work?"

"I put in some time at work, covering for people so everyone could enjoy a Thanksgiving meal with family if they wanted to." Alex shrugged. "We celebrated at Mom's on Thanksgiving Day, and the boys spent the remainder of the weekend at the ranch."

"Then did you work the rest of the weekend or join them at the ranch?"

"Work." He shrugged. "If I schedule myself off,

something always happens calling me back to town."

Nikki frowned, and they turned the corner leading to the hotel. "Isn't that tough on your family? You working every holiday?"

"When Colin and Mitch were smaller, sometimes it felt like a balancing act, deciding who would be responsible for them while I worked. Now, rather than adding to Becca's workload, they actually help with the chores."

Nikki frowned as they passed under the motion lights. "If you married again, would you want more children?" She rolled her eyes at herself, too soon in their two-date relationship to ask that question. She'd probably scared him off.

"I would really need to think on that," Alex answered. "I have two children. I'm not sure I want more."

At the back door of The Palace, Alex wrapped his arms around her, leaning down to nuzzle her neck. "I dream of you, Nikki."

"Hmm. Are they good dreams?" She breathed in his familiar scent.

"In my dreams I hold you; I feel your heart against mine." Alex kissed her gently on her cheek, her chin, the tip of her nose. Finally, their lips met, and on a breath, his tongue slipped in. He gentled the kiss, then pulled away. "The best dreams, Nikki."

She opened the door and slipped inside. Nikki admitted her feelings for Alex grew with every kiss, every touch, and every walk in the quiet night. Ambivalent about marrying, she still wanted a child. Like Kassie, she considered adoption. No more children lived in Alex's dreams, his family complete with two sons. No marriage on her horizon, but would their relationship survive if she adopted? She enjoyed his company, looked forward to his passion. She planned one day to enjoy his lovemaking. Their relationship moved slowly. She needed slow to build trust. After thirty minutes of yoga and ten of meditation, Nikki showered and, dressed in winter pajamas, climbed in bed.

During the darkest hours of the night, Nikki dreamed. A rocking chair glided back and forth. Nikki sat in the chair and held a sleeping baby wrapped in a yellow blanket embroidered with animals. Dressed in a long white nightgown, Victoria stood behind the chair, her eyes focused on the tiny child. Nikki looked up, a smile of welcome on her lips. The image of Victoria slowly dissolved.

****

Nikki woke to morning's first light peeking between the drawn curtains. Glancing at the clock, she realized the alarm was about to ring. Nikki rose and, thinking about her dream, took a moment to look around her room in an effort to determine if anything in the dream resembled this room. Was the dream a prophecy of the future, a mixing of the past when RJ was born, a subconscious wish for a child, or just a dream?

Outside, the winter sun sparkled bright yellow in a clear blue sky. Trees, their branches empty of leaves, stood completely still. Nikki turned to Eric, propped on a stool behind the front desk. "I'm out of here. Perfect weather for a day off."

"'Bout time you took a day off." He raised his eyebrows. "Big plans?"

"Just a plan to see something beside the hotel." She started down the hallway. "Call if you need me."

Gathering Georgie from the suite and waving to Eric at the front desk, Nikki and Georgie headed toward her truck. With a clear blue sky, this felt like a day to go exploring. Driving through the Sub Port a few minutes later, Nikki picked up a sandwich, pickle, chips, and iced tea, plus a slice of turkey and a bottle of water for Georgie. Deciding on North Lake, she drove out of town on a winding two-lane road, singing along to country music from the radio. A nearly empty parking lot waited at North Lake. Adding her lunch to the blanket and her reader in the backpack, Nikki hiked the graveled trail around the lake. About halfway around, she spread her blanket on a bed of pine needles and dry leaves. Georgie chose a corner and settled down for a nap. Nikki opened the chips and Georgie's ears perked up; her tail thumped against the blanket. Nikki tore the slice of turkey into small pieces and poured water into a bowl for Georgie's lunch. The spicy mustard on her ham sandwich teased her tongue. Crunching into the tart pickle, her lips puckered. Inhaling the scents of earth and pine, Nikki wondered why it took her almost a year to use her time off for a picnic at the lake. She packed the leftovers in her backpack and settled back on the blanket to watch the clouds.

Georgie's barking woke Nikki from sleep. Sitting up, she turned her head, searching for whatever Georgie considered a threat. A man, dressed in a park ranger uniform, stood a few feet away. "Sorry to wake you. You were so still, I wanted to be sure you were okay."

"Thanks for checking, Ranger." Nikki offered her

hand. "I'm Nikki Benton from The Palace Hotel in Creekside."

"William Newell." He took her hand and shook. "Is this your first visit to North Lake?"

"Sadly, yes. It finally occurred to me I should visit the area beyond walking distance of The Palace." She reached for Georgie, silencing her with a pat. "North Lake is beautiful. I bet you're extremely busy weekends and during the summer."

"True." He offered his hand and helped her to her feet. "Especially the launch ramp and picnic areas. Spring, summer, and fall there are concessions for paddleboards, kayaks, and food, and the parking area is full."

She stuffed blanket and reader into her backpack. "Do you live in Freemont or Creekside?"

"Just North of Creekside, on my family's ranch."

"If you're in the square area, stop in The Palace and I'll buy you a drink," Nikki offered. "Victoria's loves having local people mingle with our guests." With a wave, Nikki hiked around the lake to her car. She felt William watch her go.

Chapter Thirteen

"December 18, 1943, the following announcement appeared in The Reporter: 'Married in London, England, Grace Annie Blythe and Captain Robert James (RJ) Wellington Wyatt on December 1, 1943. Captain Wyatt is the son of Victoria Wyatt, owner of The Palace Hotel. The newlyweds are currently serving their country in the European Theatre of War.' "
~A Brief History of The Palace by Arthur Welles

A warm glow from the lowered lights infused the lobby, and the tiny twinkling lights wound around a miniature Christmas tree added a festive air. Dressed in a blue sweater and dark jeans, Nikki strolled into the lobby, humming along with Dr. Hook and the Medicine Show extolling the benefits of "When You're in Love with a Woman." Animated conversation competed with Dr. Hook.

Nikki settled on a bar stool, her blue sweater a colorful contrast to the red felt cover. Eric pulled a wine glass off the rack and poured a glass of Pinot Noir. Nikki lifted her glass. "Looks like you're having a busy evening, Eric. Is there anything you need before I call it a night?"

Eric shook his head. "Except save me a few minutes after closing. There are a couple of things I would like to mention."

"Of course." Nikki hopped down from the stool. "I'll be in the office when you are ready to talk."

The last notes of Gene Kelly's "Almost Like Being in Love" drifted through the now empty lobby a few minutes after nine. Eric appeared in the office, plopping into a chair across from the desk. He touched his nose. "Looks like you found some sun on your day off, Nikki."

"Yeah, fell asleep at North Lake. Do you know a Park Ranger named Newell?"

"Sure, his family owns the Falling N Ranch. Was he at the lake?"

Nikki nodded. "Caught me sleeping in the sun. What did you want to tell me?"

"Mr. Wyatt checked in this afternoon. He requested room 15, but it's still occupied by the Websters who will check out Friday," Eric answered. "Also, I don't know if she called you, but Catherine was looking for you earlier. She said there was nothing I could do and she would talk to you tomorrow. She seemed upset."

"I'll check with Catherine tonight." Nikki frowned. "Did you notice anything at the hotel that might have worried her?"

"Because I know she's hiding, I was extra vigilant about the guests in Victoria's tonight, but no one asked about her and I recognized the locals and guests." Eric paused with a sigh. "This is the most difficult part; Charlotte is pregnant. That's why we switched the schedule today."

"Congratulations."

"We just found out, and Charlotte's a little upset. The boys are barely out of diapers, and I think picturing starting all over was more than Charlotte could handle."

"Eric, that's exciting, a new baby. How does Charlotte feel?"

"Pretty good. We're hoping she has an easier time with this baby. Right now, she's pretty down about the possibility of feeling miserable for the first months, only to spend the last months walking around looking like a watermelon with feet. Her words, not mine."

Nikki grimaced. "Is that how she felt with the twins?"

"Yeah. We can't know yet, but the odds are this one will be only one baby and the pregnancy will be easier on Charlotte. She'll try to work the schedule you set up. I hope it's okay if we switch when she feels badly."

"Oh, Eric, no problem." Nikki shook her head. "I'll just put Miller on the calendar, then you and Charlotte can work out who shows up."

"We love our job. And we don't want to make it harder for you to run The Palace."

"We'll figure it out, don't worry. Please think about how much time off you two want when the baby comes. We can decide then how we are going to handle staffing The Palace."

Eric exhaled with a soft whoosh, relief obvious in his suddenly relaxed posture, the stress lines leaving his young face. "Thanks, Nikki."

Opening the calendar program on her laptop, Nikki changed the schedule. Pulling out her phone, she texted Catherine—*I'm back*—rather than knocking on her door, letting Catherine know without disturbing Lily and Hope if they were asleep. A few minutes later, Catherine entered the office and slid into a chair in front of the desk. She looked exhausted, her eyes red-rimmed.

"What can I do to help?"

"Oh Nikki, I don't know what to do. James called. Someone spoke to his receptionist today looking for me. Of course, she told him I no longer work there. James was careful to tell no one I work remotely." A worried frown marred her pretty face. "Suddenly I don't feel safe anymore, and I wonder what sort of people Craig was working with that they would trash our house and search for me so long after Craig died."

Nikki frowned. "Did you tell Chief Stark about James' visitor?"

"Yes, the girls and I walked over to the police station." Catherine's eyebrows drew down, her hands clenched in her lap. "He doesn't think the visit means much. I worked for James part-time while Craig was still alive, and Alexander seems to think whoever these people are, they are just turning over all the rocks searching for clues. Also, when I left Scottsdale I quitclaimed the house to James so he could sell it without me around; Chief Stark thinks that may be what led that man to James' office. A change of title is a public record."

"It must be awful for you not feeling safe. What did James and Alexander suggest?"

"Both said to just carry on. Neither one thinks I should move from The Palace. It's easier for Alexander to keep an eye on us here surrounded by people than if we lived by ourselves. I'm just afraid."

Nikki moved beside Catherine and took both her hands. "Catherine, I agree with Alexander and James. In The Palace you're just another guest. Someone new would find it difficult to tell if you arrived yesterday or months ago. Plus, while the locals don't know your story, Eric and Charlotte do. They'll let Alexander know if someone they are uncomfortable with shows up."

"I know, it's just I can't bear anything threatening the girls." Tears swam in her eyes.

"Is there anything we can do to help you feel safer? I'm willing to put additional locks on your doors. James has been after me to do that anyway, especially on the first floor rooms. Can you think of anything else?"

"James mentioned the new locks. He thought you were doing that anyway, so that might help." She dabbed at her eyes with a tissue. "He also said you were going to alarm the first floor windows; is he right?"

"I'd planned to put it off a while longer, but since I'm doing a little renovation anyway, this might be a good time."

With a hug, Catherine returned to her rooms. Nikki puzzled at life's occasional unfairness. Fate forced Catherine to mix fear with her grief, grossly unfair.

Nikki gathered Georgie up for their walk. When she stepped into the hallway, Victoria stood at the door of room 11, her hand poised to knock. Georgie leaned against Nikki's leg, her tail up but still. Victoria glided through the closed door. Nikki grabbed the back door handle. Anticipation flashed through her. Hers or Victoria's? Shaking her head, Nikki pushed open the door, stepping into a clear winter night lit by a full moon. The door latch clicked, and Alex appeared out of the shadow beside the door. He leaned in, placing a fleeting kiss on her lips and taking Georgie's leash. Nikki touched his scruffy cheek with the tips of her fingers and grinned. "Evening, Chief. You off tonight?"

He laid his arm across her shoulder and pulled her close. "Evening, Innkeeper." He grinned. "Been off awhile, just couldn't go home without a goodnight kiss." He matched his longer strides to hers, and they walked through the night. "You're very late, Nikki. Everything okay at The Palace?"

"If I was superstitious, I'd say the full moon got me."

"But you're not superstitious? You live in a haunted hotel in a town populated with residents who make a business out of believing in ghosts."

Nikki chuckled at his comment.

"So, what happened?"

"Fell asleep at North Lake, burned my nose, and a park ranger woke me because he thought I died on his watch." Alex chuckled. Nikki frowned. "Wasn't funny, especially the burned nose."

Alex stopped, bent down, and kissed her nose. "That it?"

Nikki continued. "Victoria's great-grandson returned, Catherine had a scare, and Eric tells me Charlotte is pregnant."

"James and Catherine both talked to me about his visitor. I've alerted the other officers to keep a watch for Catherine while they patrol. This is the first I have heard of a great-grandson for Victoria, and I'll have to give Eric my congratulations."

"Other than family, I'm probably the first to know about the baby." Nikki shrugged. "I think they didn't want me to hear it from Creekside gossip first."

Under the watchful glow of the full moon, they walked through the cold, still night. At the door, Alex handed her Georgie's leash and wrapped his arms around her. Nikki gazed into his chocolate eyes and laid her free hand against his scratchy cheek. He whispered against her ear, "Kiss me."

Nikki rose on tiptoe; her tongue darted out, touching her lips. Alex groaned. His eyes drifted shut. Nikki leaned in, placing her lips against his. She touched the seam with the tip of her tongue. He opened, and their tongues played. Her body warmed from the inside out. Georgie whined. Nikki slowly pulled back.

Alex placed his forehead against hers. "Soon, Nikki."

Nikki slipped out of his arms, yanked open the door, and disappeared inside.

****

The click of the latch announced the door locked. Zipping his jacket and shoving his hands in the pockets, Alex walked out of the light and into the deep shadows of the alley. Cold wind blew away his lingering passion, the warmth of holding Nikki in his arms. He shivered. No tourists strolled this part of town, old houses in an older neighborhood. The welcoming glow of light filtering through the curtains announced his mother was awake, probably reading in the front room. Plopped on the front porch rocker, Alex pulled off his boots and slipped inside on socked feet. Under the intense glow of a reading lamp, Beth sat curled in her favorite chair, a fuzzy white throw wrapped around her legs, a book face down on her lap, her eyes closed. On silent feet, Alex stepped across the living room, leaned down, and kissed her cheek, breathing in the familiar scent of shampoo and body lotion.

She opened her eyes. "You're home. What time is it?"

"Time for you to be in bed, or is the book boring?" He reached out his hand. "Help you up?"

"Thanks. Boys were exhausted and crashed early. House was so quiet I drifted off." Tossing the throw on the back of the chair, she placed the book on the end table. Beth reached up and patted his cheek. "Night." She started up the stairs.

Through the downstairs Alex walked, checking every window was closed tight, each door locked. Satisfied the house holding his favorite people was secure, he climbed the stairs. From the doorway of the boys' room, he watched them sleep, noticed how innocent they appeared. Full of energy and moving constantly when awake, the boys made it easy to forget they were still little. Alexander wondered if he would willingly have more children. His love for Colin and Mitch overwhelmed him and his need to keep them safe defined his life. Oh, he did his part, or thought he did after Mitch, then Colin, came into the world. He warmed bottles, rocked teething babies in the middle of the night, changed the awful diapers. Then Vanessa died, and he fell into a hell of helplessness and grief. His gun, training, and locked doors couldn't protect Vanessa from an aneurism that stole her away from him, Colin, and Mitch. Suddenly, he knew exactly what she did while he worked. Two weeks after Vanessa's funeral, Beth arrived on his doorstep, boxes and tape in hand. She pushed and prodded and moved his small family into her house. Colin and Mitch were both happy, well-adjusted boys heading toward being young men. Was he willing to start again? Would that be the tipping point with Nikki, if he were unwilling to accept another child? For a moment he pictured them spooned together, holding each other through the night, and warmth flooded him. Alex straightened his sons' blankets, moved to his room, and slid between cold sheets.

****

Slipping into her bed, Nikki said a little prayer for Charlotte and Eric, that their new baby would be safe and healthy. Three children under four years old were going to keep their parents busy and exhausted. The old pain returned—the loss of her child, then her husband, and most recently her mother. She closed her eyes, focused on her breath. Remembered pain she consciously released, returning her focus to her breath. She drifted into sleep. Just before dawn, Nikki woke from a dream of holding a tiny baby in her arms. No pain. Maybe the baby was Kassie's. She crawled from under the covers.

At five o'clock, Nikki tilted her chair back, propped her feet on the desk, and closed her eyes. The Beach Boys sang "Good Vibrations" and The Palace settled around her, the old hotel's vibrations welcoming and comforting. At the sound of Kenny Chesney's "How Forever Feels," Nikki dropped her feet to the floor and left the office, shaking her head at James' country music choice. Funny choice for her brother, the king of short-term relationships. Light danced off Charlotte's blond hair as she stood behind the bar, pouring Shelby a glass of white wine. On the other side of the lobby windows, twilight clothed the world in shadows. Inside, the low lights offered welcome. Heading up the stairs, Victoria stopped halfway, turned toward Nikki, and lifted an eyebrow. Nikki shook her head and gazed into Victoria's eyes. The spirit disappeared.

"Hi, Shelby. How's the Creekside Reporter?"

"Hi, Nikki. Doing well but discovering all kinds of things we didn't know about running a paper." Shelby sipped her wine.

"Different when you're suddenly in charge?" Nikki climbed up on a bar stool and accepted a glass of wine from Charlotte. In the gold-flecked mirror over the bar, she noticed RJ sitting alone at a table by the window, laptop open in front of him.

"Yeah." Shelby sipped her wine and frowned. "We'll get it together, though. Now I understand why you live at The Palace. Wish I had a room to sleep in at the paper when I work late nights. Going home for just a few hours' sleep seems pointless."

"Uh-huh, but living at the hotel means I take work home with me." Nikki sipped her wine. "Or at least home is not an escape." Accepting a second glass of wine, Nikki slid from the barstool. "But there are advantages, like a nearly unlimited supply of wine and conversations with friends in the bar." Nikki saluted Shelby with her glass and started down the hallway. Glancing over her shoulder, she noticed RJ, laptop stuffed in the case, moving from his table to the bar stool next to Shelby. He may not have found his great grandfather, but it looked like he may have found a friend. Who was the man in the bowler hat Victoria watched walk away? The same man she met in room 11? Was the man a friend, family member, or RJ's father? Or just a man in a bowler hat?

As Nikki slid the key into the lock on her suite, Charlotte's cheerful voice drifted down the hallway. "Well, William Newell, it's been awhile."

Relocking the door, Nikki strolled toward the lobby.

"Hi Charlotte." William's deep voice filled the lobby, accompanied by Clay Walker's "She Won't Be Lonely Long," another of James' choices. "How's the family? Your boys must be getting big."

"Big and handsome. How's your family?"

"Good. Tracey's meeting me here."

Nikki stepped into the light next to the bar. "Charlotte, his first drink's on the house. He rescued me from sunburn." Charlotte nodded. "What brings you to Victoria's?"

He slid onto a barstool. "Meeting my sister and her husband for dinner and a free drink. You working?"

"Always working, except when I'm sleeping in the sun."

William turned at the sound of bell on the front door.

A young woman wrapped in a purple puff jacket and holding the hand of a grinning man bumped shoulders with William. "There you are, brother dear. Hi, Charlotte." Her eyes roamed around the lobby and bar, settling on the drawing of Victoria. "Hey, I like this."

"Hi, Tracey. Is this your first visit to Victoria's?" Charlotte handed William and Tracey wine lists.

"Yeah, it won't be my last." She slipped off the jacket, revealing a lavender sweater. "Love the sign."

"Our resident spirit," Charlotte admitted. "Meet Nikki Benton, the innkeeper. Nikki, Tracey Alguire, William's sister, and her husband Mark."

Charlotte poured their chosen wine. Nikki enjoyed the bantering between brother and sister, especially

Tracey's quips. As the siblings walked out the front door into the cold night, Charlotte commented, "Tracey looks great. Marriage to Mark must agree with her."

"Tracey's married but William's not?"

"Right. William still lives at the ranch with his mom." Another man, her age or older, living with Mom. Nikki shook her head, wished Charlotte a good evening, and strolled toward her suite to the sound of conversation punctuated by the Beatles' "I'm Happy Just to Dance with You."

At nine thirty, Georgie in her arms, Nikki pranced down the hallway to the final chorus of "Paper Doll" by the Mills Brothers. The music ended as the door latched behind her. Above, a black velvet sky sprinkled with stars was lit by a crescent moon. A cold wind chilled her cheeks. Georgie's wiggles made her laugh, her breath a tiny white cloud.

Alex detached himself from the shadow beside the door, his voice a low rumble in her ear. "What's funny, Ms. Innkeeper?"

Setting Georgie on the cold asphalt, Nikki straightened and gazed into his chocolate eyes. "Just my silly dog. She's anxious to get going tonight."

Alex took Georgie's leash, wrapped his arm across Nikki's shoulder, pulled her close, leaned in, and kissed her cheek.

"You smell good. New perfume?"

Nikki shook her head. "Not exactly. Cinnamon and vanilla. I was making rolls for breakfast." A hint of wood smoke drifted on the air, and music punctured the quiet as they strolled near bars and restaurants surrounding the square. Nikki shivered in her leather coat. "Good night for a fire in the fireplace."

Alex pulled her tighter. "Except your Palace doesn't have a fireplace."

"True," Nikki conceded. "Does Beth's house?"

He guided them around the square, stopping at the corner, then starting across. "Yeah. A gas fireplace. Flip-a-switch heat. No wood to cut, no ashes to clean up."

"Smart. Ambience without the mess." The light over the back door welcomed them.

Looping the leash around her wrist, Alex gathered Nikki in his arms. His voice rumbled in her ear. "I want to spend more time with you. Sunday afternoon for a ride and a picnic?"

"Date three?" Nikki breathed in his scent of aftershave and soap. "I would love that."

Alex's eyes crinkled at the corners. Their lips met. He groaned and slipped his tongue inside, deepening the kiss. Nikki warmed from the inside. Slowly, he pulled back.

"Sunday. Date fifty-three." He pulled open the hotel's back door and waited while she entered. The door closed quietly with a faint click.

Climbing the stairs a few minutes later, Nikki checked that the upstairs veranda and the hallway lights were all on. The hidden door to the attic opened on silent hinges, and Nikki climbed the narrow stairs. She grabbed the attic doorknob and used her key on the lock. She wanted to look at the space one more time before she met with the contractor. Inside, moonlight filtered through the high windows, and the corners lay in shadow. Framed in light from a window, a young man dressed in a World War II uniform stood silently, a large gray dog by his side. A second young man dressed in uniform stood in front of him, hand outstretched to shake. They looked at each other and grinned, shook hands, and headed toward Nikki. She stepped aside. They passed through the closed door. The rumble of male laughter floated up the stairwell. Nikki flipped on the light, dispelling the shadows. Just an empty room lit by a single lamp. She returned to the lobby. Standing beside the window, Victoria stared out. An old black Ford car turned the corner a block away. Victoria stepped away from the window and disappeared, leaving the faint scent of lavender and a cloud of sadness.

Deep in the night, Nikki dreamed of war, the pictures black and white like an old movie. Explosions and gunfire, screams and silence. A sudden boom pulled her from sleep. Outside the window was a winter storm, flashes of lightning, thunder's boom, and rain. Thunder and lightning moved away. Only the sound of rain against glass remained. She closed her eyes, lulled to sleep by the falling rain.

****

Coffee dripped into the carafe, scenting the air, and to the sounds of the Rascals singing "A Beautiful Morning," Nikki pushed open the front doors. Water dripped from the roof, puddles dotted the sidewalk, but only a few wispy white clouds drifted across the pale blue early morning sky. She inhaled the clean scent of last night's rain. Footsteps on the wooden stairs, the hum of conversation, and within a few moments, guests filled the lobby. When only two tables remained occupied, Nikki set the bus cart aside and poured herself a second cup of coffee. RJ, laptop open and coffee mug cradled in his right hand, looked up from his seat by the window. "Do you have a minute, Nikki?"

Carrying her coffee, Nikki joined him, slipping into the chair. "How can I help?"

He turned his laptop screen to face her. "I've got some information about Victoria. Are you interested?"

"Always." A family tree lit up the screen, Victoria's name in the center.

"Victoria's maiden name was Tuley." RJ pointed to a line next to Victoria. "She married Wyatt at age seventeen, and he died two years later." He flipped to the next page, a copy of an obituary for Wyatt. "At the time of his death he owned a small hotel." RJ paged again, and the screen changed to copies of several newspaper articles. "I found a few references to Judge Welles. He was a lawyer in Phoenix before accepting the judgeship and moving to Freemont."

Victoria, a seventeen-year-old bride who became a nineteen-year-old widow. What happened during the nine years between Wyatt's death and the opening of The Palace? How did she end up an unwed mother who owned a hotel? "Where to next?"

"I'm heading to Freemont. The Freemont Journal opened in the early 1900s, so I should find information regarding the judge."

"And will you return to Creekside?"

RJ nodded. "Yep. Can't stay away from my great-grandmother or the boxes of newspapers at the Reporter." He paused, placed his cup on the table, and turned the laptop back. "Do you see her? Victoria?"

"Of course." Nikki rose from the chair. "This is Creekside. I own a hotel claiming a ghost. Do you see her?"

Standing and sliding the laptop into his case, his face split in a smile. "She's my great-grandmother." He shrugged. "Of course."

The music of a waltz played on a gramophone accompanied by the tinkling of a woman's laughter woke Nikki just before dawn. In a shadowy corner Victoria waltzed, her partner a tall man dressed in a white shirt, his trousers attached to black suspenders. Turning and swaying to the music, the couple glided across the room. The song ended, and the dancers disappeared.

Chapter Fourteen

"On March 22, 1944, Victoria Wyatt dressed The Palace in blue bunting and hosted a celebratory tea on the veranda. The Creekside Reporter stated, 'The Palace and Mrs. Wyatt wore pale blue on Sunday afternoon in celebration of Mrs. Wyatt's first grandchild, RJ Wyatt, born to Captain Robert James Wellington Wyatt and Grace Annie Blyth Wyatt on March 20. Captain Wyatt is currently serving in the U.S. Army and Mrs. Grace Wyatt is residing with family in Fallstown, North Carolina.' "

~A Brief History of The Palace by Arthur Welles

Georgie in her arms, Nikki and her dog slow danced around the suite to the Beach Boys' "Don't Worry Baby." Two days until date fifty-three. As the final note drifted away, she dressed Georgie in boots and jacket, donned her leather jacket, and slipped down the hallway humming the song, probably Patrick's choice since he claimed surfer status. Cold wind blasted her when Nikki pushed open the door. Not California weather. She set Georgie on the ground. Georgie wagged her tail so hard, her back end wiggled. Alex's deep voice rumbled in Nikki's ear. "She excited to see me or just excited?"

Nikki came up on tiptoe and placed a fleeting kiss on his lips. "Both. We were dancing. She loves to dance."

Wrapping his arms around her, he moved his lips toward Nikki's. "And I love to kiss." Their cold lips met. His tongue tickled her lips, and she opened. He slipped his tongue inside, and suddenly warmth filled her. Nikki wrapped her free arm around his neck and relaxed into the kiss. Slowly, he pulled back. "Evening, Ms. Innkeeper."

Taking a small step out of his arms, Nikki answered, "Evening, Chief. Nice hello."

His eyebrows raised. "Just nice?"

She shook her head. He wrapped one arm around her shoulder and took Georgie's leash, and they walked. Twinkle lights decorated the square's gazebo, the town Christmas tree stood a proud sentinel. Residents and businesses boasted elaborate Christmas decorations, everything from Santa's castle bearing artificial snow to reindeer grazing in a woodland scene. Conversation blended with holiday music. They walked in companionable silence, strolling around clumps of tourists.

Approaching the hotel's back door, Nikki realized Alex wore jeans and boots, no uniform in sight. "You off tonight?"

He nodded. "I'm early shift tomorrow."

"Do you have time for a drink? Since you're not working?"

"Nikki, I've spent most of our walk planning strategy on how I could invite myself," Alex admitted.

"Well, your strategy succeeded. Come in." Nikki slipped her key in the lock and pulled open the back door to a quiet hallway, the only sound the settling of an old building. Jackets hung together beside the door,

Nikki toed off her shoes, and Alex plopped in a chair and started pulling off his boots. "Hey. You don't have to take your shoes off."

"Innkeeper, you took off yours and Georgie's, so I figure that's the routine." He frowned and looked at the wood crate in the corner piled with boots and shoes. "I want to be invited back. Don't want to mess up."

"I'd have forgiven you. Boots are a special case." She pulled a bottle of wine from a small rack nestled in a bookcase. "Red wine okay?"

Alex nodded. "Perfect for a cold night." He moved to the sofa.

Nikki turned the radio to the local oldies station and Neil Diamond poured out his love for "Sweet Caroline" while she poured red wine into stemless glasses. Alex laid his arm across the sofa's back and Nikki cuddled next to him. Alex pulled her tighter into his embrace and her arms wrapped around his neck, the glasses forgotten on the table. Nikki placed her lips against his, gentle kisses. He moaned and opened his mouth, and her tongue tentatively explored. He tasted of wine and heat. Alexander's hands caressed the bare skin under her sweatshirt. Sliding her hands under Alex's sweater, she felt the muscled contours of his back and the warmth of his skin. She wished their sweaters away, allowing breast to chest contact. Instead of a disappearing sweatshirt, Nikki felt Alex's hands pull away, eventually allowing her shirt to slide back into place. Embarrassed her hands still caressed Alex's skin, Nikki pulled back as well, reluctantly breaking their embrace.

"Oh Nikki, much more and I would be carrying you to the bedroom. It's time I said goodnight."

Yanking his boots on, Alex rose from the sofa, picked up his jacket, and walked out her door, stopping only long enough to look over his shoulder and whisper, "Sweet dreams."

Nikki gathered up the wine glasses and washed, dried, and returned them to the cupboard. Alex had stopped. Why? Maybe affection and friendship was all he wanted. Perhaps there was no future with Alex. His passion felt real when they embraced, but her own attraction might blind her to his feelings. Dressed in warm flannel, Nikki slid between the sheets. Focused on her breathing, she let go of the confusion. Just before sliding into sleep, she decided instead of puzzling out what Alex wanted, she needed to figure out what she wanted. An affair? A friendship? A partner again? Not just a partner, a partner and two sons. Exhaustion claimed her, and she drifted to sleep.

****

Cold wind slapped his cheeks as Alex stepped outside the hotel's back door. Figured he deserved that for the hot and cold way he treated Nikki. As Alex meandered through the alley and streets headed toward home, he grimaced at the confusion in Nikki's eyes when he pulled away. After his push for an invitation inside, she expected more than a little making out and a quick escape. Truth, so did he. But Alex ran. It wasn't as if he'd been celibate since Vanessa died, he dated and occasionally made love to a woman he cared about. Eventually the relationship ended, no anger, no pain, just a drifting apart. He turned the last corner toward home. After they made love, would they drift apart? Would the relationship just end? He wanted to touch her everywhere and feel her gentle hands on his skin.

Listen to her plans. Support her dreams. Even wish for forever. Except he already knew forever didn't exist. All the dreams and all the plans could disappear in an instant. Inside his heavy jacket, he shivered. He was scared to death.

****

Frost clouded the glass behind the lace curtains in her suite. Outside a bright blue sky, the trees were perfectly still. Coffee's familiar scent greeted Nikki in the lobby along with Eric's off-key humming and the cheerful sound of "Day Dream" by the Lovin' Spoonful. On the veranda, she lit the fire pit and the gas heaters. Cold hit her, making her cheeks tingle. Inside, the sounds of footsteps on the wood stairs and conversation greeted her. Lots of talk about the weather as guests grabbed breakfast and settled in the library and lobby. Catherine slipped into the lobby, looked around at the crowd, and ginned at Nikki. She grabbed breakfast to go and slipped down the hallway to her rooms. As Nikki bused the table beside the lobby window, Victoria's favorite window, she glanced up. Alex, his uniform mostly covered by a heavy coat, stood across the street. Nikki shook her head. He ran last night, but he was back. A couple joined him on the sidewalk. He turned toward them. Nikki turned away, taking the dishes to the kitchen.

Immersed in drawing sketches of the new attic rooms, Nikki hummed along with Marvin Gaye's "I Heard It Through the Grapevine." Catherine's voice startled her. "Hi. Do you have a minute?"

"Of course." Nikki offered Catherine a seat. "What can I do for you?"

Catherine slipped into the chair. "I'd like to

187

decorate our rooms. Is that okay?"

"Sounds good." Nikki pictured Hope and Lily filling the room with decorations, Lily demanding each piece placed exactly how she wanted it.

"Hope doesn't remember our house in Scottsdale, but Lily does a little." Catherine frowned. "Lily keeps asking why we don't decorate. I didn't bring anything with me, so I'll have to purchase everything new. Then find a place to store it."

"I don't have another small artificial tree, but there are boxes of decorations in the basement from both our family home and my condo." Nikki rose. "Why don't we go down and look." She frowned. "Unless you're set on buying new?"

"Not at all." Catherine grinned and stood up. "Let's look now while the girls finish their rest."

They climbed down the basement steps. Nikki led Catherine to the corner farthest from the laundry. Stacked four feet tall and balanced against the wall, moving boxes labeled Christmas waited. They chose two boxes marked "small ornaments, condo" and "soft ornaments" and carried them up the stairs.

Placing the boxes inside Catherine's room, Nikki noticed a large drawing of a Christmas tree hanging on the wall. "Is that your first effort decorating your rooms for Lily?"

Catherine nodded. "Yep. She wasn't impressed."

"Well, she did help decorate the giant tree at the church, so you had a lot of competition," Nikki quipped.

"Thank you, Nikki." Catherine beamed as she started taking the paper tree off the wall. "Now Lily will have a tree."

As the sun set, conversation was a quiet hum in the lobby, competing with the sound of the Zombies singing about the "Time of the Season." Nikki stood behind the bar and watched Catherine climb the front steps, a small tree-sized box in one hand and her other holding Hope's hand. Lily carried a takeout bag from Rosa's in one hand, her other hand grasping her little sister. Nikki grabbed the front door, letting in the shoppers and the mingled scents of winter and Italian food.

"We bought a tree, Aunt Nikki." Lily dropped Hope's hand and reached for Nikki.

Nikki rescued the takeout bag before it hit the floor and lifted Lily for a hug. "That's so cool." She balanced Lily on her hip. "Was it fun, the tree shopping?"

"Wonderful," Catherine answered. Nikki released Lily, who followed Hope toward their room. "Not only did we get the tree and dinner, the girls bought a Christmas gift for Lily's teacher, and one for Georgie. A very successful trip!"

****

At nine-thirty, Georgie in her arms, Nikki slipped out of her suite and, humming "White Christmas," walked the now quiet hallway toward the back door. Stepping across the threshold, she shivered in the freezing air, her puffer jacket and new bright red knitted beanie with the white tassel no match for the shock of going from warm hallway to cold night. The door closed with a click.

Across the parking lot, Alex detached himself from the light pole and prowled to her side. Crinkles framed the corners of his chocolate eyes. "Evening, Ms. Innkeeper." He leaned in; his cold lips brushed hers in a brief kiss. He took Georgie's leash and laid his other arm across her shoulder. "Nice hat."

"Evening, Chief." Nikki touched her beanie. "Gift from James. A Santa hat." They strolled around the hotel, Georgie leading the way. *Just like all the other nights. Hum. So, they were going to pretend Friday night wasn't awkward.* Nikki shrugged. Just as well, she still had no idea what she wanted from Alex. Friendship? Love? A partner? Can't ask for what you want until you know. Nikki gazed at Alex. Maybe she just needed to know him better to decide. "What's your favorite Christmas tradition?"

They dodged a couple standing in front of the Lone Star arguing. "Opening one gift on Christmas Eve. Loved it as a kid, love it as a dad."

They turned the corner. Few tourists braved the cold. The sidewalks were nearly empty. "Does it keep the boys from getting up too early?"

"Not really, but it takes the edge off their impatience. What's your favorite?"

"I have two—putting out the nativity the week after Thanksgiving and Christmas Eve candlelight service."

Crinkles appeared next to his eyes, and he raised one eyebrow. "Does that mean you didn't believe in Santa?"

"Oh no, I believed." She chuckled with the memory. "I believed so much that the first time I remember being on Santa's lap, I screamed."

"So, no sweet smile for pictures with Santa." He shook his head and guided them across the square.

"Nope." Nikki grimaced. "Worst part? My favorite Uncle Leonard played Santa."

He leaned in and whispered in her ear, "So if I dressed as Santa would you sit on my lap?"

"Dressed as Santa? Not a chance."

"Remind me never to dress as Santa." He pulled her closer.

"Not if you want me on your lap."

Alex wrapped her in his arms, surrounding her. She felt his slightly bristly cheek against her soft cold one. "Kiss me then, if there's to be no lap sitting."

Alex held Nikki against the full length of his muscular body, bent his head forward, and placed his lips on hers. Deepening the kiss, he heard her slight hum and barely held in a moan. How he wanted to feel her skin against his, to touch her soft skin everywhere. Lifting his head to end the kiss, he stared into Nikki's passion clouded eyes. In a husky voice, Alex said, "Nikki, I'd give anything to take you home with me tonight."

Pulling further from his embrace, Nikki smirked. "Alex, home? Home to your mother? Home to your sons? Would we sneak up the stairs like guilty teenagers?"

His lips lifted in a slow smile, and he shook his head. "Not going to work, is it? We'll figure out something." Releasing Nikki, Alex watched Nikki unlock the door and slip inside.

Nikki slid under the covers, and her eyes drifted closed. She chuckled, remembering the look on Alex's face when she asked him if they would sneak up the stairs of his mother's house.

Just before dawn, Nikki woke to the sound of a woman's tinkling laughter. Victoria, seated at a small table, a box tied with a bright red bow before her, threw back her head and laughed. Standing beside her, his face in shadow, a man's deep voice joined her. Victoria lifted the box, untied the bow, and pulled off the lid. She stood and threw her arms around the man, who wrapped his arms around her. They disappeared, leaving behind the scent of lavender and laughter floating in the air.

Outside, just before noon, a clear blue sky and bright yellow sun gave a false promise of warmth. People walking by yanked their hats down and stuffed their hands into coat pockets. Dressed in layers, her warmest jacket on a chair beside her, Nikki watched for Alex's extended-cab pickup. Inside the lobby, the Doors asked a lover to "Light My Fire," which sounded like a good idea in the cold weather. Outside, the rumble of a pickup's engine announced Alex's arrival. Nikki jumped off her stool, grabbed her coat, waved to Eric, and dashed through the door and down the steps. Yanking open the passenger door, she jumped inside.

Alex asked as she clicked the seatbelt closed, "You in a hurry? I could have parked and come in." Unlatching his seatbelt, he leaned over and kissed her cheek. "Good afternoon, Ms. Innkeeper."

Nikki returned the kiss. "No hurry, but I didn't want you to turn the truck off and let the cab get cold." She tossed her jacket over the seat into the back. "Didn't want to put my jacket on."

He put the car in gear and pulled out. "You going to be warm enough on the ride? No heater on a horse."

"As long as it doesn't rain or snow, I should be okay."

"If it rains or snows, we're not riding. Horses don't like it, and neither do I." They drove through the arch announcing Windsong Ranch, and Alex stopped in front of the main house.

Four dogs and two boys hopped off the porch and raced toward the truck, and Becca walked behind them, a welcoming smile on her face. Mitch and Colin demanded their father's attention, talking quickly, describing their trail ride. Glancing over at Becca, Nikki noticed Becca laughing at Mitch's description of his friend sliding from the horse's back. Love for the boys shone in her eyes. The boys and dogs raced off toward the barn, Becca walking behind.

Alex led Nikki around the porch and through the back door into the kitchen. A young woman with a red ponytail stood at the counter, packing what appeared to be a picnic in saddlebags. "Hi, Kira, when did you start working on Sunday?"

She turned at the sound of his voice. "Special occasion. Becca and Cody are taking an adult group out on the ridge for a sunset party to celebrate an engagement. Luke and your boys are taking a family group the other way." She beamed. "I volunteered to put together food for the engagement party in exchange for Luke including Katie and Micah on the family ride."

"Kira, meet Nikki Benton. Nikki owns The Palace Hotel; Nikki, Kira Mathews, our chef and housekeeper." He raised an eyebrow. "So, you traded food prep for time without twins. Good move."

"Sounded good to me. It's nice to meet you, Nikki. Becca's mentioned you a couple of times. I hope you enjoy your ride today." Kira finished packing the food and with a wave, slipped out the door.

After they packed sandwiches into a saddlebag, Nikki and Alex strolled toward the barn. Inside, the scent of horse mixed with the scent of hay. From the other end of the barn, they heard Becca talking to a horse, her voice mixed with the sounds of animals shifting in their stalls. "Whose engagement party, Becca? Are they local or tourists?" Alex grabbed a saddle from the rack and tossed it over the blanket on a large black horse.

Leaving him to handle that horse, Becca opened the next stall and led out a second horse, exchanging the halter for a bridle. "Do you remember Cynthia Lyons? She was in my high school class. After graduation she attended college in California and her parents left Creekside. Cynthia wanted something different for an engagement party."

"Well, a weekend at a ranch is different." Alex grinned and tightened the girth on a saddle.

"Cynthia and her fiancé rented bunkhouse two for tonight. We're providing the trail ride, food, and drink on the ridge, beer, wine, and an appetizer board tonight, and breakfast tomorrow." Becca saddled the second horse. Nikki admired how she made tossing the heavy saddle onto the blanket look easy. "Colin and Mitch set up a couple of games outside bunkhouse two for entertainment after the ride."

"We'll wait until Mitch and Colin's group leave, then we'll head out; that okay, Becca?"

"Sounds good. Take Blue and Comet. They need the exercise."

After the boys' group left, Nikki and Alex walked their horses away from the barn in the opposite direction. "Where do Kira and her family live? Windsong's a long commute to work from Creekside."

"In the foreman's house, just through those trees."

Alex pointed toward a stand of pine trees. "It's not visible from the main house."

Nikki searched the trees and caught a glimpse of a brick chimney. "Is her husband the foreman?"

"Mark died in Afghanistan when the twins were two, and Kira asked Luke Mathews, Mark's brother, if he knew of a job. Luke suggested we hire Kira and offer the house as part of her salary."

"Luke is one of your employees, right?"

Alex guided them around the corral. "More than an employee, Luke is Becca's foreman, friend, and probably a lot more."

Watching rabbits and squirrels scamper out of her path, enjoying the clear sky and quiet, Nikki admired Alex, so comfortable in the saddle he could be part of the horse. "Is it difficult living in town when you could be on this beautiful ranch?"

He shook his head. "Not really. I love Windsong because I grew up here, but until my father died, I hadn't lived in Creekside since leaving for college." Alex led them along a path through the trees. "Becca finished college and couldn't wait to return to Windsong." He shrugged. "I finished college and started with the Chandler Police Department."

"Sounds like a perfect solution. You each got what you wanted."

"Then my dad died. Mom fell apart for a while, and Becca held Windsong together alone." Nikki heard the underlying sadness in Alex's voice. First, the death of his father, forcing Alex to abandon his career in the city, then the death of his wife. Alex's path to police chief included its share of sadness.

Cantering toward the stream stopped conversation,

and Nikki focused on her riding and enjoying the scenery. At the stream, they slowed the horses to a walk, then to a stop. Dismounting, Alex grabbed the saddlebags and tied the horses to a tree. With a wink, he grasped Nikki around the waist and brought her to the ground. She clutched the saddle horn, surprised by her legs' stiffness. Alex raised an eyebrow. "Starting to feel the ride?"

Nikki stepped away from her horse. "Yep. More than I thought I would." Together they spread the blanket and unpacked the picnic. Sated and lazy after consuming everything packed in the basket, Nikki stretched out to watch the white clouds skim across the sky. A comfortable silence embraced them. Drifting in the place between waking and sleeping, Nikki relaxed. Alex rolled onto his side, reached for her, and drew her into an embrace. His hands roamed her body, stroking. Her eyes opened slightly. "Oh, I feel like a cat, my fur stroked in exactly the right way."

Alex's hands moved to her face, his fingers sliding through her silky hair. "Will you purr?"

"Mmm, don't you hear me?" She raised an eyebrow.

"I do." He kissed her cheeks, chin, forehead, and the tip of her nose. She lifted her arms and pulled him closer. Their lips met, a soft touch, a firm kiss, finally a long, deep, warm kiss. His hardness nestled against her belly. She gazed into passion-filled chocolate eyes. Alex groaned. The kiss gentled, his hands slid from her hair, he rolled away. Alex laid his forearm over his eyes and groaned. "Just give me a minute." Silence. Their breathing settled. He reached out and took her hand. Nikki watched white clouds drift across the sky. She looked over at Alex; he stood and pulled her up with him. They packed up blanket and food and mounted Comet and Blue. Returning to the stable via a different route, they could hear the conversation of other riders heading toward the summit.

Everything put away, they grabbed bottles of water from the fridge and moved to the porch swing. Kira walked toward them from the trees. "How was your ride? Did Comet and Blue behave?"

Alex nodded. "Excellent ride. Are you back to greet the returning twins?"

"That, and I need to put the lasagna in the oven for the staff dinner and assemble the salad. Will you join us?"

"No, but thank you. Mom's making Sunday dinner. Colin and Mitch have school tomorrow." The sounds of horses and riders returning interrupted them. The twins spotted Kira and shouted hellos. Everyone dismounted. Lemonade, iced tea, or water was offered. Nikki and Alex helped untack and groom the horses. By five thirty, the horses meandered in their corral, the tack put away, and Nikki, Mitch, Colin, and Alex climbed into the pickup. Mitch and Colin kept their father's attention the entire trip, describing the wildlife, the picnic, and the behavior of the guests.

"Dad, you should have seen this little kid," Colin commented with a giggle. "He rode with his mom, but as soon as we stopped at the creek, she put him on the ground. He walked right over and fell in."

"Yeah, and was his mom mad," Mitch added and shook his head. "I don't know why; she had a backpack with a change of clothes for him."

"Then there was the little girl who climbed the tree

and couldn't get down," Colin announced, and both boys broke into giggles.

"So, who rescued her?" Alex asked.

"Luke," admitted Mitch. "He wouldn't let us go after her."

The truck slid to a stop in The Palace's parking lot. Alex reached for the door handle. Nikki touched his hand and shook her head. She pushed open the passenger door and jumped down. "Thanks for ride, Chief. Bye, boys."

To a chorus of goodbyes from Mitch and Colin, Nikki slammed the truck door shut and dashed toward the hotel's back door. As she slipped inside, she heard the rumble of the engine, tires crunch on the asphalt, and date three was over.

Nikki stepped inside the suite, and at the click of the closing door, Georgie bounced up, dragging her tug toy. "Ahh, did you miss me?" Nikki snagged the end of the toy and pulled, shaking her head at ten pounds of doggie pulling against her. Nikki let go. Georgie sat on her haunches and popped back up, her tail wagging as she pranced toward her bed. "You know, Georgie, I could learn a lot from you about celebrating every moment."

Nikki stepped out of a hot shower to Old Dominion asking, "Are we written in the stars, baby, or are we 'Written in the Sand'?" Good question. Dressed in clean jeans and a red sweater, Nikki pulled open the suite door and strolled the hallway to the lobby.

Conversation drifted from the lobby, the Turtles sang "Turn, Turn, Turn," and Victoria stood on the threshold, a tender expression on her face. Against her shoulder, a tiny baby wrapped in a blue blanket fussed.

Victoria glided toward Nikki down the hallway. The scent of lavender drifted by, and Victoria disappeared. Nikki stared at the now empty space. Did spirits in a haunted hotel foretell the future or merely reenact the past?

Nikki slipped up on a barstool and greeted Eric. "Busy night."

He nodded and placed a wine glass in the sink. "Too cold to wander Creekside tonight." He lifted the lid of the slow cooker, and the scent of cinnamon and cloves floated in the air. "The mulled wine is really popular and almost gone." He pulled a wine glass from the rack. "Pinot Noir?"

"You know me so well. You'd make a good boyfriend if you weren't married."

Eric placed the wine glass in front of her. "Nope. Just a good bartender." He shrugged. "You're easy. Pinot Noir when it's cold; Riesling in summer."

She lifted her glass in toast to Eric's cleverness and slid off the barstool. At a table beside the window sat RJ, a nearly empty wine glass beside his open laptop. He looked up and waved her over.

"Hi, RJ, how was your Sunday?" Nikki slid into the empty chair.

"Productive." He pulled a familiar red bound book from his backpack. "Have you seen this book?"

"I have a copy; it came with the hotel." Nikki accepted the book from his hand, noticing the pristine condition, the pages stiff. "Where did you find this?" She handed the book back.

"Amanda Welles Kendrick." He returned the book to his case. "She's a docent at the Historical Museum of Freemont and a descendant of the author."

"Are there other copies?"

"Arthur Welles gave each of his children a box of books. Amanda's mother, Victoria Welles Kendrick, split her copies between Amanda and her sister Anne."

"And she gave one to you because of your connection to The Palace?"

"Exactly. I started asking questions about Judge Welles, and she offered me a copy. Arthur Welles passed away this year."

"Do you think Amanda would sell me a couple of copies of the book for the hotel library?"

RJ dug through his backpack, finally unearthing a business card from Amanda Kendrick, Docent. "Amanda says if you're interested in a copy of the book just call her. She has most of her box left."

"Does Amanda know why her grandfather wrote about The Palace?"

"No idea. Judge Welles inherited the property in 1949, the same year Amanda's mother, Victoria Lynne Welles, was born. The name is something of a coincidence. I've no idea what relationship Victoria and Judge Welles had." He paused, a smile lighting his face. "I have an explanation for Victoria's will, though."

"Amanda had information about the will?"

"Yep. According to Amanda, and verified by my father, Victoria left Judge Welles in charge of finding a way to use The Palace to help Grandmother Grace and my father."

"But you didn't know that when you started looking."

He shrugged and sipped his wine. "My father neglected to mention it. From almost the moment RJ died, Grace received a monthly check, first directly from Victoria, and after 1949 from Judge Welles."

"Victoria's will wasn't a scandal then, just an attempt by a grandmother to take care of a grandson she never met." Now she haunted The Palace, watching her great grandson. Did RJ know Victoria slipped into his room at night? Did he feel Smokey's presence when he climbed the stairs and Smokey bounded after him? Her wine glass empty, Nikki rose, thanked RJ for the information, and wished him good evening. Handing Eric her empty glass, Nikki strolled down the hallway to the mellow sounds of Bing Crosby's "Swinging on a Star." Inside her suite, she dressed herself and Georgie in red jackets and boots and slipped out the back door. Soft white snowflakes fell. She pulled out her phone, took a short falling snow video, and texted it to Sheri with a note.

—White Christmas, almost. You're still coming for Christmas and New Year's, right?—

The response came immediately.

—Yes, Yes, Yes.—

The sound of a squeaky rocking chair woke Nikki. In the shadows gently rocking, Victoria gazed with wonder at her nursing child. A male voice whispered from the shadows, "Vicky, if only…"

"Shhhh," Victoria answered quietly, "things are as they are, and this precious moment is enough. No regrets, our child is perfect." They disappeared, and Nikki returned to sleep.

Chapter Fifteen

"January 1, 1945, Victoria's white star changed to gold and the following appeared in the Reporter: 'January 5 at 10:30 in the morning, Emanuel Lutheran Church, Pastor Douglas Williams presiding, will host a memorial service for Corporal Wesley Aaron Greene and Captain Robert James Wellington Wyatt of the United States Army. Wesley and RJ are Creekside's first casualties of war. Wesley is survived by his parents, Aaron and Rebecca Greene, and sisters Kathleen and Amanda. Robert is survived by his wife, Grace Annie Blythe Wyatt, son Robert James Wyatt, and mother, Victoria Wyatt. As a community, our hearts ache for the families and friends of these brave soldiers.' "

~A Brief History of The Palace by Arthur Welles

Thursday night, Nikki shoved open the hotel's back door and entered a white world lit by a full moon. The door clicked behind her, and Alex appeared from the shadow beside the door. His lips icy against her cheek, she felt his kiss and a smile. His deep voice mumbled in the still night. "Evening, Innkeeper."

Nikki turned and gazed into his chocolate eyes. "Evening, Chief. I'm surprised to see you." She looped her arm through his and inhaled his familiar scent. "Winter Wonderland and the first snow fall brought so many visitors I doubted you'd have time."

He took Georgie's leash. "I made time, Nikki." They strolled around the building, Georgie in the lead. "All day I look forward to our walks."

Holiday music and animated conversation greeted them when they walked near the square. Tourists thronged the streets closed for Winter Wonderland. Every business boasted elaborate decorations, miniature villages, and animated elves. Groups of carolers strolled along the sidewalks, stopping to serenade clusters of visitors. Houses near the square competed with each other, each one telling a story through Christmas decorations. The Creekside Christmas Tree lit the square, the star illuminating the black velvet sky.

They wove their way around a group stopped in front of an elaborate display in the Lone Star window and retraced their steps to the hotel.

"My favorite part of the evening." Alex wrapped his arms around Nikki, pulling her against his body. "Holding you is a nearly perfect ending to my day."

She laid her free hand against his scratchy cheek, stared into his eyes, and inhaled his scent. He grinned, pulled her tighter against him, placed his lips on hers, and closed his eyes with a low moan. She answered his pressure and her body warmed, and she relaxed into the embrace. Nikki groaned slightly, and Alex released a sigh. Pulling away, Nikki gazed into Alex's eyes, finding a mixture of passion and longing in their depths.

"Good night, Nikki."

He wanted her. His passion screamed it. She wanted him. Her body responded to each touch, each caress, each kiss with longing. When they finally came together, would it be a beginning or an end? Nikki shook her head. The Palace boasted a ghost but no crystal ball.

After releasing Georgie into her suite, Nikki checked the lobby a last time. RJ sat in a chair at the game table, immersed in his notes. Nikki pictured Victoria's RJ as a child living in the hotel, getting ready for Christmas. No regrets. Victoria raised her son alone with no regrets. If today's RJ found his great-grandfather, would he have regrets?

Dressed in a flannel nightgown, Nikki slipped between cold sheets and drifted off to sleep. A scraping sound coming from the lobby woke her. Nikki grabbed her robe and slippers, put her cell phone in the pocket, and hurried toward the lobby. Though the clock showed three in the morning, Victoria stood on the veranda surrounded by daylight. A black car pulled in front of the hotel and out hopped several young men. One rushed up the steps, grabbing Victoria in a bear hug and twirling her around. Victoria laughed. They disappeared. Nikki stood silently. She turned, and returned to her room. The sheets were cool when she slid into bed. Georgie snored softly. Nikki drifted into a dreamless sleep.

Bright golden sun glinted on pristine snow, frost decorated the edges of the lobby windows, and Nikki swept snow from the veranda to the beat of Aretha Franklin demanding "Respect." Inside the lobby, the scent of coffee and cinnamon rolls greeted her. Conversation hummed and combined with the scrape of chairs on wood floors and the clatter of dishes.

From a table in the corner, Hope's voice rang. "Aunt Nikki, Aunt Nikki, we're going to play in the snow."

Grabbing a cup of coffee, Nikki joined Catherine and the girls. "Wow, I'm jealous. You get to go play, and I have to work."

"We're going to be gone all day today, Nikki. Maryanne Milke invited us to a day of fun at the lake."

Admiring the parkas hanging on the back of the chairs, Nikki gave a single nod. "Lily and Hope will look like miniature snow bunnies. Can't wait for your pictures."

Eventually, only Charlotte and Nikki remained in the lobby. "I can finish this, Nikki. Isn't this your morning off?"

Louis Armstrong's raspy voice demanded she notice "What a Wonderful World" she lived in. Yep, time to check out Winter Wonderland in daylight. "Great idea." She waved to Charlotte and strolled down the hallway to her suite.

Her loafers replaced with boots, Georgie in jacket and boots, Nikki grabbed her heaviest coat and headed toward the square. She stepped carefully on slippery sidewalks. Locating a taco vendor at the square, Nikki purchased lunch, and strolled around the square admiring the homes and businesses dressed in holiday finery. A live band on the square filled the air with holiday music with a rock and roll flavor. Visitors crowded the sidewalks, laughing, talking, and checking out the businesses. Creekside celebrated Winter Wonderland in full tilt.

As the sun set, the bell over the front door tinkled, announcing a visitor. Nikki glanced up from restocking Victoria's with lemon and lime slices and greeted a very tall, dark-haired visitor dressed in jeans and a heavy overcoat. "Welcome to Victoria's. What may I pour for you?"

He leaned on the bar. "Coffee and information. Are you the hotel manager?"

"Nikki Benton, the owner, and you are?"

"Bill Meyer." He focused hazel eyes on Nikki. "I'm looking for a young woman and two children, her name is Catherine Jessup."

Surprised by the request after all this time, Nikki poured Bill's coffee and pointed him toward the cream and sugar on the side table. When he turned away to fix his coffee, Nikki grabbed her cell and texted Alex.

"Where are you from, Mr. Meyer, and why are you looking for Catherine Jessup?"

"Phoenix, I'm a PI, and my client asked me to locate Catherine Jessup." Bill Meyer pulled his ID from his pocket. "Do you know her?"

Alex walked in the front door. "How can I help, Nikki?"

"Chief Stark, I'd like you to meet Bill Meyer, a PI from Phoenix looking for Catherine Jessup." Nikki frowned. "Mr. Meyer, Creekside Police Chief Alexander Stark."

"May I see your identification, Mr. Meyer?" Bill handed the ID to Alex. "Shall we step away from the bar?" Alex indicated an area to the side.

"Of course." He stepped to the other side of the room. "Is there a problem with my speaking to the innkeeper?"

"None at all." Alex returned the ID. "Why are you searching for Catherine Jessup?"

"Finding people is what I do." Bill sipped his coffee. "My client wants to talk to Mrs. Jessup about documents her husband may have kept at home.

Apparently, Mrs. Jessup left town before my client could contact her after the funeral."

"Did you check with Mr. Jessup's partner about the missing papers?"

"Craig Jessup's partner claims he doesn't have anything." Bill frowned. "Catherine's former neighbors told me after the house was vandalized, Catherine packed up her girls and drove away. She hasn't returned, the house is for sale, and the Realtor handling the sale never met Catherine."

Alex thought for a moment. "How did you end up in Creekside, Mr. Meyer?"

"Catherine's former boss owns part of the hotel." He set his coffee cup on the table. "I thought someone here may have seen her."

"Mr. Meyer, come to the office tomorrow morning at ten. I'll see what I can do about contacting Catherine Jessup."

After Bill Meyer left The Palace, Alex returned to his office. His first call was a contact at the Phoenix Police Department about Bill Meyer, his second to Catherine. "Hello, Chief."

"Hello, Catherine. Where are you?" Alex heard the high-pitched voices of young children in the background.

"Just leaving North Lake after a full day of fun in the snow."

"Nikki had a visitor today asking about you. Don't panic; it was a Phoenix PI. Phoenix Police Department says he's a legitimate PI and they've had no complaints."

"How did he find me?"

"Someone retained him to search for you and his

only lead was James' ownership of The Palace. Instead of returning to The Palace, can you bring the girls to the station?"

"Of course, do you think we're in any danger? What did the PI want?"

"I'll explain when you arrive. Are you driving?"

"No, but I can have my friends drop us off at the station. We should be there in a few minutes."

Through his office window, Alex watched Catherine unloading a stroller, her two girls, and backpacks from an SUV. Joining her in the parking lot, he offered his help and they pushed and carried everything to the station. Alexander carried a sleeping Hope, Catherine holding a whimpering Lily. Settling Hope in the stroller, Alex glanced up to find Catherine rocking Lily in her arms and everything else piled in the corner. Pulling his chair away from the desk, he offered it to Catherine, and she settled. He slid into the chair behind his desk. "I don't know who hired the PI, Catherine, but he's here to ask you about something his client believes Craig left in your house. Did Craig have a safe at home?"

"Yes, and there were several envelopes inside." Catherine shrugged. "I didn't bother to open them. Anything stamped with Jessup and Phelan I sent to Craig's partner. All the other envelopes were marked with their contents, the trust, life insurance, house title, passports."

"Was that before the vandalism or after?"

"After." Catherine shook her head. "Whoever vandalized the house didn't find the safe. Craig hid it in the entry closet, but it was up high. He kept a gun in the safe, and we didn't want the girls to find it."

"What about a safe deposit box?"

"We had one, but it contained only copies of the girls' birth certificates, our marriage license, our diplomas from college, stuff we thought we wouldn't need often but didn't want to lose."

"So, anything relating to anyone other than immediate family went to the partner?"

"Yes. Craig rarely brought work home. When he did, he returned it to the office the next day. If something's missing, it probably burned up in the car accident. There were only three envelopes from the partnership in the safe, but I didn't bother to open them."

"Do you remember what Craig had with him the day of the accident?"

Catherine shrugged and frowned. "He carried his black briefcase, so his laptop was probably inside," she explained. "He loved that briefcase. His grandfather gave it to him."

"But nothing unusual?"

"No. Craig loved computers and everything they could do. Whatever he worked on was stored on the computer or backed-up somewhere."

Catherine's eyes shone with unshed tears. "Do you think I should move again, Alex? If the PI found me here, I'm not as safe as I thought."

"Let's see what the PI has to say tomorrow. Do you want to meet him, or shall I just talk to him and let him know what you said?" Alex rose and lifted a sleeping Lily from Catherine's arms. "He'll be here at ten, so you have a little time to think about it." Alex slung a diaper bag on his shoulder. "I'll walk you and the girls to the hotel. Do you have the code for the back door?"

"I do, Nikki gave it to me since sometimes getting the stroller up the front steps when Hope is asleep inside is more than I can handle." Catherine opened his office door and pushed the stroller through. "Tonight, I'll call James for his opinion about meeting the PI tomorrow."

****

Returning to The Palace was uneventful. Winter Wonderland visitors crowded the sidewalks and the square provided the perfect cover for Catherine's walk. Nikki met Catherine at the back door. Alex handed the still sleeping Lily to Nikki and bid them good evening. After pushing Hope's stroller inside, Catherine lifted Lily from Nikki's arms and carried her to the bed. "Thank you, Nikki. Once the girls are settled for the night, I'll call James, if I can stay awake. Chasing Lily and Hope in the snow wore me out."

"Victoria's is still open, but I'll leave the fire door shut between the hallway and lobby," Nikki offered. "Is there anything you need before I go back to the bar?"

Assuring Nikki she was fine, Catherine locked her doors and woke Hope, giving her a quick wash, brushing her teeth, and slipping her into clean pajamas. Repeating the process with Lily, Catherine thought about what she should do next. Would it be safer to let Alex handle the PI or was she just delaying the inevitable? Would he go away after talking to Alex or would he continue to search for her? If she stayed in Creekside, eventually he'd find her, everyone in town knew Catherine with the two little girls who lived in The Palace. What could Craig have had that was important enough to vandalize her home and send a PI after? Why didn't this person check with Craig's partner first? Logically, anything relating to a client would be in Craig's office rather than his home.

With the girls settled for the night and herself finally wearing comfortable pajamas, Catherine phoned James. After a lengthy discussion, James finally said, "What we have are more questions than answers. If whatever they're looking for was in the house, it's gone now; you emptied the safe and stored everything you didn't sell. What did you do with the personal papers from the house and safe deposit box?"

"Safe deposit box in the Creekside bank," Catherine answered. "I thought I might need the girl's birth certificates and social security cards eventually, and it seemed silly to have boxes at two banks." Catherine paused. "You have the title to the house."

"Did you open the envelopes or just assume they contained what was listed on the outside?"

"Every envelope, both business and personal, was marked. The personal ones listed the contents so I didn't open them, except the one with the house and car title since you are selling the house for me and you sold the car. Should I go to the bank and be sure nothing was mismarked?"

"The bank isn't open till Monday, but I think you should check, maybe have Alex accompany you just in case there's some surprise. If you meet with the PI, I suggest the girls stay with Nikki. Whatever you decide, I'll help."

"But what else can you do?"

"If you feel unsafe now in Creekside, we'll find you something else. I don't have any other innkeeper sisters, but Patrick in San Diego would be a safe place, and he has lots of room."

"I feel like I am taking advantage of your family, James."

"Catherine, I promised Craig I'd take care of you. He was worried about something. Anyway, marrying Craig made you a Benton. We take care of our own."

Catherine rolled her eyes. "Craig was a Jessup."

"In name only." James chuckled. "In truth he was a Benton. Let me know when you decide about tomorrow; you may have a better feel for any potential danger if you talk to the PI."

The feel of a tiny soft hand patting her on the cheek woke Catherine from dreams full of racing vehicles, fiery crashes, and gloomy funerals. "Did you have a nightmare, Mommy?"

"Yes, Lily, thank you for waking me." She lifted Lily into her bed. "Did you sleep well?"

Lily nodded. "Hope is awake too. We're hungry."

Smiling at Lily and grabbing her for a hug, Catherine started her morning routine, dressing everyone for breakfast in the lobby. She would feel more informed after meeting with the PI. She was an adult and a mother, and she was tired of being afraid. Maybe the PI had answers.

Gathering toys and a favorite DVD after breakfast, Catherine started second-guessing herself. Would it be better to just pack up and run or maybe let Alex handle the PI and hope he would go away? Catherine, with Lily one step behind, carried Hope and the bag of toys to Nikki's sitting room. Kisses and goodbyes given, Catherine started the walk to the police station under a cloudless, pale blue sky. She walked carefully on the wet sidewalks. Yesterday's blanket of snow melted in the sun, leaving behind puddles.

Two men rose as Deputy O'Neil ushered Catherine into Alex's office. "Good morning, Catherine. May I introduce Bill Meyer, a PI from Phoenix? Mr. Meyer, Catherine Jessup."

Alex motioned Catherine to a chair next to his, placing her facing the PI, the desk between them. "What is it you want, Mr. Meyer?"

"My client believes you may have something your husband was holding for him." Mr. Meyer slipped back into his chair.

"Did your client vandalize my home, Mr. Meyer?"

"He claims not, Mrs. Jessup. That happened before he hired me."

"If he did, he belongs in jail. What is your client looking for?"

"Mr. Jessup was putting together a property deal for my client. My client would like access to your husband's notes regarding which investors were considering participation and what financial support they were offering."

"Craig rarely brought work home. Everything business related I found in the house was returned to Jessup and Phelan." Catherine frowned. "If Craig's partner doesn't have the file, then it was destroyed in Craig's accident."

"What about his computer?"

"Craig's personal computer was in his car at the time of the accident, so even an electronic file doesn't exist. I can't help you, and I would appreciate you not telling your client where I am."

"Would you be willing to meet with my client?"

Catherine shook her head. "No. I believe your client vandalized my home rather than approaching

Jack Phelan about his paperwork, which doesn't sound like an honest business practice to me."

"You understand why Mrs. Jessup is concerned about your client," Alex commented. "The vandalism right after the funeral may have been a coincidence, but perhaps not."

"I understand your concern. I'll tell my client you have nothing regarding his land development. I won't tell him where you are."

"Do you think your client will leave me alone now?"

"After I talk to him, I'll call Chief Stark." Bill shrugged. "My client couldn't find you on his own so maybe this will be the end of it." He stood. "Thanks for your time." He nodded at Catherine and Alex and stepped out the door, closing it softly behind him.

Catherine rose. "Do you think I'm safe now, Alex?"

"Let's wait until Mr. Meyer calls to make a decision." He pulled out her chair, and they walked to the office door. "My police department contact claims Bill's a good PI and a decent guy. I figure you can trust him not to tell his client where you are."

Returned to The Palace, Catherine walked into Nikki's sitting room to the cheerful sound of Lily's giggles. "Hi, everyone. Let's go home." She helped Nikki gather the girls' toys. "Thank you, Nikki."

Nikki shrugged. "Anytime, Catherine." She lifted Hope. "I love having playmates and an excuse to avoid laundry."

While Hope and Lily napped, Catherine called James.

"What do you think, Catherine? Should I talk to

Patrick about moving you to San Diego?"

"Bill Meyer seemed trustworthy, and Alex said his contacts claim he has a good reputation." Catherine curled up in the wingback chair. "He's looking for something Craig was working on, which sounds innocent enough."

"But you gave everything to Craig's partner. Are you and Alex going to check the contents of your safe deposit box in Creekside?"

"As soon as the bank opens on Monday. Craig was so careful keeping his business out of our personal lives, I can't imagine that we'll find anything," Catherine explained. "I'll hold up for a little while on moving. I hate disrupting the girls again."

"Just know I'll help you move. I called Patrick and he's happy to have you as guests."

After a few minutes more of conversation, Catherine hung up, powering up her computer to work while the girls napped.

Nikki watched out the front window on Monday as Catherine's small family started their walk first to preschool, then to the police station. Perhaps Bill Meyer finding Catherine would mean an end to mystery, and Catherine could make plans for her future. Nikki turned from the window and started breakfast clean up. Her cell phone rang just as she turned the dishwasher on. "The Palace Hotel, this is Nikki. How may I help you?"

After a moment's pause, the voice on the other end asked, "Are you Nikki Benton?"

"Who is calling please?"

"Ms. Benton, this is David Treat. I'm representing SheriLynne Larsen."

"What do you mean, representing? Is SheriLynne

all right?"

"I'm sorry to tell you Ms. Larsen was involved in an automobile accident on Saturday." His voice breaking, he cleared his throat. "Ms. Larsen appointed me executor of her estate."

"Where is Samuel Larsen?" Tears silently ran down Nikki's face. "Was he in the car?"

"No. Samuel was home with the nanny. How soon can you be in Phoenix?"

"Tomorrow, I'll be there tomorrow. Where's Samuel now?"

"Mrs. Treat and I took him home with us until you could be contacted. Sheri appointed us emergency contacts, and Samuel knows us."

"I'll be there tomorrow, Mr. Treat." David rattled off his office address and phone number, asking Nikki to call when she arrived.

Nikki took deep breaths, forcing back her tears. She speed dialed James. "James, can you drive up tonight and stay in The Palace for a few days? I'm driving to Phoenix as soon as I pack a few things."

"What's wrong, Nik? I can hear the tears in your voice."

"It's Sheri. She died in a car accident Saturday night. I have to meet the attorney and pick up Sam."

"Oh, Nik. How awful. I'll leave as soon as I can. Call me when you leave Creekside and again when you get to Phoenix so I know you're safe."

Nikki disconnected from James and the tears started again. Catherine and her girls walked in. "What's wrong, Nikki?"

"First, what happened at the Bank?" Nikki took more deep breaths, trying to control her tears.

"Nothing, the envelopes in the safe deposit box contained exactly what was listed on the outside." Catherine reached for Nikki, wrapping her in a hug. "What happened? What can I do to help?"

"Car accident Saturday. My friend Sheri Larsen died, and I have to go pick up Sam in Phoenix."

Catherine squeezed her hard once and stepped back. "I'm so sorry. Hope and I will watch the desk until Eric comes, or at least while you pack. Go ahead, get started."

"Thank you, Catherine." Nikki sighed, comforted by the hug. She dashed to her room. Suitcase plopped on the bed, she pulled clothes from the closet and drawers.

When Eric arrived at two thirty, Nikki explained she was going to Phoenix for a few days and James would be arriving tonight sometime. "Don't worry, Nikki; I'll work with James and we'll cover The Palace. Is it okay if I ask Shelby to help if she has time?"

"Sure. There are breakfast casseroles in the freezer and the recipe for Crock-Pot oatmeal inside the cupboard door. Just call me if you need anything."

Her suitcase in his hand, Eric walked Nikki to her truck. He tossed the case inside the back seat. "Drive carefully, Nikki. James and I'll take care of The Palace." Before she could climb into the driver's seat, he grabbed her in a hug. "Be safe."

She climbed in. He slammed the door. Nikki drove away, and on the radio Scotty McCreery asked for "Five More Minutes." She thought of Sheri and Sam, and tears silently coursed down her face. Nearly one hundred years after RJ, The Palace would be home to another little boy.

Chapter Sixteen

"PEACE! was the headline appearing on the Creekside Reporter on September 2, 1945. According to the Reporter, 'The Palace Hotel, the St. George Hotel, the Birdcage Saloon, and Courthouse Square are decorated with festive red, white, and blue, celebrating the end of a conflict which took many of Creekside's favorite sons, including Corporal Wesley Aaron Greene, Captain Robert James Wellington Wyatt, Midshipman Walter Benson Stark, Sergeant Ronald James Donovan, and Corporal John Donald Miller. Victory required a high price from Creekside, not only in loss of our sons, but also in the years lost by those who will be returning. As we celebrate the end of war, let us never forget its cost.' "

~A Brief History of The Palace by Arthur Welles

"For the Lamb in the midst of the throne will be their shepherd, and he will guide them to the springs of living water, and God will wipe away every tear from their eyes. Revelation 7:17."

Standing in front of the Columbarium, at the edge of the church's garden, Pastor John, white vestments a beacon against the Columbarium's gray marble, spoke of peace, a life lived with joy, and the security of belief in grace. Sam, a comforting weight against Nikki's shoulder, slept, his breathing even, his little boy smell a counterpoint to the perfume of flowers warming in the winter sun. The weight of Patrick's arm around her shoulder comforted her. Sheri's brother Max shifted in his seat. Nikki focused on Pastor John's words. Familiar words, words spoken when her mother died not so long ago. Memories pulled her away, memories of Sheri's twinkling eyes. Memories of Sam's birth. Ending the short service with a prayer and sign of the cross, Pastor John walked toward Nikki and Sam.

"Thank you, Pastor John."

He took her hand, bringing her forward for a hug, Sam nestled between them.

"I'll miss Sheri and Sam. They're integral members of our congregation."

Other mourners approached Nikki, expressing condolences and confirming attendance at the small reception in the church hall.

Hours later, Nikki, Scott, Patrick, and Max sat in James' condo. Sam slept. Patrick, a glass of red wine in his hand, looked at Nikki, concern clouding his blue eyes. "You're returning to Creekside tomorrow?"

Nikki lifted her teacup, sipped, and nodded. "Charlotte, Eric, and James each called assuring me everything is fine, but I'm ready to go home."

Scott set his water bottle on the table. "It's nearly Christmas, Aunt Nikki. Are we still visiting you over the holiday?"

"Please come. This is my first Christmas as a guardian-mom. I'll need all the support I can get." She turned to Max. "You're welcome to join us for Christmas. In fact, please let me know anytime you want to visit Sam."

"Thank you, Nikki. I'll let you know where I'm

stationed and when I can get back to Arizona." He lifted his beer and sipped. "How are you going to manage Sam living in a hotel?"

"I'm still working on that. Have you ever been to Creekside and stayed at The Palace?"

"No." He shook his head. "I know it's a small town because Sheri talked about your big move."

Nikki pulled her tablet out. "Here's the website. The Palace is small, sort of a cross between bed and breakfast and boutique hotel."

"So, Sam's home is a very large house with a constant stream of guests." Max shook his head. "Do many children stay at The Palace?"

"Not many." Nikki shrugged. "The rooms are pretty small. I have a two bedroom with a sitting room suite, so Sam will have a bedroom and a place to play."

"At least Sam will grow up in one place." Max flipped through the hotel's website. "Sheri wanted a sense of roots for Sam. Not the nomadic Air Force life we had."

Nikki sipped her tea. "Creekside's a good place for families. Low crime, good schools."

Max raised his eyebrows. "Sheri didn't tell me your hotel's haunted."

"That's part of its charm. Creekside's small enough the residents know each other, yet because the town depends upon tourism, there's always something going on. The resident ghosts are part of the draw."

"Yeah," Scott added. "After spending the summer in Creekside with Aunt Nikki, my social life in San Diego seems a little boring."

"That's because Patrick doesn't work you as hard as I did. I'm expecting a lot of help over Christmas."

With a last hug for Nikki and a final moment in the bedroom watching Sam sleep, Max left for his flight.

Patrick sat down again next to Nikki. "Why isn't Max Sam's guardian? He's a blood relative."

"He's also career army. Sheri couldn't wait to grow up and live in one place. She wanted a permanent home for Sam." Nikki placed the tea things on the tray.

Patrick picked up the tray and headed toward the kitchen. "When Max leaves the army, do you think he'll petition for custody? It could get ugly if he does."

Nikki frowned and followed Patrick. "I can't worry about that." She filled the sink with hot water and soap and washed the dishes. Patrick picked up a towel and dried. "Anyway, by the time Max retires, Sam might be old enough to make his own decisions. Right now, I've enough to do worrying about being Sam's guardian." Nikki knew she lied to herself and her brother. If Max attempted to take Sam, she'd fight.

Bright blue sky, yellow sun, and puffy white clouds greeted Nikki as she and Patrick loaded her truck for the return to Creekside. Nikki lifted Sam into the backseat. He climbed into his car seat and buckled himself in. Scott lifted Georgie into the back seat; she sat up beside Sam, leaning her head against the car seat. Patrick pulled open the driver door, and then pulled Nikki in for one more hug. She relaxed into his comforting arms and breathed in the familiar scent of his shaving soap. She stepped away and climbed behind the wheel.

"Yes, Nikki, I'll do everything on my list and keep you posted." He grinned and shook his head. "There has to be some advantage to having an attorney brother. I'll take care of the legal details. You worry about

Sam." He pushed the door closed. Her last sight of Patrick and Scott in the review mirror was of their identical blond heads glinting in the sunlight.

From behind the front desk, James grinned at his sister. "Welcome home." He grabbed her in a bear hug. "We're glad to see you."

Balancing a sleeping Sam on one shoulder and Georgie's leash, Nikki hugged him back. "We're glad to be home. My truck's out front if you'd like to start unloading. I need to put Sam down."

When she entered her second bedroom, Nikki's eyes opened wide in shock. Sam's furniture waited, his favorite big truck comforter covered his bed, and toys lined the shelves. After gently removing Sam's shoes and covering him with a blanket, Nikki whispered, "Sam, you're home." Quietly setting up a monitor in Sam's room and slipping the receiver in her pocket, Nikki slipped out of the bedroom. Feeling blessed Sam's furniture arrived so quickly and that James set everything up, Nikki greeted Eric and James as they unloaded her truck. "Thank you, Sam's room looks awesome."

"We wanted Sam to know he was finally home. You mentioned he keeps waking in the night and asking for Sheri." James shrugged. "Maybe waking surrounded by his own stuff will help."

Nikki pulled the monitor out of her pocket. "We're about to find out how Sam feels." She dashed inside.

Sam sat on his bed, looking around the room. His brown hair was tousled from sleep, one sock covered a foot, and the other sock lay on the bed.

Sam frowned and climbed off the bed, his feet hitting with a soft thump. "Where am I?"

"Home." Sam moved around the room, touching familiar things. Georgie walked beside him. Each time Sam stopped, Georgie leaned against his leg. He reached down and scratched her behind the ears.

Sam stopped in front of Nikki. "It's all my stuff?"

She kneeled. "All yours."

Sam wrapped his arms around Nikki. "So I don't live with Mommy anymore? I don't live in our house?" His voice broke on the last word.

Sam in her arms, Nikki slid into the rocking chair. "Mommy is with the angels now. She's in heaven keeping an eye on us. You're safe here with me."

Tears slid slowly down his cheeks. "But I want Mommy."

Nikki's voice broke, and she hugged him tighter. "I know. Me too." She handed him tissues and slowly rocked. When his tears stopped, she set him on the floor, took his hand, and walked through the suite. In the sitting room, James waited, a pizza on the table in front of him. He rose and lifted Sam into a chair at the table. They held hands, said grace, and ate. James drew giggles out of Sam with stories of eating pizza with Patrick when they were kids, always arguing about the toppings and fighting over the last piece and then one of them giving it to the dog. Who always threw up the pizza a few minutes later. Their mom making them clean it up together, saying it wouldn't have happened if they didn't argue.

Later, when Victoria's closed, Sam fell asleep and James returned from walking Georgie, James and Nikki sat in the sitting room with glasses of wine. "Thank you, dear brother. Thank you for dinner and making Sam laugh."

James shrugged and sipped his wine. "Patrick spoiled pizza for me. I think of him every time I bring a pizza home."

Nikki sipped her wine. "Thanks for setting up Sam's room. Which room are you using?"

"Six." He lifted his glass and sipped. "When Sam's furniture arrived, I realized I needed to get out of his room. Wasn't space for both of us." James grinned and took another sip. "Will you start looking for a place to rent, or are you going to raise Sam in The Palace?"

"I'd rather stay in The Palace." Nikki frowned. "Sam won't be the first boy raised in the hotel."

"True. Eric wondered if you'd be hiring a nanny."

"Definitely. Sam needs someone focused on him all the time; he's three." She frowned, wishing she had a neighbor like Miss Effie. "I'm afraid he won't get the attention he needs from just me. I don't suppose there's a Miss Effie clone living in Creekside."

James lifted his glass in a toast. "Doubtful. I'd bet there's not another Miss Effie anywhere." He sipped and set the glass on the end table. "Regular child care isn't going to work with your hours."

"We were so lucky with Miss Effie," acknowledged Nikki. "She was like having a grandmother living next door."

"Do you think having someone live in is better?"

"Yeah, I think so." Nikki took a sip and plotted how she could entice someone to live in a haunted hotel. "I'm going to connect Sam's room with the one you're in and see if I can hire a live-in nanny. Salary, room, and board. Think I'll find someone?"

James nodded. "You may have just gotten lucky. Talk to Eric. He mentioned a relative."

Low gray clouds filled the sky when Nikki woke. The click and slap of the doggie door and the click of Georgie's toenails on the wood floor announced her return from the veranda. Dressed in jeans and a long-sleeved red Palace shirt, Nikki poured kibble into Georgie's bowl in the sitting room and opened Sam's door. He sat in the middle of his bed…silent.

"Morning, Sam. I was just coming to wake you." She lifted him into her arms for a hug and a smacking kiss on the cheek. His lips turned up a little, and he pecked her on the cheek.

"Morning, Aunt Nikki." She set him on the floor. "I'll get dressed now. I can dress myself."

Nikki ruffled his hair. "I know. We'll get breakfast when you're ready."

Georgie slipped into the room, following Sam back and forth as he found clothes. Nikki left him to get ready.

Eric strolled into the kitchen just as Nikki finished filling the coffee maker with water. "Good morning, Nikki." He glanced through the door to the library. "Looks like Sam finished breakfast. I can finish here."

In the library, Sam sat at his table waiting, hands folded in his lap. She recognized the perfectly behaved Sam. Sometimes when Sheri took him visiting or out to a restaurant, this Sam appeared. Nikki missed the other Sam, the running, playing, wiggling, chattering Sam. After she explained that Sheri was in heaven, Sam was an almost eerily quiet and well-behaved child. Not a positive sign. "Looks like you finished breakfast. I'll return your plates to the kitchen, and we'll stop at your room for toys."

"Okay."

In the basement, Nikki folded towels, Sam playing with his trucks on a mat beside her. Sam crashed his toy vehicles into each other and one always rolled over and over. Sam must have heard exactly what happened to Sheri, how a truck barreled through a stop sign and hit her broadside, her compact car rolling over and over. Nikki grimaced. Looked like they needed a counselor. She understood a mother's grief for an unborn child and an adult daughter's pain at the loss of a mother. She watched Sam move his truck into position again. She felt way over her head with a small child's loss of his mother.

Sam and Nikki ate lunch in the library. When the meal ended, they walked to the suite.

"May I play with Georgie, Aunt Nikki?"

"Good idea." Georgie waited with a toy in her mouth, her tail wagging. "Georgie loves when you hold her rope and play tug-a-war." At a tentative knock, Nikki let Eric into the suite. "What's up?"

"James says you're interested in a live-in nanny."

"I'm considering it. Do you know someone?"

Eric nodded. "My cousin Megan just moved in with us. I'm sure she'd be interested."

"Tell me about Megan." Nikki led Eric to a small table and chairs beside the window.

"She's twenty-two, working on her degree in early childhood. She's been taking the classes on-line the last two years, living in Flagstaff, caring for Aunt Mary."

"And she's living with you now?"

"Aunt Mary died six months ago, and Megan sold the house in Flag." Eric shrugged. "She needs a fresh start and a place to live."

"Would she be willing to live in a hotel?"

"She'd probably enjoy living in The Palace. I was going to suggest she apply here for a part-time job, but a nanny position would work better if she had a place to live."

"Okay, bring her by sometime tomorrow if she's interested." Nikki glanced over at Sam and watched his eyes drift shut. "Come on, Sam; let's read a story in your room."

The family of bears just started setting up the tent when Sam and Georgie fell asleep.

Nikki fell into bed exhausted. She dreamed. Dim lights bathed Sheri's room at St. Joseph's Hospital in shadows. Tiny Sam wore a little blue cap and lay in Sheri's arms. Propped up in bed, Sheri gazed into the face of her son. Nikki placed a spray of yellow roses on the bedside table and handed Sheri a small bag. Using one hand, Sheri opened the gift bag and pulled out a blue onesie, a truck graphic on its chest. "Thank you, Nikki. Wait, I have something for you."

"Why?"

"For being my labor coach, for being a godmother." Sheri handed her a small jewelry box. Inside on a silver chain, a heart was engraved with "I love Sam." Nikki woke. Outside, yesterday's promise of snow came true. White flakes drifted through the sky and settled on the ground. Bing Crosby promised "I'll Be Seeing You," and Nikki replenished the food on the bar and watched Sam eat breakfast with Catherine, Hope, and Lily. His posture not as stiff as yesterday, he teased Lily. Grateful for his hesitant smile, so much like Sheri's, Nikki turned as Eric entered the hotel. "Good morning. You're off this morning, aren't you?"

"Yeah. Charlotte's on this afternoon. I wanted to

introduce you to Megan. I thought I'd take over breakfast while you talked." He moved behind the bar and took the package of bread from Nikki.

A petite young woman waited beside the door.

"That's an excellent idea. Hello, I'm Nikki Benton, and you must be Megan Lake."

"It's nice to meet you, Ms. Benton." Megan joined Nikki beside the bar. "Is this a good time to talk?"

"Perfect, since Eric is taking over breakfast. Let me tell Sam we'll be in the office." Nikki walked over to Sam and knelt to his level. "Sam, I'll be in the office for a few minutes."

Catherine looked at Nikki. "He's fine with us."

They walked to the office, and Megan took the chair across from the desk. "Have you any experience as a nanny, Megan?"

"Here are my references." Megan handed Nikki a few sheets of paper. "Until I took over care of my mom, I was interning at the day care on campus at N.A.U. I'm still working on my degree in early childhood education on-line."

"The hours are erratic. I want to spend as much time as possible with Sam, but I need someone available whenever I'm working." Nikki glanced at the references. "Sam starts preschool soon, and the nanny will take him and pick him up when I can't."

"That's why you're offering room and board, right?"

"Exactly. Of course, I'll respect any time off we agree to. As soon as the renovation's completed, the nanny's room will connect with Sam's."

"What's Sam's schedule? Does he take naps or eat at a particular time?"

"Sam's only been with me a few days." Nikki laid the references aside. "The nanny's going to need flexibility as we figure out schedules and duties. Since the hotel offers breakfast to guests, I'll expect Sam and the nanny to eat with guests most of the time."

"That's why he was in the lobby this morning. He seemed comfortable with the other children."

"He played with Hope and Lily for a little while yesterday." Nikki stood. "Let's introduce you to Sam." Megan rose and followed Nikki to the lobby. "This is Miss Megan, Sam. Miss Megan, this is Sam."

"Hello, Sam." Megan slid into a chair beside Sam. "I understand you live with a dog named Georgie. What does she look like?"

Sam looked up at Nikki, frowning,

"It's okay, Sam; you can tell Miss Megan about Georgie."

"Georgie is little and white." Sam's dimples appeared. "She likes to play with me." Within a few minutes, Sam was offering to show Megan his room and Nikki knew she'd found the perfect nanny.

****

Winter sun glinted through the lobby windows, turning the wooden floors the color of honey. Perched on a stool behind the front desk, Nikki hummed along with Elvis Presley's version of a "Winter Wonderland." Car doors slammed, and James, Patrick, and Scott raced up the steps, yanked open the front door, and chorused, "Merry Christmas." Nikki jumped off her stool and dashed into a group bear hug, laughing as Patrick turned her in a circle. They all talked at once.

"Creekside looks like a Christmas card or the movie set of *White Christmas*."

"Is this our first white Christmas?"

"Is Sam excited about Christmas and Santa?"

Nikki stepped back. "Thrilled is a better word. We visited Santa last weekend, and while Sam was concerned about sitting on a stranger's lap, he screwed up his courage enough to give Santa a list." She reached behind the desk and handed them keys.

Patrick took his key. "Where is Sam?"

"At the square with Megan. There are games, food, and a carousel. You can probably find them at the carousel after you drop your bags in the rooms." The bell on the front door tinkled; Sam raced in, then slid to a stop in front of Patrick, James, and Scott. Nikki bent to Sam's level. "Remember Scott, James, and Patrick?"

"Yes! You came for Christmas."

Nikki started unbuttoning Sam's jacket and helped him pull off his gloves. "How was the carousel?"

"I rode the unicorn, Aunt Nikki," Sam boasted. "Miss Megan got dizzy, we rode so many times."

Nikki stood. "Is that true Miss Megan? Did the carousel make you dizzy?"

"Not the first time." Megan shook her head. "But after five times, yes, I was dizzy."

Sam frowned at the suitcases in front of Patrick, James, and Scott. "Did you bring presents for under the tree?"

"We did." Scott tousled Sam's hair. "Will you help me put our presents out after Dad gets them out of the car?"

"Yes." Sam pulled Megan toward the sitting room.

"Go ahead, Miss Megan. I'll send James along in a minute with hot chocolate and snacks."

Looking around the sitting room after Sam and

Megan were off to bed, James commented, "Where's Georgie? It's not like her to miss a Benton family meeting."

"She's moved in with Sam," Nikki answered. "I bought her a second bed when I realized she was splitting her nights between my room and Sam's."

"Do you think Georgie realizes Sam needs comfort?" Scott asked, sipping hot chocolate.

"Probably…she's a therapy dog." Nikki shrugged. "One night right after Sam moved in, Georgie woke me before I heard Sam on the monitor. He was having a nightmare."

"Did you talk to a counselor?" Patrick asked. "I know you considered it."

"Yeah, I found a grief counselor," Nikki confided. "She thinks Sam is a little young yet for individual sessions, but we'll start seeing her together about once a month after the holiday."

"I like your fireplace." Scott touched the electric fireplace. "That's new, right?"

"Just delivered last week." Nikki smoothed the stockings hanging on the mantel. "With Sam, I felt a need to decorate the sitting room and put up stockings. In fact, Sam wanted to know if Santa could get down the chimney."

"What did you tell him?" Patrick asked. "I vaguely remember Mom telling you she left the back door unlocked since we didn't have a chimney."

"Sam now understands we give the code for the front door and a magic key for the sitting room to Santa." Nikki took a sip of red wine. "Megan and I carefully demonstrated how Santa opens the front door."

"How's Megan working out?" James asked. "She seems to really like Sam."

"At the moment, Megan is my favorite Christmas blessing," Nikki admitted. "She's great with Sam and Georgie, plus she enjoys the hotel guests."

They cleared the room of dishes and carried them to the dishwasher. Patrick followed Nikki around while she checked the windows and doors. With Georgie dressed in a red jacket and black boots, Nikki and Georgie headed toward the back door for a last walk. Only the sound of her boots and Georgie's toenails on the wood floor broke the silence in the hallway. Nikki yanked open the back door, moved outside, and listened for the lock's click. Stars studded a black velvet sky. White light from half a moon glinted on the snow. A familiar shadow detached from the corner of the hotel and glided toward her.

"Evening, Innkeeper." First time she'd heard that rumbling voice or seen this particular shadow since Sam moved in a few weeks ago. He took Georgie's leash and looped his arm through hers.

"Evening, Chief." No hello kiss. "It's been an age since we've walked."

They walked through the night, each motion light a yellow glow on white snow as they passed. "I noticed someone else usually accompanied Georgie at night, Nikki. I gather you've been staying in because of Sam."

"Yes." He could have visited her. Her other friends found time to stop by, meet Sam, offer advice, and make Sam welcome. "It feels like Sam's adjusting a little."

"How's Megan working out?" Alex led them toward the square, the Creekside Christmas tree a beacon of light against the black night. "I've seen them around town quite a bit."

"She's awesome." Nikki tugged them back toward the hotel. "Sam adores her. I'm not sure how I would have handled living in the hotel with Sam without her."

At the back door of The Palace, Alex drew Nikki into his arms. She laid her head against his shoulder, comforted by his familiar warmth, his scent blended of aftershave and soap. He squeezed her once and pulled away, planting a brief kiss on her forehead. Looking into his chocolate eyes, Nikki recognized regret.

"Goodnight, Nikki."

"Night." She opened the door, slipped inside, and heard his boots on asphalt walking away. Tonight, he'd answered her question without a word. No passionate kiss or lingering embrace, only a brief, friendly hug and kiss on the forehead. No longer an unencumbered, potential lover operating a haunted hotel, the moment she held a tearful Sam in David Treat's office she'd become the parent of a very young boy. Alex wanted a lover, not more children. A companion, not a wife. Holding Georgie in her arms for comfort, Nikki walked toward her suite. At the door to Sam's room, Victoria stood in a shadow. She turned and glided through his closed door.

As Nikki slid under the blankets, she felt Alex's arms around her. She tasted his lips and longed for his gentle touch. For a moment, she smelled again his familiar scent. With an exhale, she consciously released those sensory memories, letting go of what might have been. She pictured instead Sam's glee as he explained that Megan got dizzy and heard his giggles when he and Scott played tickle war on the rug. A part-time lover wasn't enough. To take on a lover, she would need him to want Nikki and Sam, package deal. Nikki pictured the Christmas tree with gifts piled high and drifted off to sleep.

She woke startled by a whining Georgie standing beside the bed. She tumbled out of bed, pulled on fuzzy socks, and followed Georgie into Sam's room. Sam thrashed through a dream, totally uncovered, the blanket tangled on the floor. Straightening the covers, Nikki gathered Sam in her arms and moved to the rocking chair. With an afghan wrapped around them and Sam nestled against her heart, Nikki rocked, singing softly until Sam quieted.

"Ahh, Georgie," Nikki whispered as she laid Sam in his bed. "Thank you for warning me Sam was restless. You are the very best of guards for a grieving little boy."

Nikki walked through the sitting room, moonlight through the window lighting her way. When she reached her bedroom door, she glanced back at the window. Victoria stood at the window, her hand on the glass. She turned toward Nikki, a tear sliding down her cheek. She looked into Nikki's eyes and disappeared, leaving only a profound feeling of loneliness and the drifting scent of lavender.

****

Activity filled the days leading to Christmas Eve. James, Patrick, and Nikki attended a holiday party at the St. George, leaving Scott and Sam at The Palace. After food, drinks, fun, and adult conversation, the siblings walked the few blocks home.

"Are you still dating Alex, Nikki?" James asked as they walked in the cold, clear air.

"No. We only had a couple of dates, mostly we're just friends."

"Oh." Patrick frowned. "He seemed interested in more than friendship when I was here at Thanksgiving."

"Well." Nikki climbed the steps and reached for the front door. "Not that it's any of your business, but I don't think Alex is interested in dating a single mom."

"Nikki, don't give up your social life because of Sam. You need the company of adults; everyone does."

"I agree." Nikki read the concern in Patrick's blue eyes. "I'm surrounded by adults, all of my guests and my Creekside friends." She shrugged. "Anyway, I admit I don't know much about your love life, but I haven't seen you get involved since your divorce."

Changing the subject, the siblings discussed Nikki's plans for the attic, the basement, and what special she meant to offer for New Years.

Later, the brothers lounged in the library drinking a final brandy before bed. The Palace was quiet, the guests tucked in for the night.

"Nikki's right, Patrick," James commented. "You haven't been serious about a woman since your divorce."

"True," Patrick admitted. "Amy was a lesson I'd prefer not to repeat. But that doesn't mean I haven't dated. Just that I haven't found the one I'm looking for. What about you?"

"Seeing Nikki with Sam, I'm thinking about looking for someone finally." James sighed. "I don't know that I'm cut out for marriage, but I'm finally ready to find a partner."

"Nikki's right about something else. She's a single

parent. I know from experience from now on she'll look at guys differently. Her first thought will be how they'll interact with Sam."

"Having a kid would change your priorities." James changed the subject, and eventually the brothers wished each other good night.

Surrounded by family willing to help with Sam and The Palace, Nikki released Megan to spend three days at Eric's and cut Eric and Charlotte's hours so they could be together with their children. Christmas Eve, Nikki's family walked to Emanuel Lutheran Church through the cold night air for the candlelight service. A sprinkling of white flakes drifted on the breeze, melted as soon as they hit the ground. Sam peppered the adults with questions about the service and his chances of holding a candle. Sam's biggest concern was if Santa would come while they were gone. By the time they started the return to The Palace, Sam slept on Patrick's shoulder.

Sam tucked in bed, the family met in the sitting room and filled Sam's stocking. Nikki placed the last of the gifts under the tree. "It looks like Santa filled his sleigh with gifts just for Sam." She frowned. "Do you think we may have gotten carried away?"

"Probably," Patrick admitted and picked up his wine glass. "Do you remember what Mom's tree looked like when Scott was little?"

"Oh yeah." James grabbed a Christmas cookie, crunching it between his teeth and dropping powdered sugar on his black shirt. "When he was Sam's age, we had so many gifts, we had to put a few behind the sofa. There just wasn't room."

"And the year Mom hid some of them in the

bathtub, Scott found them Christmas Eve before church." Nikki slipped a small box into Scott's stocking.

"Jeez." Scott blushed. "You guys are embarrassing me. I think you're making that stuff up."

"Not a chance." James shook his head and brushed off the sugar. "You were Mom's only grandchild. She was determined you have every wish come true."

Nikki raised her wine glass in a toast. "To Mom, who loved us best of all and filled every Christmas, every birthday, and every holiday with love." Their glasses clinked. Out of the corner of her eye, Nikki caught a glimpse of Victoria standing in the shadow. She lifted a wine glass in toast and disappeared.

Chapter Seventeen

"From the Creekside Reporter, Monday, April 25:
'Celebration of Life scheduled Wednesday, April 27, at
five in the evening, at Emanuel Lutheran Church for
Victoria Jane Tuley Wyatt (12/2/1887 to 4/24/1949).
Mrs. Wyatt's grandson, Robert James Wyatt, survives
her. Reception on the veranda of The Palace Hotel
immediately following the celebration. In lieu of
flowers, donations to either Creekside Ladies Aid
Society or Creekside Helping Hands are
appreciated.' "

~A Brief History of The Palace by Arthur Welles

"Merry Christmas, Megan," Nikki greeted from the
front desk.

"Merry Christmas, Nikki. I've a gift for Sam. Is he
in the sitting room?"

Nikki nodded. "Assembling a race track with Scott.
How was your Christmas?"

"Excellent." Megan rolled her eyes. "Zane and
Zack are buried in toys." Megan opened the sitting
room door. Heads together discussing the finer points
of racetrack assembly, Scott and Sam sat on the floor.
"Merry Christmas."

"Merry Christmas," they chorused.

"Look what Santa brought, Miss Megan," Sam
said.

"Wow, that's a big racetrack." Megan knelt down to Sam's level. "It must have filled the sleigh all by itself." She pulled a small, wrapped gift from her bag. "Here's one more from me."

"Can I open it now?"

Megan nodded.

"Wait, here's your present." Sam pulled a small package from the tree's lowest branch. "Let's open them together."

Megan pulled the bow from her package. Inside the box rested a pair of earrings shaped like tiny bows. "Thank you, Sam. These are perfect."

Sam lifted a bright, red car just the right size for his racetrack from the box. "Thank you, Miss Megan." He hugged her.

The time between Christmas and New Year's flew. "Happy New Year, baby sister," James greeted Nikki when she answered her cell.

"Happy New Year to you. Are you on your way?"

"Almost. I'll see you in a few hours. Is Scott ready to go home?"

"Yeah. I'm not sure we're ready to let him go."

"Will they be back?" Sam asked, his face wreathed in a worried frown as they watched James and Scott drive away the next morning.

"Yes, Sam." Nikki hugged him. "They'll be back. Let's check on Georgie."

At eight-thirty, a tiny creak and the door to Sam's room opened. Nikki peeked in, Sam slept on, but Georgie lifted her head in question. Of course, Georgie curled up on the foot of Sam's bed instead of her brand new dog bed. Sam lay still, though his blankets hung precariously at the edge of the bed and his feet poked out one side.

On quiet feet, Nikki slipped into his room, one last check on her sleeping child. Pulling his blue blanket carefully back from the edge, Nikki covered him and silently promised him her best and her unconditional love. His feet covered, Nikki blew him a kiss, Georgie laid her head down, Sam slept on, and Nikki slipped away.

Voices from Victoria's greeted her when Nikki entered the hallway. Eric's low voice in conversation with another familiar deep voice, Alex. Nikki stopped, wrapped her slightly bruised heart in cotton wool, and, chin up, entered Victoria's. The hurt and betrayal she felt was ridiculous. They'd only dated a couple of times, walked Georgie together, and shared a few kisses. And then nothing…he'd ghosted her.

"Evening, Chief." He nodded in reply and she turned to Eric. "Thanks for coming back to close. I promise we'll figure out a schedule eventually."

Eric shrugged. "No problem, Nikki. I don't mind the extra hours. It'll work out."

Nikki slipped back into the kitchen, pulled tomorrow's casserole from the freezer, and slid it on the refrigerator's bottom shelf. Yeah, eventually a schedule. For now, she walked Georgie a different time and different route every day. Some days Megan and Sam joined her, sometimes just Sam. No walks through the night with Alex. At the kitchen's threshold, Nikki stopped. Victoria glided ahead of her. Though it made no sound, at the door of room 11 she raised her hand and knocked. She disappeared through the closed door. No doubt Victoria's lover waited in room 11. Nikki silently wished her a lovely evening in the arms of a faithful lover.

****

"Good morning. I'm Nikki Benton. I have an appointment with Mrs. Golding." Nikki greeted the receptionist at Emanuel Lutheran Church Preschool on Monday. Moments later, Sam's registration complete, Nikki walked him to class. "Megan will walk you home, Sam." His grip on her hand tightened when they reached the classroom. Nikki pulled the door open. A young woman walked toward them.

"Good morning. You must be Sam. I'm so happy you're in my class."

Sam leaned against Nikki's leg.

"Look, Sam, Lily's waving at you."

Sam pulled on Nikki's arm. She crouched to his level.

"Can I go by Lily?"

Nikki looked at Ms. Compton, a question in her eyes.

"Of course, Sam," answered Ms. Compton.

Sam headed toward Lily. Nikki waited.

"He'll be okay now." Nikki followed Sam across the room, touching him on the shoulder. "I'm going, Sam."

"See ya, Aunt Nikki."

Catherine and Hope waited in the lobby. "How did it go? Sam okay on his first day of school?"

Nikki held the door, and Catherine pushed the stroller outside. "It was harder on me than him. Lily replaced me."

"Oh, I remember Lily's first day." Catherine shook her head. They easily slipped around the few tourists on the sidewalk. "I'm sure it was harder on me. She told

241

me I could leave almost as soon as we walked in the classroom."

"Yeah, Lily's independent."

"And flexible. Now we're making another change."

"Ah. Did you find a house?"

"I did, and it's perfect, two bedrooms, a little backyard, and the best part, it's within walking distance of preschool."

"Congratulations, Catherine." Nikki frowned. "Is James okay with you leaving the hotel? Does he think it's safe?"

"He thinks we're safe as long as we stay in Creekside."

"When are you moving?"

"About February first," Catherine explained. "As soon as I get a firm date from the moving company, James promised to help us move."

The front door buzzer's annoying sound woke Nikki from a dreamless sleep. She threw a sweatshirt over her T-shirt, slipped into sandals, grabbed cell phone and keys, and carefully opened the door to the hall. Softly, she closed it behind her, hoping the other guests and Sam wouldn't be disturbed. At the front door stood a very large man, black scruffy beard darkening his cheeks, a frown on his face. Not one of the guests. In his arms he cradled a woman, her fingers grasping his shirt. Her, Nikki did recognize, Jeri Knowles, room 15. Unlocking the door, Nikki motioned him inside toward the library. The low lobby lights illuminated Jeri's face, scraped, bruised, and starting to swell.

"Lay her there." Nikki motioned toward the sofa. "Tell me what happened."

"Don't know. Found her behind the big tree on the square." He carefully laid her down and started backing out of the room.

"No, wait. I'm calling the cops; they'll want to talk to you." Nikki covered Jeri with the afghan.

"Don't know anything." He took another step back.

"They'll want to know where you found her." Nikki didn't want him leaving. "What's your name?"

A whisper came from the sofa. "Stay, please."

He stopped, looking down at Jeri. "Okay, guess I can wait." Like a balloon with the air released, he folded into a chair. He held out his hand to Nikki. "Jude Healy."

The EMTs arrived, and close on their heels, Alex. "Ms. Benton, what happened?" So formal, but that's who they were now, Ms. Benton and Chief Stark.

"The doorbell woke me. Mr. Healy carried Ms. Knowles inside and laid her on the sofa. I called 911."

Jude Healy handed his driver's license to Alex. "I was crossing the square to the St. George. Heard a moan. Curious, I found Ms. Knowles curled up under a tree. Thought she might have had too much to drink. Asked her if she was okay, did she need help. She wanted me to bring her here. When I realized she wasn't drunk but hurt, I carried her. Pushed the bell, Ms. Benton let us in."

Alex looked over at Jeri Knowles, now strapped on the gurney, covered in a blanket. "Not him. He just helped," she whispered. Nikki realized she'd not only been beaten but probably raped. She grabbed a pair of Palace sweatpants and a T-shirt from the cupboard beside the fireplace and set them on the gurney.

Jeri looked in Nikki's eyes. "Thank you."

Nikki felt tears rise but refused to let them fall. Her tears wouldn't help.

Finally, the EMTs left, carrying Jeri to the hospital. When Jude said he needed a room for the night, Nikki checked him in. Officer Corbin and Jude left, Jude to point out exactly where he found Jeri. Alex surprised her, waiting in the library until she'd sent Jude off. So badly, Nikki wanted to wrap her arms around Alex, lean against him, lay her head on his shoulder. Couldn't happen. Now Chief Stark and Ms. Benton, innkeeper and police chief, were barely friends. Nikki asked, "Did you need something else, Chief?"

"You and Georgie still take the same routes on your nightly walk?"

"Uh-huh."

"You shouldn't. Start changing the time you go and the way. It'd be safer."

Hearing the concern in his voice, Nikki nodded. "Good idea. You think whoever hurt Jeri is still around?"

"Don't know, but better safe."

"Sure. That it?"

He looked in Nikki's eyes. Whatever he searched for, he didn't find.

"Goodnight," and he was gone. Again.

****

Cold air whacked Alex in the face when he stepped out the back door of The Palace and strode to the square. Corbin's flashlight cast a small yellow circle around the oak tree. He sent Jude back to the hotel, back to Nikki. Not much to see beside the tree, just dead grass smashed in a circle the size of a grown woman curled in a ball. At first light, they'd come back.

Through the night, Alex walked Creekside's familiar streets, senses alert for anything that didn't belong. Finally, Creekside settled for the night, music turned off, lights dimmed as people left the sidewalks, headed toward their homes or hotels. Quiet, too quiet. No distractions. Alex needed distractions to avoid remembering his panic when he heard dispatch call for an EMT at The Palace and then an officer. His first thought was Nikki opened the door to the wrong person. Relief when he realized she wasn't hurt nearly brought him down. Then, she looked at him like a stranger, greeted him as though he'd never held her in his arms. His fault, his decision. Was it a mistake, letting her go?

Alex slipped through his mom's back door, pulled off his boots, locked up his gun, turned off the light in the entry, and climbed the stairs. Inside the boys' room, Mitch slept sprawled across his bed, covers and pillows on the floor, while Colin curled in a ball buried under his blankets. Both hanging on the edge between boys and young men. Such a struggle for the family getting here, Mom, Becca, Alex. Could he start over with a four-year-old? Alex changed into sweatpants and slipped between cold sheets, stretching out in the king-size bed. Could he begin again? Did he have a choice? Could he really let Nikki go? No answer, Alex drifted to sleep. His dreams were a kaleidoscope of remembered emotions. Worry when the doctor explained Vanessa's illness. Tearing pain when he held her the last time. Terror when he realized he was suddenly a single parent of two young boys. His mother's calm advice, moving from his apartment to her house, the sound of his sons' sobs in the dark. Their nightmares.

The enticing scent of coffee and the familiar sound of his boys arguing, no real anger in their voices, woke Alex. Entering the kitchen a short time later, the comfort of familiar smells and sounds surrounded him. Toast popped, his mother sat at the table reading the newspaper, coffee in her hand, while Mitch and Colin shoveled cereal into their mouths.

****

For the third night in a row, Alex leaned against the hotel wall waiting for Nikki in the shadows. All day she filled his thoughts. She drew him back each time he decided to stay away. Without conscious thought, each night at nine o'clock, he leaned on a wall behind the hotel and waited. The first night he waited a half an hour. She'd listened to him and changed the times. Second night she didn't show at all. He figured she left the hotel early and got back before he found his spot against the wall.

The motion light cast a yellow glow as the hotel's back door opened. Nikki stepped out, and the door closed with a loud click. Georgie whined, and Nikki stopped, searching the shadows. Dog and woman turned away from him headed down the alley. Alex peeled himself away from the wall and took one step to follow her. His earpiece clicked, followed by the dispatcher's voice. Alex turned the opposite direction, heading toward the square, wishing he could join Nikki instead.

Next morning, Nikki stood on the veranda and watched Catherine, Lily, Hope, Sam, and Georgie stroll down the sidewalk. Catherine dodged clumps of tourists, easily sliding the stroller along, Lily and Sam hung onto the handle, their rain boots bright pops of color. Sam lifted one leg high and stamped into a puddle, and the sounds of their giggles drifted in the air. They disappeared around the corner. Grinning at Sam's silliness, Nikki turned toward the front door and nearly bumped into Carol Harvey.

"Hey, Carol. What can I do for you?"

"It's what I can do for you." She pulled a box from her bag and handed it to Nikki. "Have a great day!" Carol trotted down the stairs and dashed down the street.

Nikki took the box to her office and pulled off the attached card.

I miss you. Alex.

Nikki shook her head. She missed him too, but there was no point hanging onto a relationship going nowhere. She opened the box; inside, Harvey Truffles nestled against each other, colorful wrappers a counterpoint to the shades of chocolate. She grabbed her phone and texted Alex.

—Thank you for the truffles. Nikki.—

"Welcome to The Palace," Nikki greeted a tall, blond man as he strode toward the front desk. "How can I help you this afternoon?"

"I have a reservation, Stephen Redfield, three nights." He handed Nikki a credit card and driver's license. "Are you the owner?"

"Yes." She handed the printed reservation to Stephen. "How did you hear of The Palace?"

"Max Larsen suggested I stop by." Stephen's dimples winked in his cheeks. "I'm hoping to spend some time with Sam since Max won't be around for a while."

"Will Sam recognize you?" Nikki frowned. "I don't remember meeting you."

"I'm not sure. It's been several months since Max and I stayed with Sheri."

"We're about to find out." She smiled at Megan and Sam when they entered the lobby.

Running full tilt toward Nikki, a laughing Sam threw himself into Nikki's arms. "Aunt Nikki, I brought you a picture." He pointed at a black and white circle with black eyes. "Look, there's Georgie, and Miss Megan, and you, and Uncle James, and Scott, and Uncle Patrick, and there's The Palace."

"Wow." Nikki hugged him. "You drew the whole family."

"No." Sam shook his head. "I left off Hope, Lily, and Miss Catherine because they're moving."

"I know, and you're not happy Lily's leaving. You'll still see her at school." Nikki took Sam's hand. "Sam, this is Stephen Redfield." Nikki watched Sam's face for a reaction. "He's a friend of your Uncle Max."

"Where's Uncle Max? Is he going to live at The Palace too?"

"No. Uncle Max didn't come this time. Do you remember Mr. Redfield?"

"No." Sam asked, "Where is Uncle Max?"

Stephen explained Max was working. Sam and Megan headed to the sitting room, and Nikki handed Stephen his key.

Key in hand, Stephen offered, "May I take you and Sam to dinner?"

"Why don't you join us instead," Nikki suggested. "We'll eat in room 10 about six thirty. Dinner's already cooking, and there's plenty."

"Thank you. I don't want to put you out."

"No problem." Nikki shrugged.

****

Gathered at the table in Nikki's sitting room, Megan and Nikki encouraged Sam to talk about his day at preschool and his afternoon playing with Georgie. "What did you like best about today, Sam?"

"Playing freeze in the gym. We stayed inside because the playground's wet."

Nikki nodded. "Recess can be the best part of school."

Dinner over, Sam and Megan retired to his room for a bath and story time.

Stephen watched Nikki move the dishes to the bus cart, grabbed his dishes, and added them. "Sam seems happy with his school."

"He is. His preschool in Phoenix was similar, so this feels familiar. The grief counselor suggested I surround him with as many normal experiences as possible. Would you like to wish Sam goodnight? It sounds like he's out of the bath." Stephen nodded. "He's right through that door."

Sam finally asleep, Megan retired to her room to study, and The Palace closed up for the night. Nikki and Georgie, both dressed in a heavy jacket and boots, slipped out the back door. Nikki shivered in the cold air and turned up her collar. She searched the shadows and then looked at Georgie. Her tail wagged, but she stood still waiting. Shrugging, she accepted no one waited, her imagination responsible for the feeling of being watched. Uneasy with the idea of Max sending someone to check on Sam without giving her notice, by the time she returned to The Palace she decided

249

confrontation was the best tactic for dealing with Max. Can't get an answer unless you ask.

After checking on a sleeping Sam, Nikki texted Max.

—Who is Stephen Redfield, and why is he here?—

Then she slid under the blankets and drifted off. She woke with a start. Three in the morning, shadows filled the room. Beside the window, Victoria stood. A man, his face hidden in the shadow, held her hands. His deep voice rumbled in the dark. "Ask me to stay, Vicky."

"You can't, so I won't. Go." Victoria pulled her hands free.

"I'd rather stay."

"You can't."

The man's shadow disappeared. Victoria turned and faced the window. She disappeared, leaving only a sense of sadness and warmth in the air.

Next morning Nikki greeted Stephen in the lobby. "After your breakfast, please meet me in the office."

"Of course."

As she sat across her desk from Stephen, Nikki wondered why she hadn't noticed the sadness in his eyes yesterday. "I talked to Max this morning. He was surprised you were here."

"Yeah." Stephen shrugged. "He didn't send me to check on Sam. This was all my own idea."

"Why, Stephen? What's your interest in Sam?"

"When Sam was about two, I dated Sheri. I know I was more into her than she was into me. In fact, when I got my transfer orders, she dumped me. I kept thinking if I had a little more time, I could change her mind."

"What happened?"

"The army…I just couldn't get back to Phoenix." Stephen shook his head. "By the time I was ready to try again, Sheri was gone."

"You weren't at the funeral. Why now?"

"I didn't know about Sheri's accident until Max returned from the funeral. I guess this was just my clumsy way of saying goodbye. It's hard accepting she's gone."

"I can understand your grief." Nikki shook her head. "If Sam wasn't here, I'd probably be picking up the phone to chat with Sheri. Sam's my reminder she's gone."

"Thanks for understanding, Nikki. I'll just check out today, if that's okay."

"Sure," Nikki agreed. "We don't keep our guests prisoner. Do you want to say goodbye to Sam?"

"No." Stephen shook his head. "He didn't remember me, so a good-bye might be disruptive."

Snuggled under her quilt, Nikki remembered Sheri's determination to give Sam roots. She understood Sheri's willingness to let Stephen go when his chosen career demanded a nomadic lifestyle. Would Sheri be happy with Sam living in The Palace, surrounded by both strangers and friends? Just before dawn, Nikki dreamed again of climbing the stairs to the attic. She pulled open the attic door and found four young men, teenagers probably, lounged on the bare floor playing Monopoly. Their words indistinct, their voices no longer the high-pitched sound of small children, instead the deeper tones of young men. Nikki recognized RJ the minute he looked up from the game and smiled. Before she could return his smile, she woke.

Outside her window, water dripped off the roof; snow melted in the sun. Dressed in a long-sleeved Palace shirt, Nikki checked on Sam and Megan, who were laughing as they debated which shirt would look best in Sam's school photos. Nikki opened the door to the scent of coffee, the sound of Billie Holiday admitting "I Can't Give You Anything But Love." Smiling at Eric's cheerful singing along with Billie, she grabbed the casserole from the oven and joined him at the bar.

"Hey, Eric."

He nodded and continued singing. He set the toaster up and pointed toward the front desk. A snake plant wearing a bright blue bow sat in the center of the desk. The music switched to the Rascals claiming today "A Beautiful Morning," and Nikki pulled a small white card from the plant.

I miss you. Walk with me tonight? Nine o'clock? Alex.

"When did this come, Eric?"

He shrugged. "Was on the porch when I got here." Nikki carried the plant to her office, pulled out her cell phone and texted.

—Thanks for the snake. Okay, nine o'clock. Nikki—

****

The lobby filled with cheerful conversation punctuated by the clinking of glassware. Megan and Sam sat at a table with Catherine, Lily, and Hope. Nikki grabbed a mug of coffee and joined them, admiring Lily's description of the pose she planned for school pictures. Time plodded on. The preschool contingent headed out, their piping voices drifting on the breeze as they walked away. Eric finished his shift and, with a wave goodbye, dashed down the stairs headed toward home. All day Nikki worried. What should she say to Alex? What did she need from him? What did Sam need?

At nine o'clock, she placed the last wine glass in the rack and started the dishwasher. After she checked Sam once more, she dressed herself and Georgie in leather jackets and slipped out of the suite, down the hallway, and through the back door. A click announced the door locked, and Georgie whined, wagging her tail so hard her backend shifted from side to side.

Alex strode toward her. "Evening, Innkeeper." He took Georgie's leash. "Thank you for coming." He looped his arm through hers.

"Evening, Chief." They took a few steps. "I'm not sure why I'm here."

The parking lot lights came on and flicked off, marking their progress. "To forgive me?"

Nikki frowned, and they stepped around a small puddle. "For what, exactly?"

Alex guided her across the square to a shadow beside the gazebo. He stopped and turned her to face him. "For running hot and cold. For not being there for you when you came home with Sam." He took a big breath and released it in a sigh. "I'm sorry."

Nikki inhaled his familiar scent, gazed into his chocolate eyes. "Why?"

Alex tilted his head, a confused look on his face. "Why should you forgive me? Or why am I apologizing?"

Nikki slid her arm through his again. "Let's walk." They strolled toward the hotel. "From the beginning, I knew you wanted a companion, a friend, a lover at least for a while." She shrugged. "But I'm no longer available to fill those roles."

"Because of Sam." His tone was flat.

"Yeah." They reached the hotel's back door. Nikki leaned against the door and gazed at Alex. "Sam and I deserve more. If I add someone to our family, that someone must want both of us. Oh, I get that only this moment is a guarantee, but we need someone we can count on at this moment. Someone who is a friend every day." She shrugged. "I'm sorry that's not you." She lifted up on her toes, placed a soft kiss on his cheek, pulled open the door, and slipped inside.

Tears coursed down her cheeks. She hated goodbyes. She shook her head. Funny for an innkeeper who made her living from hello and goodbye.

****

Cold air swirled around Alex, lifting the tail of his jacket, sneaking underneath to chill his back, but he walked on. Was that it then? Were they over just that fast? His boot heels made a soft clink on the sidewalk, his chest tight, his breath a white puff in the cold air as he strolled familiar streets. Without any idea how he got there, Alex climbed the steps to his mother's house. He sat on the porch swing and yanked off his boots, slipped his key in the front door, and padded into the hallway. The standing light beside Beth glinted on her silver hair. She raised her head from her book. "Late night. Everything okay?"

"Sure." He padded into the front room and sat in a wing back chair facing her. "Mom, how come you don't date? Dad's been gone a long time."

"Small town. Busy helping you raise the boys. Set

in my ways." She shrugged and raised an eyebrow. "How do you know I don't date?"

Alex frowned. "Do you?"

"None of your business. I don't comment on your love life."

"Don't have a love life." He dropped his head in his hands.

Beth set the book down and grabbed his hands, concern written on her face. "What's wrong? You fight with Nikki?"

"Not exactly. She basically told me to go away."

Beth let go of his hand and sat back. "Why? I'd think she'd need more support now she's taken on raising her friend's son." Beth stopped. "Oh. You told her you didn't have any support to offer."

Alex groaned. "Not in so many words." He looked up at Beth. "When I met Vanessa, I saw forever."

"Instead, you had a few years and a lot of pain."

He nodded. "With Nikki, I pictured one day at a time, living in the moment, no plans for the future," he confessed. "It was working really well. She's so much fun, so smart, so warm."

"But now there's Sam."

"Sam." He nodded again. "She says she and Sam are better off without anyone else unless that person wants them both. Only interested in someone she can count on."

"And that's not you."

Alex stood, leaned over, and kissed Beth's cheek. "I guess not." He climbed the stairs and quietly opened the door to his sons' room. Mitch slept spread-eagled and uncovered. Alex pulled the covers over his son. Colin hid under the covers, curled into a ball. Love for these boys soon to be men filled him. Is that what Nikki felt for Sam?

Wearing old sweats and a T-shirt, Alex slipped between cold sheets and stretched across the king-size bed. Was he wrong to want Nikki on his terms? If the tables were turned, if she chased him but didn't want anything to do with his sons, would he be okay with that? He shrugged, probably not, at least not if he expected the relationship to last very long. What did he want from Nikki? Did he dare wish for forever when he knew forever was a lie? He slid into sleep.

On the last day of January, sun glinted off the lobby windows and white puffy clouds drifted across the sky. The coffee perked, filling the lobby with its warm scent, and conversation and the clink of glassware combined in a familiar song of morning at The Palace. Taking two steps at a time, James bounced onto the veranda, yanked open the door, and grabbed Nikki from her perch behind the front desk, wrapping her in a bear hug.

"Welcome back, James."

He set her on the floor and looked into her smiling face. "You look good, happy. No tears then, losing your long-term guests?"

"No tears." She shook her head. "After all, Catherine's moving exactly three blocks away, so I'm not really losing her."

"Let's get her moved. Her furniture arrives in a couple of hours. We're hauling her stuff from here in your truck, right?"

"Exactly." Nikki pulled her keys from her pocket. "Here."

In a flurry of activity, one truck and an SUV,

Catherine, Lily, and Hope moved from The Palace. Just before closing, James joined Nikki at Victoria's for a nightcap.

"Did everything arrive safely at Catherine's?"

"Nothing missing, and the movers were exactly on time," James answered. "Perfect location. Catherine can still walk to the preschool. Have you seen the house?"

"Yeah, last week. She's excited about the back yard and her own kitchen. It's smaller than what she had in Scottsdale, isn't it?"

"It's about half the size, but Catherine sold most of the furniture after the vandalism. She just kept her favorite pieces and the girls' furniture. Everything fit in the little house."

"And she's finally safe."

James confided, "I hope so. The PI was working for one of Craig's legitimate clients. The police department claims they have a lead on the accident." He downed the last of his wine, grabbed Nikki's empty glass, and rose. "You close, I walk Georgie, or I close, you walk Georgie?"

Nikki grabbed the glasses. "I'll close. You walk." She rose.

James frowned. "That's a surprise. Thought you and the local chief walked Georgie?"

Nikki reached over and kissed him on the cheek. "Nope. You walk." She disappeared into the kitchen.

James dressed Georgie for the cold, grabbed his heavy jacket, and pushed open the back door. Cold wind blasted his cheeks. He turned up his coat collar and listened for the click of the door latch. Georgie frantically wagged her tail, and a shadow pulled away from the wall.

"Evening, James."

James nodded. "Alex." They strode across the lot. "Nikki said you don't walk with her anymore. You and my sister have a fight?"

"Nope." At the sidewalk, Alex turned right and strode down the block, disappearing around the corner.

Georgie whined. "Too cold out for you, huh?" James retraced their steps. "Don't suppose you can tell me what that was all about?" Georgie wagged her tail. "Guess not."

Chapter Eighteen

"From the Creekside Reporter Monday, May 1, 1949: 'Reopening today, The Palace Hotel. According to Judge Welles, The Palace will continue to provide the superior lodging experience guests have come to expect. New Managers Kathleen and Amanda Greene promise to uphold the traditions of grace, style, and service to the community previously established by Mrs. Victoria Wyatt, original owner and innkeeper of The Palace.' "
~A Brief History of The Palace by Arthur Welles

Outside, the early morning sun hid behind a dense gray cloud cover and snow clumped in small drifts under trees and next to buildings. Cars inched their way along Beatrice Street, the hum muted. Inside The Palace lobby, Bing Crosby promised the threatened rain was really "Pennies from Heaven." Nikki grabbed a second cup of coffee and slid it in front of Catherine at the game table.

"Accept it, Nikki. As long as Sam walks with us to preschool, I'm going to be helping myself to your breakfast." Catherine reached over and righted Lily's cup before it could spill.

"Hey. As far as I'm concerned you can come every morning."

The bell on the door jangled, and Becca Stark

strolled over carrying a small box.

"Morning, ladies." Her eyes widened, and with one hand, she grabbed Hope's glass before it toppled off the table.

"What brings you to town, Becca?" Nikki asked.

"Favor for my favorite brother." She handed Nikki the box and sauntered out the door.

Lily slid off her chair, dashed around the table, and reached for the box. "Open your present, Aunt Nikki."

Nikki shook her head at Lily's impatience. "Too busy. I'll open it later." Nikki stood. "Don't forget your backpack, Sam. It's behind the front desk." She moved away and slipped down the hall to the office. She set the box in the center of her desk. Not afraid of the box but worried about what might be on the card. She told Lily the truth, but she was too busy now to open the card and face the emotions. She left the box in the center of the desk.

Catherine zipped Hope's jacket just as Nikki returned to the lobby. Grabbing Sam's backpack, she strolled over and ruffled Sam's hair. He grimaced. "Aunt Nikki, you messed up my hair." He reached up and patted down the soft brown strands.

Nikki held the backpack in one hand. "Give me a hug?" Sam wrapped his arms around her waist. Nikki hugged him back and slid the pack on his shoulders. "Have a great day." From Victoria's favorite lobby window, Nikki watched them walk away.

The kitchen cleaned up, the dishes washed, the lobby straightened, and checkouts completed, peace filled the hotel to Fred Astaire's cheerful advice, "Let's Face the Music and Dance." Nikki accepted she needed to face the gift and the card. She pulled open the office door, moved behind her desk, and plopped in the chair. The shiny red bow waited. Nikki untied the bow and lifted the lid. Inside, a card rested on white tissue paper.

Nikki, I can't promise forever or even tomorrow, but from now on I promise you can count on me. These are for Georgie; she can count on me too. Alex.

Nikki peeled away the paper. Inside, four Georgie-sized black cowboy boots nestled together. Each boot bore the Windsong brand. Nikki lined the little boots up in a row at the edge of the desk. The front bell rang, interrupting her planning what to text to Alex.

"Welcome back, RJ." Nikki slipped behind the front desk. "Did you have a good holiday?"

"An excellent holiday. How about you?" He handed her his credit card.

"Excellent." Nikki processed the card and grabbed a key from the box under the desk. "Are you still working on family history?"

RJ nodded, accepting the key. "I have lots of new information about Victoria."

"When you're ready, I'd love to hear it."

He grinned. "Later then." Suitcase in hand, he climbed the stairs. Smokey appeared, tail wagging, and bounded after him. At least for Smokey, love didn't die when he lost his people. Instead, his love and loyalty expanded to include the living.

She pulled out her cell phone and texted Alex.

—Georgie and I thank you for the boots. She'll be wearing them tonight at nine thirty. Nikki—

Conversation hummed, glasses clinked, and the Andrews Sisters claimed they'd danced the whole night through and it was now "Three O'Clock in the Morning." At nine o'clock, last call over, Nikki and RJ sat at the game table, RJ's research spread out before them. "Victoria was the only child of Cora Lynn Tuley and Jackson Able Tuley. Cora and Able divorced in 1889, and Cora raised Victoria alone. Cora was a florist in Phoenix. She owned a small shop on Central Avenue named Palace Flowers."

"So, Victoria honored her mom by naming the hotel The Palace," Nikki concluded. "Not exactly the information she gave the Reporter."

"True." RJ pulled copies of marriage and death certificates from the stack. "Cora died in 1904, and Victoria married Benjamin William Wyatt a few months later. He was thirty-eight. Benjamin died in 1906, and there isn't any mention of Victoria in any public records or newspapers until she built the hotel in 1917."

"Did you locate any family for Wyatt?" Nikki stared at the marriage license, but the witness names were illegible.

RJ shook his head and pulled another sheet of paper from the pile. "No, the obituary stated 'survived by Victoria' but no siblings or parents. It looks like two people without family found each other."

"What next?" Nikki gathered the scattered papers and handed them to RJ.

"I'm going back to Freemont tomorrow to visit with Amanda Welles." RJ stuffed the papers into a folder. "She found some information about Judge Welles, and she asked if I'd bring a few copies of Arthur's books to you."

"I'd appreciate that." Nikki sipped the last of her tea. "I told her I'd come get them when I had time, but it's nice of you to bring them."

"No problem. It's my thank-you for being such a good listener." RJ chuckled. "Nice to have an audience who actually cares about my subject."

Nikki rose. "Oh, I definitely care about this subject." She pushed in her chair and gathered their empty teacups. "RJ, what do you do when you're not researching your family? When do you have an audience who doesn't care?"

He raised his eyebrows. "Can't you tell? I teach American History at a college." He grabbed his backpack, tossed it over his shoulder. "I'll see you tomorrow." With a wave, RJ climbed toward room 15, his shoes a soft thud on the stairs. Out of the shadow beside the stairs, Victoria appeared. She glided behind him, disappearing around the first landing without a sound.

The lights in the lobby dimmed, the music silent, as Nikki carefully opened Sam's door. He slept curled in a tight ball, Georgie on the foot of the bed, her head on her paws. Georgie lifted her head, stood, stretched, and hopped off the bed, landing with a soft thud. Tail wagging, she trotted over to Nikki and slipped through the door to the sitting room. Nikki dressed them both in black jackets and black boots and slipped into the hallway.

The Palace sighed in relief at the end of the day, the only sounds a low hum from a television set in an upstairs guest room and the whir of the central heater. Nikki pushed against the back door, leaning against the emergency handle. The motion light above the door flicked on, and she stepped into a black night. Clouds covered the sky, no moon and no stars. A familiar shadow pulled away from the lamp pole and strode toward her.

Alex took the leash, leaned in, and kissed her lightly on the cheek. "Evening, Innkeeper."

The scent of soap and aftershave warmed her, his rumbly voice enticed. Nikki looped her arm through his, noticing the muscles in his arms. "Evening, Chief."

Georgie leading the way, they strolled through the night, the motion light marking their progress in the dark. Silence. Night sounds surrounded them, music and conversation. Between them silence.

His rumbly voice whispered in her ear. "This is hard." They turned toward the square. "Harder than I thought it would be."

They stepped off the sidewalk and moved under a tree. "What's hard?" Nikki turned to face him.

"Apologizing. Asking for forgiveness."

Nikki frowned. "You already apologized. I already forgave." She shrugged. "Again, I'm not sure why I'm here other than to thank you for the boots."

He grimaced and took both her hands. "I wasn't even a decent boyfriend, running scared, pushing forward, and jumping back."

Nikki shrugged. "Hey, I allowed it, figured there was plenty of time to discover what we had, what we could be. No hurries. A relationship wasn't even on my priority list."

"But things changed."

She nodded. "Yeah. Sam changed everything, except relationship still wasn't on the list." She gazed into his chocolate eyes. "But Alex, friend moved up the list all the way to the top. Real friends I could count on for emotional support, advice, or just a shoulder when things went wrong."

"And I disappeared." He hung his head.

"Yep. Ghosted me. Something my single girlfriends talked about. A new experience for me." She lifted an eyebrow. "Maybe appropriate for someone living in a haunted hotel."

He winced and shook his head. "It should never have happened. I should have been there for you. Please, can we start again?"

She frowned. "Start what again?" She shook her head. "Alex, I'm not up for hot and cold. Either I can trust you or I can't. If all you want is a casual friendship then let's just part now, no blame, no shame."

He shook his head. "I want more. I need more. You can trust me as a friend. I'll have your back, be on your side. Let me prove it." He took a deep breath. "Let me court you, woo you, slip you and Sam into my family. Let me prove I can be who you need."

She pulled her hand from his, looped their arms. "Let's walk." They strolled across the square, onto the sidewalk, and retraced their steps to The Palace. At the door under the glary yellow light, they faced each other. Beneath his chocolate eyes, she noticed faint dark circles.

Nikki sighed. "Okay. I may be a fool, but I'm also a believer in second chances."

Alex wrapped his arms around her, lifted her off the ground, and pushed his lips against hers. He gentled the kiss, touched his tongue to her bottom lip. She opened, and their tongues played. Their lips parted and she slid down the length of his body, landing with a soft thump. The night no longer felt cold, she felt warm from the inside.

"You won't be sorry. I promise."

She shook her head and tugged open the door. "Night, Chief." She disappeared inside. The warm glow of low lighting beckoned from the lobby.

In the silent hallway, Nikki lifted Georgie in her arms, pulled off the tiny black boots, and stuffed them in her pocket. Georgie nestled against her shoulder. "Let's check the front door, Georgie. Just to be safe." The hall carpet absorbed the sound of her footsteps. Inside the lobby, she checked the front door lock, moved behind the bar, and checked the refrigerator lock. All secure. Outside, antique streetlights punctured the black night. Small clusters of visitors strolled on the sidewalk. "Bedtime, doggie."

Georgie whined.

Nikki glanced at the stairs. Smokey sat on the bottom step, his ears pricked. Another guard dog protecting a boy. Nikki shook her head. Not a boy, a man. Smokey stood, turned a half circle, and silently bounded up the stairs. Inside her suite, Nikki pulled Georgie's jacket off and hung it on the hook. Georgie waited, her focus on Nikki.

"Yes, you may go." Georgie trotted toward Sam's room, Nikki trailing behind. The dog slipped inside, hopped delicately onto the foot of the bed, turned two circles, and curled into a ball. Sam slept on. Nikki knelt and placed a kiss on Sam's forehead. "Night, Sam."

Nikki flipped the bedroom light off, leaving the room in shadow broken only by the faint glow of the hallway light through the transom window over the door. Plopped on the edge of her bed, she kicked off her slippers and slid beneath the covers. The faint scent of lavender drifted through the room. Beside the window Victoria stood, light reflecting off tears on her cheeks.

A man wearing a long coat and holding a bowler hat, his face in shadow, lifted his free hand. He touched her cheek, turned her head toward his, and placed a fleeting kiss on her lips. He dropped his hand, turned, and walked through the closed door. Victoria looked at Nikki and disappeared, leaving behind a lingering scent of lavender.

****

Keith Urban's "Wasted Time" yanked her from sleep. Nikki grabbed her cell phone and popped out of bed in a practiced move. "Morning, James." At the window, sunlight just barely peeked through the lace curtain. "It is morning, right?"

James laughed, the familiar sound bringing Nikki fully awake. "Did I wake you?"

"Yeah. What's up?"

"Nikki, I'm headed your way this afternoon. Do you have room for me?"

"Of course. Try to remember you own part of The Palace. There will always be room for you. What's the occasion?"

"I wanted to deliver some information to Catherine in person. It's about Craig and the vandalism."

"Did you warn her you were coming?"

"Of course, her and Chief Stark."

James arrived late afternoon, and they walked to Catherine's house, finding Alex waiting on her front step.

"Come in. The girls are playing in their room. May I offer you a drink?"

"Let's just go in the living room." James placed his hand on the small of Catherine's back, guiding her toward a wingback chair. Alex and Nikki settled at

267

opposite ends of the sofa. "I know you're dying of curiosity." He sat on the ottoman in front of her. "I can't think of a way to say this except just to spit it out." He took both her hands. "This morning, Scottsdale Police Department arrested Craig's business partner, Daniel Phelan."

Catherine's eyes widened. "For what?"

"Murder, embezzlement." James shrugged. "There may be other charges."

"Did you know this was going to happen, James?"

"Not really. About three months before Craig's death, he came to me, worried about his business. He wanted my opinion more as a friend than accountant, but he wanted me to look at some information he'd gathered. You know Craig and Daniel didn't do the same type of work or have the same clients. Craig was the real estate business and Daniel the financial advisor. Anyway, just before he left my office, he asked for my promise that I would take care of you and the girls if something happened to him."

"That's why you already knew where we should go when I called."

"Yeah, I was on my way to convince you to leave town for a while until I could figure out what was going on. The vandalism scared you and me. You came to me before I could get to you."

"You thought we were in danger even before the vandalism?"

"Honestly, I just didn't know. I'd promised Craig to protect you, and he died so soon after our conversation." He shook his head. "I couldn't believe it was a coincidence."

Catherine focused on Alex and frowned. "So, Alex,

does that mean we're really safe now?"

"I think so, but no one's keeping me in the loop about the charges against Daniel. I'll keep checking with my contacts in Phoenix though and let you know."

Lily and Hope wandered into the living room, running straight to James.

"Whoa there, ladies. Hop up here and tell me about your day."

Eventually Nikki and Alex left, leaving James to visit with Catherine and the girls. When he rose to leave, Catherine walked him to the door.

"Thank you, James. You've been more than a friend."

"Oh, Catherine. I am more than a friend. Craig was like a brother, so you're a sister. I would have protected you even if Craig hadn't asked." With a parting hug, he headed for The Palace.

"I love it! The blanket's perfect." Kassie laughed into the phone the moment Nikki answered.

"Oh, it got there. Text me a picture."

"You've never seen it? But you bought it."

"Sight unseen. Ainsley, the artist, described her idea. She said you'd love it, and it was perfect. So, I ordered it made for your daughter."

"I'll text the picture. The dragons are darling. Where did you find the artist?"

"Met her in Wickenburg at an art fair years ago. She sold every blanket that day. Her website's called Serendipity."

"It's perfect. Thank you, thank you. The dragons will protect our beautiful Zoe. When can you visit?"

"Not anytime soon. But whenever you feel like traveling, come to Creekside." She quipped, "I've lots of room, a whole hotel."

"How's Sam?"

"Adjusting. Doing well."

"And you? How are you?"

"Better. All the counseling after Aaron left made me stronger. Plus, Sam's a delight. He keeps me happy and keeps me busy."

"Can I do anything to help? Is there anything you need?"

"I'm good. Just love that baby and send me pictures."

Nikki admired the picture on the text. As Ainsley promised, a mother, father, and baby dragon stood together in the blanket's center. The father obviously prepared to fight off any warring knights. Around the edge, baby dragons danced. Perfect for Kassie, a dancer since the age of three.

Outside, night fell, the sky a black velvet blanket studded with a few stars peeking through the clouds. Inside Victoria's, Nikki lowered the lights as the last guests slipped away, either into the night or moving to the library. Bobby Hatfield hit the final notes of "Ebb Tide" and only the latching of the dishwasher broke the silence. Nikki strolled down the hallway in time to the music still playing in her head. She pushed open the back door, the motion light a brief glare in her eyes. From the shadow a familiar deep voice offered, "Evening, Innkeeper." His large hand took the leash. She felt a whisper of warm breath and then a fleeting kiss on her cheek.

"Evening, Chief." She looped her arm through his, and they strolled through the quiet night. The wind picked up, ruffling Georgie's ears. Nikki shivered. Alex wrapped his arm around her shoulder, pulling her against his warmth. They retraced their steps.

Under the hotel's glary light, Alex pulled her gently into his arms. "Would you and Sam come for lunch Sunday at Windsong?"

Nikki laid her cheek against his chest and relaxed into his warmth, his familiar fragrance. "Is this a special occasion? Your mom rarely stays at Windsong through Sunday."

"It's Mom's birthday." He pulled back slightly and gazed into her eyes. "Kira's doing the cooking, and I'm bringing the cake from Grandma's," he coaxed. "It's time you and Sam were included in my family."

"Are you sure you want that, Alex?" Nikki frowned. "Including us in a family event might create expectations." She shook her head. "You were clear in the beginning that you didn't want any more complications. A single mother with a four-year-old living in a haunted hotel is a major complication."

"Yeah, Nikki." Alex tapped her nose with one finger. "You're a complication, but one I can't get enough of. Join us for lunch. It will be our first date." He lifted her off the ground, and their lips met. The gentle kiss held no demand, just a gift. Slowly, he lowered her feet to the ground. "And that was our first kiss."

She shook her head. "You win. Sunday lunch for Beth's birthday."

He held the door open, and she slipped inside.

Sunday found Nikki strapping an excited Sam in his car seat for the ride to Windsong. Sam's chatter filled the air with questions: Were there horses? Would there be cake? Could he pet the horses? Could he ride?

Sam rarely took a breath between questions, so no answers required. Nikki nodded her head in response, but most of the time Sam's happy chatter was a counterpoint to Nikki's internal dialog. Reservations tightened her stomach. Tension pulled her shoulders and stiffened her neck. Starting over with Alex, what did that mean? Were they headed for making love? Was that the end goal? Would he ghost again after? Was it fair to Sam to bring him to a family event when they weren't part of the family and very likely never would be? She shook her head. No, that part was okay. Sam lived in the hotel. He already understood some people came to stay and others came and went away, didn't return. Some, like Catherine, left but still lived nearby, visiting all the time. They were still friends. They just didn't live across the hall anymore. Is that what the future held with Alex? Friends, nothing more.

Pulling into the drive, Nikki discovered the party was not family only, and she breathed a sigh of relief. The drive was full of cars and trucks, the yard dotted with picnic tables, white tents with gas heaters, and barbeque grills. Children of all ages ran laughing through scattered groups of adults. Nikki felt Sam's sudden tension as she lifted him from the truck. "Hold my hand for a while, okay? I don't know all these people, and you can help me remember names," she whispered.

Sam let out a breath and grinned. "Sure, Aunt Nikki. I'll help you. There's a lot of people here."

Making their way toward the porch and Becca, Nikki nodded toward familiar faces, all the while keeping a running commentary going for Sam. "Hello, Becca, Happy Birthday, Beth. Have you met Sam?"

"Thank you, Nikki," Beth answered. "Hello, Sam, thank you for coming to my birthday party. Have you met Luke? He's a real cowboy."

Sam's eyes widened, and shock crossed his face. "Really, with guns and horses?"

Bending down to greet Sam at eye level, Luke stuck out his hand, prompting Sam to shake. "It's nice to meet you, Sam. I have guns, but they're all put away today. Would you like to meet the horses?"

Sam dropped her hand and, a pleading look on his face, looked up at Nikki. "Could I?"

Nikki bent to Sam's level. "Yes, but stay with Mr. Luke, and do exactly what he says. Horses are big, so we need to be careful around them."

Off they went, Sam nearly bouncing with the excitement of holding the hand of a real cowboy.

Hours later, Alex lifted an exhausted Sam into his car seat. "Thank you for an excellent Sunday afternoon, Alex. We had a great time."

"I'm glad you came, Nikki." Alex leaned in and kissed her cheek. "Will you bring Sam out again when it isn't such a mob scene?"

"We'd love it." Niki shook her head. "Living with a ghost is going to seem tame compared to meeting a cowboy with real horses." With a wave, Nikki pulled her truck out and headed toward Creekside. The day hadn't been what she'd expected. Becca and Mrs. Stark were both warm and friendly. When Nikki first joined Luke and Becca on the porch, she wondered if they were connected, possibly lovers. But during the afternoon she saw nothing to confirm a connection. Mitch and Colin were polite and friendly but more interested in their friends than either Nikki or Sam.

273

Nikki remembered being very young and trying to keep up with her older brothers. James and Patrick were rarely interested in entertaining their much younger sister.

Sam asleep, Nikki got ready for bed. She moved her photos from phone to laptop. Sam's day captured in a slideshow, Nikki watched Sam sit proudly in the saddle on a very large horse and walk around the corral. Next photo caught Sam his mouth open in a scream as he headed down the slide. Sam in serious focus as he carefully held his hand out to give a horse a carrot. Then Sam playing hide and seek with Kira's twins and the other young children. Very last picture, Sam sound asleep in his car seat on the ride home. Only one moment was missing from the pictures—Sam dressed in pjs, his hands folded, asking God, "Please take care of my mommy. Make her have fun like I did today."

Wiping away tears, Nikki composed an email to Max. "I thought you might like to see Sam's introduction to a working ranch. Sam's favorite part was the real cowboy with the real horses. I'm planning a small party for his birthday in April. I hope all is well with you. Nikki."

Nikki climbed the steps to the attic. She opened the door. The renovated rooms were gone; instead the attic was nearly empty. Victoria stood beside the open doorway and chuckled as boys slid across the polished floor in their socks, landing with a thump on the wood floor and ending their game in a pile of children and dog. Nikki blinked. Victoria and children disappeared. The renovated rooms were just as she'd left them earlier. Nikki closed the door and headed back toward the lobby. When the rooms were ready for guests, anyone staying there should feel surrounded by boyish glee.

Nikki finally settled between cold sheets and drifted into a dreamless sleep. The sound of Georgie's whimpers woke her. Surprised Georgie didn't just come in the bedroom, Nikki crossed the sitting room to Sam's room. He slept soundly, Georgie asleep on the foot of his bed. Georgie whimpered in her sleep.

"Are you dreaming of RJ and his friends?" Nikki gently stroked Georgie. "You can rest now, Georgie; they're gone and Sam's asleep."

Georgie settled, and Nikki returned to bed. Sliding between the sheets, her mind circled with questions. Did Victoria haunt The Palace because she was happy here? Were the visions of RJ and his friends merely a manifestation of Victoria's memories? RJ died somewhere in Europe. Did that mean ghosts don't necessarily haunt the place they died? Her last thought before sleep took over: some day would she join Victoria in haunting The Palace because of her own happy memories?

****

Thursday, Nikki yanked black wool slacks, a peach silk blouse, and a white fuzzy sweater from her closet and tossed them on the bed. She pulled out black boots and purple socks. Her date with Alex. A real date. Where was this relationship going? Alex had run hot until Sam, and then he ran cold. Now the heat was back and a rush. He waited the nights she walked Georgie. He invited her to Beth's birthday party. Not exactly home to meet the family because half the town attended. Still, it was a party she didn't have an invitation to except through him. He promised she could count on him as a friend. And she admitted they both wanted more than friendship. Would they end and still be friends? Would that be awkward in a small town? Or would they drift along, lovers like Victoria and the man in room 11? Alex had all the children he wanted. She had custody of a child. Alex couldn't want her in his future. Stop! He said he wouldn't ghost her again. She could trust him. She wasn't going to sleep with him tonight. He lived with his mother and sons, and she lived in a hotel with Sam. Another time she'd worry. Tonight, she'd enjoy. She lifted her lips in a smile and stared into the small mirror over the sink. Grateful. Isn't that what she'd learned in therapy after Aaron? What she'd learned in the caregivers group when she took care of her mom? Be grateful for every good moment. No two were exactly alike. None would ever come again. She chuckled. Unless you were Victoria, destined to live them over and over.

Sam and Megan sat cross-legged on the sitting room floor, Candyland spread before them. Sam jumped up, dashed over, and wrapped his arms around her waist. "You look pretty, Aunt Nikki."

"Thank you, Sam." She hugged him back, and he returned to the game. "Are you winning?"

He giggled. "I am. Miss Megan's not very good at this. Not as good as Scott."

Nikki raised her eyebrows at Megan's exaggerated frown. "You'll be asleep when I get back. But I'll stop by with a kiss anyway."

To a chorus of good night, Nikki danced down the hall, her steps keeping time with Gene Kelly admitting it's "Almost Like Being In Love." She waved to Eric at the bar, pulled open the front door, and walked right into Alex.

"Isn't this how we met?"

He grinned and wrapped his arms around her. "Yep." He stepped back, leaned in, and dropped a fleeting kiss on her lips. "Ready?"

Cloudless sky, an almost full moon, and a blanket of stars, perfect night for a walk to dinner. He took her hand, and they strolled. Conversation ebbed and flowed; the topics varied. She laughed at his anecdote of the visitor who filed a complaint because she didn't see a ghost. Through the appetizers and the salads, they chatted, and Nikki noticed people stopped by the table a lot. Greeted her, talked to Alex. Mentioned concerns, thanked him for help. The waiter placed the entrées on the table, poured more wine in their glasses, winked at her, and moved on. Nikki took a bite of chicken and nearly moaned at the taste. She sipped her wine. "Alex?"

"Hum?" He looked up from the trout on his plate.

"How did you end up police chief?" Nikki took another sip. "I know why you came back to Creekside. But how did you end up chief?"

Alex set down his fork. "A chance convergence of events? A perfect storm?"

Nikki frowned. "Really, I'd like to know."

He sipped his wine. "You know why we moved back to Creekside?" She nodded. "Once she had Mitch to focus on, Mom bounced back pretty quickly. She found the house in town. Donaldson started the renovations. It was all good." He took another bite of fish. "Except Windsong. Mom didn't want anything to do with the ranch, which left Becca managing with no support."

"So you stepped in?"

He sipped the wine. "Yeah. You ever work for Patrick or James?" She shook her head. "Don't. I worked for my younger sister." He grimaced. "We were both miserable."

"And then?"

He sipped the wine. "And then Luke. Thank God for Luke."

"He didn't already work there?"

"Nope." Alex shook his head. "But as soon as I remembered where he was working, we stole him away."

"You knew him before?"

He shrugged. "Sure. He's from Creekside. Childhood friend."

"So, you left ranch work for police work, again."

"Yep." He lifted his glass, his eyes focused on the red liquid. "Vanessa died, and I found myself a single father of two very young boys. So, I stayed where Beth and Becca could help." He set the glass down. "Perfect storm, the former chief retired, and I was next in line."

They finished dinner and walked toward the hotel holding hands. "Your turn. How did you end up in Creekside?"

"Abridged version. Ready?" He nodded. "I took a leave of absence from my job to care for Mom. Discovered I missed working but not my job. Decided I wanted to recreate the fun we had when Mom and I would travel about Arizona with Andrea staying off season in tiny B and B's and small historic hotels."

"Off season?"

"Always. It's cheaper. Patrick and James were in college, so it was just us girls." She raised an eyebrow.

"Ever stayed in Tucson in summer?" He shook his head. "Anyway, I researched historic hotels and B and B's in Arizona and took hospitality classes online," she explained. "Patrick and James insisted on providing some financing. I found The Palace for sale. We bought it."

"Why The Palace?"

"Three reasons. Creekside's cooler than the desert. Price was good." She shrugged. "It's haunted. How cool is that?"

The yellow light over the hotel's back door glinted on Alex's dark hair. His arms surrounded her. Warm breath tickled her cheek. "How am I doing?" He placed tiny kisses on her cheek, beside her ear. "With my wooing you?" She felt the tip of his tongue against the top of her ear.

She hummed under her breath, and warmth spread under her skin. "Mmmm." She tilted her head, allowed him access to her neck. "Good. Great."

He gazed into her passion-filled eyes. "Thursday night. Dinner, Mom's house." He nibbled on her ear lobe. "Just you and me."

She kissed his lips. He opened for her, and their tongues played. She forced her eyes to open, forced herself to gaze into his chocolate eyes. "Okay, Thursday."

He picked her up and swung her around. "Thursday."

She shook her head and slipped inside. "Night, Chief." The door closed with a quiet smack.

Under the covers, Nikki's eyes drifted closed. She woke to the sound of muffled voices. In the soft light of a winter's dawn, a man and a woman danced, moving to the music of a silent waltz. The woman, Victoria, threw back her head and laughed. They disappeared. Could she find a love with Alex full of Victoria's exuberant joy?

****

The truck-shaped night-light in the corner threw a red glow on the wood floor. Sam slept, a curled ball in the center of his bed, the only sound his quiet snore. From her curled position on the foot of the bed, Georgie lifted her head. Nikki shook her head, and Georgie dropped her head to the quilt. After placing a brief kiss on the top of Sam's head, Nikki glided out of his room, closing the door silently behind her. She zipped her jacket, grabbed a small backpack, and moved into the quiet hallway, texting Megan as she walked.

—*I'm leaving*—

Smiley face attached, Megan text back.

—*Have fun!*—

Hand resting on the back door latch, Nikki glanced over her shoulder for a last look at the quiet lobby and Sam's closed door. Hand on the doorknob, Victoria stood at Sam's door. Their eyes met, Victoria lifted an eyebrow, nodded, and glided through the closed door.

****

Nikki pushed open the back door, slipped through, and listened for the lock's click. A shadow beside the door moved next to her. She breathed in his familiar scent, and his voice rumbled, "Evening, Innkeeper." Warm breath tickled her ear and a fleeting kiss touched her cheek.

"Evening, Chief." He took her hand and they strolled into the cold, quiet night. "This feels a little awkward. I'm not sure why."

He guided her down the alley onto a sidewalk. Houses marched on either side of the street, their lights shining behind curtains and shutters. "Because it's our first time and we had to work so hard to arrange it." Under a streetlight, Alex shook his head. "I haven't put this much planning into a date since my high school prom when I thought if the date was perfect, I might finally get lucky."

Nikki felt the tension in her shoulders relax. "And did you, get lucky?"

"Nope. All I got was grounded for a curfew violation. My dad was strict."

Picturing a disappointed Alex, Nikki grinned. "We don't usually put much thought into dates as adults, do we?"

"One of the perks of adulthood." Alex let go of her hand and laid his arm across her shoulder. "Usually, all you have to do is offer dinner or a movie, and either the other person is interested or not. For us, interest isn't the issue."

They crossed the street, and Alex guided her up the sidewalk of a two-story Victorian. A soft light glowed through lace curtains, welcoming them.

"Lovely house." Nikki walked into a tiled entry and then a great room stretching the depth of the house. "Did you remodel it?"

"Mom did." Alex took her hand. "Come back to the kitchen, and I'll pour you a glass of wine."

"Wow." Nikki touched the granite countertop and admired stainless appliances. "That's quite a kitchen. Your mom must love to cook."

"She does; in fact this is the kitchen she dreamed of when she lived at Windsong." Alex shook his head.

"Becca and I couldn't imagine what she needed the giant kitchen for when she was going to live here alone, but it's been a blessing since the boys and I moved in."

Accepting a glass of wine and a stack of vegetables, Nikki sipped and started assembling a salad. The scents of Italian seasoning and tomatoes filled the kitchen. "Did you cook the lasagna?"

"Well, I put it in the oven, if that counts," admitted Alex. "Mom made the lasagna and left it for me with complete directions."

"You told your mom I was coming to dinner. That surprises me. What's Mom think about you dating an innkeeper with a small son?"

"She and Becca have been after me to date for years," Alex admitted. "You're the first woman I've invited into Mom's house."

Nikki found it hard to believe Becca would willingly share her nephews.

Cuddled together on the great room sofa, Nikki and Alex watched the flames in the fireplace dance. "Come here, Nikki." Alex pulled Nikki against his chest and slid down until they lay together on the sofa. "I knew you'd feel this good in my arms."

"We almost got this far once before." Nikki kissed his check, laid her hand on his smooth cheek. "What made you pull back?"

"Sometimes I'm such a mess." Alex shook his head and wrapped his arms tightly around her. "I wanted you too much. More than I expected."

"Umm, and do you still want me too much?"

"Now, I need you." His lips met hers. He licked the seam. She opened for him. "Too much to turn away. Let me see you."

Alex helped Nikki pull her sweater over her head, running his hands from her shoulders to her waist; he unhooked her bra and tossed it away. His callused hands gently cupped her breasts. He lifted himself away and suddenly they were skin to skin, their clothes a tangled puddle on the floor.

"Nikki, look in my eyes. Let your eyes tell me what pleases you." He gently touched her everywhere. "Such pretty skin, so soft."

Nikki ran her hands across Alex's back, along his shoulders, down his arms. She gently squeezed his muscular biceps.

Alex slid down her body, placing random kisses, sucking briefly on her belly button, and finally his tongue found that spot. Alex licked and sucked and licked again until Nikki came apart, then, pulling a condom from the pocket of his jeans, he sheathed himself and entered her, slowly giving her time to adjust. He gazed into her eyes. "It's been a long time for you?"

"Yes."

Suddenly, he was in all the way.

Alex set a rhythm, watching Nikki's eyes. She moved in counterpoint, pushing back, taking him further until they both exploded.

They dozed, the only sound their quiet breathing. With a sigh, Nikki rolled away off the couch, gathered her clothes, and headed for the bathroom. Groaning, Alex picked up his clothes and dressed. Dressed, Nikki watched Alex straighten the cushions on the couch and turn off the gas fire. Through the quiet night they walked. Was tonight a beginning or an end? At The Palace door, Alex pulled Nikki into his arms and whispered, "Letting you go is tough."

"And are you, Alex?" Nikki touched his now scratchy cheek. "Are you letting me go?"

"Only for tonight." Alex caressed Nikki's cheek with one finger. "Tonight, I'll let you go. Just for tonight."

****

The hum of conversation spilled from the Opera House, puffy clouds drifted in front of a full moon. Alex glanced at the marquee. Again, the Opera House hosted a traveling Shakespearian company performing on the Ides of March. He mentally patted himself on the back. Creekside had made it through another traditional day of disaster without disaster. No freak rainfall, cyclone, or deadly blizzard. The only death a pretend demise of Julius Caesar on stage. He counted his blessings. Weather hinting at spring, healthy mom, happy sister, profitable ranch, well-adjusted sons, Nikki back in his arms. Life would be perfect if he could hold her more often, spend more nights beside her. Alex entered his mother's house. Boots left at the front door, he climbed the stairs to the boys' room. Before he could enter, he heard Colin's voice. "Do you think Dad will marry her?"

"Who, Nikki?" responded Mitch. "Nah, he's just sleeping with her. Dad doesn't want any more kids. That's what Aunt Becca told Grandma."

"Yeah, but that was a while ago," Colin argued. "He spends all his time with her. Randy asked me if I was getting a new mom."

"No," Mitch answered. "Just tell Randy no, we had one mom, and now we're too old to need another one. We've got Grandma and Aunt Becca."

"Do you think Aunt Becca will marry Luke?"

"Yeah," Mitch admitted. "They don't have kids, and Aunt Becca wants a kid."

"How do you know what she wants?"

"Heard her talking to Grandma. You can learn lots of stuff once you stop talking and listen. Grownups forget you're there if you're quiet."

"I feel sorry for Sam sometimes," Colin commented sleepily. "We at least had Dad, Grandma, and Aunt Becca. All Sam has is his Aunt Nikki."

"Yeah," Mitch responded. "Don't feel too sorry for him. His Aunt Nikki acts like a mom. And Scott's his cousin. Scott's cool. Anyway, Dad doesn't want Sam. That's how I know he won't marry Nikki."

"If he married Nikki, he'd get Sam too?"

"Yeah. He's got us; that's enough kids."

"Time for sleep, boys," Alex said as he opened their door. "School tomorrow."

Leaving his sons with a goodnight, Alex walked down the stairs and into the kitchen. Beth sat at the table, a cup of tea in one hand and a couple of her excellent chocolate cookies on a plate in front of her. She looked up. "Quiet evening in Creekside?"

"Yeah." Alex pulled open the refrigerator. "Lots of tourists, but they're happy behaving themselves. Any beer in the fridge?"

"In the back. Unusual for you to ask for beer."

"I'm worried about Mitch and Colin." Alex plopped into a chair. "Am I setting a bad example? How did Mitch figure out my relationship with Nikki, anyway?"

"He's thirteen. He's just started paying attention to girls, and he's looking to you to figure out how that works." Beth sniggered. "Plus, Creekside's a small town; nothing stays a secret for long."

"Well, Nikki was never a secret." Alex frowned. "But we didn't exactly announce we were sleeping together."

"Does it bother you that the whole town's watching to see what happens next?" Beth asked.

"Not really." Alex shrugged and sipped his beer. "But Mitch told Colin I wouldn't marry Nikki because I didn't want more kids. That I didn't want Sam. I was already sleeping with her, so why marry. Like the only reason to marry was children and sex."

"Think about it, Alex." Beth reached across the table and touched his hand. "The important adults in Mitch's world are single."

"But I don't want my boys to think the only things women are good for are sex and babies." Alex frowned. "It's not what I believe. Maybe I should have married after Vanessa, but until Nikki, everyone else bored me."

"Mitch hears everything, Alex. You probably told Becca you'd never marry, and I know you mouthed off about no more kids."

Embarrassed, Alex mumbled goodnight, finished his beer, and left the kitchen. Coming from Mitch, no more kids and no marriage sounded stupid. He sounded like a jerk who used women rather than a man who loved. Yeah, at one time his life was a mess, his heart battered from losing Vanessa, two little boys needing constant attention, a job working weekends and nights. By the time Nikki arrived, life was perfect. Becca and Mom took the pressure off with the boys, the job was better, or he was better at the job. Perfect. Now an uneasiness crawled up his skin, his only relief walking with Nikki, holding Nikki, loving Nikki. Could he love another child, not his own child, not even Nikki's child? The child of a woman he'd barely met. And what about another child, Nikki's child? At thirty-two, Nikki might want a child. But what were his choices? He couldn't leave things as is, bad example for Colin and Mitch.

Anyway, he wanted more time with Nikki, more than walks, dinner dates, and rare nights in his bed. He wanted everything. Nikki's present and her future. Alex showered, the hot water easing his tense shoulders. He pulled on old sweatpants. He checked on the boys. Mitch lay crosswise on the bed, covers kicked to the floor. When had he grown so tall? Colin curled up in the middle of his bed, only the top of his head visible above the blankets. Not grown up, but no longer little kids.

Alex slid between cool sheets. Exhausted, he fell into sleep. A kaleidoscope of moments filled his dreams. Dancing with Vanessa at their wedding, her laughter when he tried a fancy turn, holding tiny Mitch a few minutes after birth, Mitch trying to climb into Colin's crib, at the hospital holding Vanessa in his arms as she slipped away, Colin propped in front of him on Midnight, Mitch balanced on a pony. A kaleidoscope.

Chapter Nineteen

"From the Creekside Reporter: April 24, 1975: 'Today the National Historic Register added The Palace Hotel to its roster. Built in 1917, The Palace was home to Mrs. Victoria Wyatt until her death in 1949. The smallest of the three hotels operating in Creekside in 1917, The Palace contained twenty-five rooms and a small lobby bar.' "
~A Brief History of The Palace by Arthur Welles

Under a clear sky and warm sun, Nikki strolled the three blocks to Catherine's, humming "April in Paris" under her breath. The slight garlic scent from sub sandwiches blended with the spring scents of flowers and new grass. She raised her hand to knock, and the door of the little blue house opened. Nikki grinned at Catherine standing in the doorway. "Lunch delivery."

Catherine waved Nikki inside the entry. "We'll eat on the patio. Hope's down for a nap, so we have a little time for adult conversation."

"Good." Nikki set the bag of sandwiches beside a tray holding a pitcher of iced tea, lemon, sugar, and two glasses. "I'm hoping for experienced mother advice, and you're the experienced mother I know best." She slipped into a chair at the patio table.

"As long as you stick to experience with very young children, I'm good." Catherine poured glasses of iced tea while Nikki moved the sandwiches from bag to plates. "How can I help?"

"Sam's birthday is the twenty-fourth, and I'd like to give him a party." Nikki sighed and stirred sugar into her tea. "But I don't know where or what exactly we should do at a party for a four-year-old. Alex suggested a party at Windsong since Becca handles birthday parties, but I don't think that's appropriate for Sam."

Catherine nodded, sipping her tea. "Sam's a little young for a Windsong party. Better might be my backyard."

"Are you sure you're willing to let me use your yard?" Nikki frowned. "I'd try to keep the guest list down, but it still might be too many people. Plus, do you think some parents will stay through the party?"

"If this were Scottsdale, I'd say only a few parents, but you might get some uninvited siblings." Catherine picked up her sandwich and frowned. "I took Lily to a birthday party once that had twelve three-year-olds, and only two parents stayed. Plus, one guest was accompanied by an older sibling who didn't want to be left out."

"I could use the basement for the party. The apartment is finished but doesn't have furniture yet." Nikki shrugged. "But the weather's too nice to confine children indoors."

"Let's combine Sam's birthday with Lily's," Catherine suggested. "Lily turns four on the tenth of May. They have some of the same friends from preschool, and we can join forces. We'll prepare enough food for any stray adults but not plan to entertain them. How does that sound?"

"I knew you'd be a great help," Nikki declared and

sipped the cold tea. "How do you do it? Single parenting is tough. I'm not sure what I'm doing and sometimes it feels like I'm running backward."

"I was lucky," Catherine admitted, her voice wistful. "When Lily was born, I switched to part-time, and while Craig worked a lot of hours, at least he shared in the decision making. By the time he died, I felt comfortable being a mom, though I'll admit it's lonely." She patted Nikki's hand. "You were thrown into motherhood. You didn't even get nine months to prepare."

"True." Nikki shook her head. "I wasn't prepared to be a mom, but at least I'd known Sam since birth. I attended birthing classes with Sheri and was her labor coach. Even when I moved to Creekside, Sheri and I talked every week."

"It sounds like Sam's not the only one grieving," Catherine said, quietly. "You probably haven't had time to deal with your sadness." Before Nikki could answer, Hope's giggles rang through the monitor. "Sounds like nap time is over."

In the bright sunshine, Nikki strolled toward The Palace. She focused on plans for Sam's party, but thoughts of grief distracted her. Too many losses for being only thirty-three. First her baby, then Aaron, her best friend and husband, then her profession when she stopped working to care for Mom. Mom's memories were lost to Alzheimer's, then Mom to cancer. Finally, Sheri, her best friend, lost to an accident. She slipped through the back door, and Louis Armstrong serenaded her with "What a Wonderful World." Losses? Yep. But gains too. She gained a new profession, a hotel, new friends, a lover, and best of all, a son. Perched on her stool behind the front desk, she watched puffy white clouds drift and sun glint on the wood floors, turning them the color of honey. She waited for Sam and Megan's return from preschool, and her heart eased.

"Hooked on a feeling, high on believing..." Nikki swayed to the Blue Suede's sound and gathered the last of the wine glasses from the library, lowered the lobby lights, checked the front door lock, and silenced the music on the song's final note. Georgie in her arms, she pushed open the back door, and strong arms surrounded her. A familiar rumbly voice spoke in her ear. "Hello Innkeeper, how about a kiss?"

Nikki gazed into his chocolate eyes and inhaled his scent of aftershave and soap. "A bribe, Chief, are you asking for a bribe?" He leaned in and their lips met. He tasted of mint. She kissed him back, pulled away, and raised an eyebrow. "So, what am I buying with my bribe?"

"Escort on your walk? My jacket if you're cold? My hand to hold Georgie's leash?"

"I'll take it all, except the jacket." He took Georgie's leash; they looped arms and strolled through the parking lot.

"Heard you humming when the door opened. Was it a good day?"

"Excellent day. Catherine and I are joining forces combining Sam's and Lily's birthdays at a party in her backyard," she admitted. "A major relief."

At the corner, they crossed the street, the hum of slow-moving cars an accompaniment to the music from a band on the square. "Not Windsong? Sam really loves horses."

"He does." Nikki shrugged. "I think Windsong

would be too much."

"At Windsong, Becca would help. So would Beth."

"I'm not comfortable asking Becca. Even if I just scheduled the party there and paid her like everyone else, it would feel awkward."

"She wouldn't want you to pay. She thinks of you as a friend."

"More like potential friend." Nikki shook her head. "We haven't spent enough time together to be friends."

They circled the square and retraced their steps. "Marry me. Then you'd be family. Birthday parties no charge."

"First, you haven't asked me." Before Alex could respond, Nikki placed a finger on his lips. "And don't ask now. I do love you." She shrugged. "Relationship still not on the priority list."

Alex pulled her into his arms. She could feel his heartbeat through their sweaters. Her body warmed, and she wrapped her arms around his neck. He gazed into her eyes. "I want you, not just sometimes in my bed, but in my life."

She placed a fleeting kiss on his lips. "You said no kids, no wife."

"I was wrong. Believe me, I rarely say that." Nikki chuckled. "I thought my life perfect before we met. Everything was organized, all my bases covered, but it was gray. You brought back the color." He put his lips against hers, gently at first, then more firmly, finally slipping his tongue inside. Nikki responded, answering his tongue by gently sucking. Alex moaned and pulled back slightly. "I'm not giving up."

Alex took his boots off on the front porch and entered his mom's house, following the light from the kitchen. "Hi, Mom. You're still up?"

"It's early. I'm just doing the prep for tomorrow's dinner. How's the law? You off tonight?"

"Yeah. Quiet night, no crime. Mom, I asked Nikki to marry me."

"And…"

"She's fighting it."

"She doesn't want to marry you?" Beth's eyes widened.

"Nikki claims a relationship is at the bottom of her priorities. We both have jobs that require nights, weekends, and holidays. Nikki has Sam, and I have two sons, one a teenager. She lives in a haunted hotel, and I'm thirty-nine years old living with my mom." Alex groaned. "Guess I'm not really much of a bargain."

"Nikki's smart and ambitious. If it was just those complications, I bet the two of you could figure a way around them." Beth pointed out thoughtfully. "There has to be something else holding her back."

"I screwed it up when we met. I told her I didn't want any more kids or a wife."

"Should have listened to your mom; better to keep some opinions to yourself." Beth shook her head at his hangdog expression.

"Who knew I'd scare off the first woman I've been really interested in since Vanessa."

"Karma? Kismet? Bad luck?" She patted his shoulder.

"Not encouraging, Mom."

"I'm encouraging. I have faith you'll work it out. Might have to grovel though."

"Not a bad idea," Alex agreed. "Or maybe I just need to be so persistent she gives in to shut me up."

Wishing Beth goodnight, Alex headed for bed. "She loves me," Alex thought as he climbed into bed. "Why isn't that enough?"

At The Palace, Nikki slipped into Sam's room for a final good night. The truck night-light glowed on the wooden floor. Georgie slept in a curled ball at the end of the bed. Pulling the covers over Sam, Nikki knelt beside him and placed a kiss on his cheek. "Night, Sam. I'm sorry Sheri's gone, but I'm so glad you're here."

****

Blue sky decorated with a few puffy white clouds. Yellow sun, blooming flowers, and grass turning dark green in the spring warmth. Sam's birthday. Sam skipped, hopped, and bounced. Megan and Nikki held his hands, and they walked to Catherine's. Sam's excited chatter included a steady stream of questions, though he left no time for answers. Lily stood on the front porch, Catherine in the doorway behind her. "You're here finally. It's time for our party."

Catherine rolled her eyes. "Not quite time. They're early." She ruffled her daughter's short hair.

"But I've waited forever," Lily whined.

Nikki stepped onto the porch and lifted Lily up. "I've waited too. Waited for a birthday kiss." She planted a smacking kiss on Lily's cheek.

Sam made a yucking sound. "I won't give you a kiss, but we have a present for Lily even though it's my birthday." Sam grinned. "We brought Hope a present too so she wouldn't feel left out. Is that okay?"

"Hope loves presents." Catherine led them inside. "Hope's in the playroom."

Megan, Hope, Lily, and Sam stayed in the playroom while Nikki and Catherine set up games in the yard.

"Let's put a sign on the door sending everyone to the back gate," Nikki suggested. "Otherwise we'll spend so much time running back and forth, we'll miss the party."

Final preparations completed, the first guests arrived. Sam and Lily welcomed their friends at the gate. Parents stayed, helping direct games, serve food, and wipe up spills as eighteen preschoolers pinned ears on a rabbit, fished plastic ducks from a wading pool pond, froze on command during a game of statues, and played Simon Says. After pizza and sandwiches were devoured, cake and ice cream enjoyed, and gifts opened, parents gathered their exhausted offspring, coaching them in thanking Nikki, Catherine, and Megan for a great party and wishing Lily and Sam happy birthday.

"Wow, Nikki." Catherine looked around the yard, picked up a stray paper napkin. "That went better than I expected. We had almost as many adults as kids and the adults helped. Some even pushed their kids to help with clean up."

"I was prepared for most of the parents to leave the kids and run. It has to be hard finding time to do things without the kids when you work." Nikki gathered the last gifts from the table, carrying them inside. "Instead the parents seemed to have a good time helping the kids with the games. Looks like I'll have lots of great parent examples in Creekside."

Pulling a wagon full of exhausted birthday boy Sam and his loot, Nikki and Megan returned to The Palace. They helped Sam find places for his new toys. After a light supper, Nikki tucked Sam into bed.

"Thank you, Aunt Nikki. Great party. I wish my mom could have come."

"Oh, Sam." Nikki pulled Sam close for one more hug. "I wish she were here too. But I'll bet she's watching. She must be so proud. You were a great host."

"Goodnight, Aunt Nikki." He yanked the covers up, leaving only his brown hair showing.

"Sleep tight, Sam." Nikki slipped out his door.

Nikki opened the back door and discovered Alex leaning against the building. "Evening, Innkeeper." He placed a soft kiss on her cheek. "I'm a little surprised you're walking tonight. Aren't you exhausted after Sam's party?"

"I'm beat," Nikki agreed. "I thought the quiet night might help me settle. How was your day?"

"Quiet." Alex took her hand. "How was Sam's birthday party?"

They strolled toward the square. "According to Sam, great." Nikki shook her head, still surprised by the helpful Creekside parents. "The party went better than Catherine and I expected. The kids' parents stayed and helped. All the guests had a great time and avoided any meltdowns. Do Colin and Mitch have birthday parties?"

"Not so much anymore." Alex guided them around a cluster of tourists in front of The Lone Star. "Last birthday, Mitch wanted a movie with a couple friends and pizza, and Colin wanted an expensive new saddle and no party."

"Well, I'll enjoy this time then," Nikki remarked. "When Sam still thinks a party thrown by his Aunt Nikki is great."

At the back door of the hotel, Alex wrapped his

arms around her, pulling her against him. She leaned her head against his chest and accepted his warmth and comfort. "Mitch knows we're sleeping together. Apparently, everyone in town knows or thinks they know. Is that going to be a problem for you?" he asked.

"No, not for me." Nikki shrugged. "We're both single adults, and Sam's little enough it won't mean anything to him. What about you?"

"Oh, Nikki," Alex admitted. "I'd rather you'd commit to me. At least let me buy you a ring so everyone knows this is permanent."

"But we are committed." Nikki frowned. "I love you, and that's a commitment."

"I know you keep saying you weren't looking for a relationship." Alex tipped her chin up with one finger and gazed in her eyes. "But you found one anyway, with me." He released her chin and leaned in, placing his lips on hers in a gentle kiss. "I want you and Sam in my life, committed and legal."

"Alex." Nikki whispered, "I need to think this through."

"While you're thinking, remember I love you." Alex placed a fleeting kiss on her lips. "I'm not going to give up."

"I wish you'd been there, Sheri," Nikki thought when she checked one last time and discovered Sam sound asleep with Georgie curled on the end of his bed. "Sam is such a great kid. You would have been so proud. He played and shared the attention. Thank you for letting me raise him when you couldn't."

Sliding between her sheets, Nikki's mind filled with gains and losses, blessings and disasters. Did she put off Alex because she feared another loss? He'd spent the last months slowly rebuilding her trust. She trusted he'd be there for her. Be there for Sam. Today he claimed he wouldn't give up, but how long before she lost him because she was afraid to move forward? When she finally slipped into sleep, Nikki dreamed a kaleidoscope of scenes from Victoria's life in the hotel. Victoria laughed on the veranda during her first interview with the reporter, watched the man in the bowler hat walk away, held an infant RJ while she rocked, watched from the veranda as a group of young people drove away. A white star appeared in the window. It changed to gold. Nikki woke to the soft squeak of a wooden rocker on the wood floor. Beside the window, in the faint light of dawn, Victoria, her hair glinting silver, rocked slowly, and gazed out the window. Nikki sat up, and Victoria disappeared, leaving behind a drifting scent of lavender. Nikki accepted Victoria and Nikki's mom had something in common. They lived life with enthusiasm and during times of loss they moved forward. Fear couldn't stop them from giving and accepting love.

****

After breakfast, Nikki sat down at her desk, downloaded the photos from her camera, and composed an email to Max:

Hi, Max. Hope all is well with you. Sam loved your gift, and he's working on his thank you notes. Attached is a slide show. First part is Sam opening the family gifts from you, Patrick, James, Scott, and me. Pictures of his birthday party fill Part Two. He had a great time. You can probably tell that by his smiles and the chocolate cake he's wearing on his shirt. Sometimes he's almost too fearless. Notice the picture of him leading several boys in a tree climb. Please let me know when you can visit. There's always a room ready at The Palace for you. Be safe, Nikki.

Low lights bathed the lobby in a warm glow. Nikki gathered the last wine glasses, locked the front door, and cruised into the kitchen. In the library, a couple of guests remained curled up on the sofa with their tablets. Wishing them good evening, she sauntered down the hallway, humming along with the Beach Boys' claim that "Every night's a special occasion..." as they extolled the joy of "Spring Vacation." Not exactly a May Day song, but close enough. The antique Tiffany lamp cast a soft welcoming glow in her sitting room. The truck night-light in Sam's room illuminated Sam's bed, his brown hair on the pillow. A boy-size lump in the center reassured her he slept on. Georgie leaped down from the bed with a soft thud and trotted behind Nikki into the sitting room. Dressed in matching blue sweaters, they slipped out of the suite. Nikki pushed the back door open; the security light came on, the yellow glow glinting on Alex's deep brown hair. He pulled her into his arms and placed a fleeting kiss on her lips.

"Will you stay the night with me on Friday?"

Sinking into his embrace, Nikki wrapped her arms around his waist. "Sounds lovely. Is this a special occasion?"

"Yes," Alex admitted. "We'll have a late dinner at home and talk. For the rest of the night, I'll hold you in my arms. My definition of special."

Friday night, Nikki stood in front of her closet, pulling out first one shirt and then another, finally deciding on a silver T-shirt and black skinny jeans. After adding a Palace shirt and underthings to a small backpack, Nikki checked once more that Sam slept and the monitor to Megan's room was on.

"Wow, you look great," Megan commented, looking up from her laptop. "That's a pretty shirt. Is it new?"

Nikki shook her head. "No, it feels new though. Sometimes it seems I wear nothing but Palace polo shirts. I forget there's anything else in my closet."

"So, are you and Alex doing something special?" Megan looked Nikki up and down. "You look like you should be going to Wellington's for dinner."

"No Wellington's. But hopefully something special." Nikki sauntered out of Megan's room to the sound of Megan's cheerful giggle. Victoria faced Nikki from the doorway of room 11. Her right eyelid slowly lowered in a wink. She disappeared through the closed door, and a scent of lavender drifted in the hallway. Shaking her head at Victoria's wink, Nikki pushed the back door open, slipped through, and listened for the click of the latch. Beside her, a shadow leaned down and pressed a kiss on her cheek. Nikki inhaled his familiar scent. "Evening, Chief. Nice greeting."

"Evening, Innkeeper." He slipped his hand in hers, and they strolled through the cool summer evening. Music floated from the live band playing at the square, the sound disappearing as they turned onto the residential street. Scents of new grass and flowers surrounded them. Nikki breathed deeply and sighed with pleasure. Special occasion. A perfect spring evening and the company of her friend and generous lover. In this place, in this moment, she felt overwhelming gratitude for the blessings in her world. Sam, her friends, her family, and Alex. She stopped, lifted up on tiptoe, and kissed his cheek.

"What was that for?"

She shrugged. "Because I could, because the night's perfect, because it's spring."

After a dinner filled with conversation, Nikki and Alex took glasses of wine into the living room. Setting their glasses on the table, Alex pulled Nikki into his arms and gazed into her eyes. "Say you'll marry me, Nikki. Take a chance on us." Nikki opened her mouth to respond, and Alex shook his head. "Please let me finish. You don't have to marry me today or tomorrow. Just agree we'll marry when you're ready."

Nikki gazed into his chocolate eyes and let one finger stroke his scratchy cheek. "Marry?" She shook her head. "But what about no more children? What about no wife? What about your almost perfect life?"

Alex tugged her closer, his arm heavy across her shoulder. He shook his head. "Never going to let that go, huh?"

"Hey, those were your words." She kissed his cheek.

Alex grimaced. "And after our romantic dinner I'm eating them. Again."

"Oh, Alex." She laid her head against his chest. "What if you change your mind? What if your boys hate me?"

He pulled her onto his lap. "What if I love you forever? What if the boys love you and Sam loves me?" He protested and kissed her cheek. "What if we marry and we spend our lifetime wrapped in each other's arms?" Leaning in he kissed her, teasing kisses on her cheek, chin, and forehead. "Say yes. I warn you if you say no, I'm going to ask again, and again." He hugged her tighter. "Not letting you go. No giving up."

Nikki placed her hands on his cheeks. She shook her head. "You leave me no choice." She kissed him. "Yes, Alex, I'll marry you."

In room 15 of The Palace Hotel, Victoria gazed out the window, watching the street. She smiled.

A word about the author…

An Arizona native, Stella spent her childhood visiting small towns and campgrounds all over the state and entertained herself on long car trips writing stories.

Married, she lives in Scottsdale, where she still imagines every new acquaintance's story and spends her free time traveling, reading, walking her tiny dog, meeting up with friends, and practicing yoga.

http://stellajaynephillips.com

Thank you for purchasing
this publication of The Wild Rose Press, Inc.

For questions or more information
contact us at
info@thewildrosepress.com.

The Wild Rose Press, Inc.
www.thewildrosepress.com

To visit with authors of
The Wild Rose Press, Inc.
join our yahoo loop at
http://groups.yahoo.com/group/thewildrosepress/

www.ingramcontent.com/pod-product-compliance
Lightning Source LLC
Chambersburg PA
CBHW070051030726
47506CB00002B/427